Conditional Love

L.A. Arbuckle

Published by L.A. Arbuckle, 2025.

CONDITIONAL LOVE

First edition. April 30, 2025.

Copyright © 2025 L.A. Arbuckle.

ISBN: 979-8992891218

Written by L.A. Arbuckle.

In Honor and Memoriam
Terence (Terry) Donnelly (1941–2024)

• • • •

This novel exists because of Terry
—my mentor and beloved friend—
who believed in me, and this story.
From its screenplay origins to this book,
his encouragement fueled every step.
His quote graces the back cover, as I promised him it would.
Thank you, Terry, for inspiring me to write the novel version of Conditional
Love.
I promise to pay it forward in your honor.

DISCLAIMER

Be advised: violence, sexual content, and coarse language run through these pages. Dive in if you're up for it; turn back if you're not. There is no handholding here.

As Neva would say, "Cowboy up or you'll miss the whole damn rodeo."

PROLOGUE

June 1994

Neva Stevenson lay sprawled and still on the living room floor, a child's jump rope wound tight around her neck. Fresh bruises in hues of purple and blue were already visible, marring the ivory skin around her eye and along the delicate jawbone of her swollen face. Blood oozed into her blonde hairline from a cut above her left eye. The house, like Neva's body, was still and it, too, showed signs of being battered. Pieces of broken dishes and overturned furniture lay strewn throughout the dining and living room. A fist-sized hole decorated one pastel-yellow wall, and a red vase lay broken on the floor, shards of its glass scattered like rubies near Neva's head.

A loud thud from the floor above echoed through the still room. Neva's body jerked in response. Her eyes snapped open, hands flying to the rope at her throat. She couldn't breathe, couldn't think. Her mind struggled to clear itself, even as her fingers scratched and scrabbled to loosen the rope.

Within seconds, she had loosened it enough to release some of the pressure. She gasped in a breath and rolled onto her stomach. The motion made her dizzy and set off a violent spasm of coughing and gagging. The stabbing pain that punctuated every cough made her see stars. She rested her forehead on the cool hardwood floor and attempted a deep breath. The air felt like fire as it made its way into her lungs, and she winced from the burn.

Summoning all her strength, Neva pushed herself onto her knees. With shaking hands, she unwound the rope from her throat, exposing a deep, blood-soaked groove cut into the skin beneath. It oozed blood and burned like a fresh brand. Trying again to swallow, she triggered another wave of nausea. She covered her mouth, fighting the urge to gag.

She had lost consciousness twice as he dragged her through the house by the rope around her neck. Then he had stopped to finish the job. As blackness seeped into the corners of her vision, she had been sure she wouldn't be regaining consciousness again. But she had. Somehow, she had.

Neva panted in shallow gasps, trying to get enough air into her lungs without setting off the pain and nausea. She raised her hand and delicately touched the wound. Bright spots swam in and out of her vision as her fingers made contact.

Neva gritted her teeth, willing her head to clear, and scrambled shakily to her feet. A sharp stab of pain in her right ankle sent her staggering, and she grasped the door frame to keep herself upright. The room swayed, and she hesitated, waiting for the spots in her vision to clear. Breathing in quick gasps, she put all her weight on her uninjured foot, scanning the living room and adjacent dining room. Her eyes darted around the space like a rabbit seeking an escape route. She could feel her heart pounding, fast and erratic, in her chest and the awareness of it fueled her panic.

Neva forced herself to focus. Where is he? Did he leave? Does he have the kids?

Heavy footsteps thudded across the floor of the room above her. She flinched, ducking away from the sound as if it could inflict physical pain. More footsteps sounded from above. Her eyes fastened on the ceiling. Oh my God, he's still here. The son-of-a-bitch is upstairs! The kids must be up there!

The realization hit her like a blow to the stomach, and she doubled over from the overwhelming fear it brought with it. She couldn't leave them there. She had to get them out. Get them far away from him.

Neva steeled herself and straightened to her full height. Pushing hard off the door frame, she limped toward the stairs.

· · · ·

Upstairs, eleven-year-old Kris and her six-year-old brother, Tom, clung to each other, silent and terrified. When their mother had intervened between Tom and their father, they knew it would be bad. Real bad. Kris had panicked, scooping up her three-year-old sister, Rachel, and half-dragging Tom by the back of his shirt up the stairs. Once on the upper level, Kris assessed the area for the best hiding space. Spotting the wicker hamper just inside the bathroom, she stumbled toward it, both siblings clinging to her like drowning swimmers to a life raft. Reaching the hamper, she threw open the lid and pulled several towels from inside. Setting Rachel down in front of her, Kris knelt and brushed the blonde wavy locks back from her sister's tear-stained face. She looked into the little girl's huge green eyes, swimming with fear and confusion.

"Rachel, we're going to hide until Mommy and Daddy feel happy again. Like last time, remember?" Kris asked, forcing steadiness into her voice.

Their father's deep voice boomed from somewhere below. "What are you gonna do, Neva!? What!? Call the police!?" he bellowed, the rage in his voice vibrating through the floorboards.

Rachel whimpered, her eyes darting toward the stairs, her tiny body tensing.

Kris gently turned Rachel's face back to hers, distracting her from the sound. "Do you remember hiding last time?"

Rachel nodded, tears streaming down her flushed cheeks.

"Good. You'll be in the best hiding spot in the world. Daddy will never look for you in here. Tommy and I will put towels on top of you and nobody will see you. You just have to be still like a statue and quiet like a mouse. Like when you're sleeping, okay?"

Rachel shook her head, a nervous frown pulling at her lips as she glanced toward the stairs, her small hands clutching at Kris's shirt.

Kris took Rachel's face in her hands and met her gaze. "Yes. If you don't, he'll find all of us. He's mad at Mommy, and Tom, and me. Not you. You'll be safe in the hamper, I promise."

Tom danced from foot to foot beside them, whimpering with every thud or thump they heard from below.

More yelling and the sound of breaking glass echoed up the stairs from the battle waging below. A strangled scream from their mother brought Tom to his knees next to Kris. He took Rachel by the shoulders, giving her a little shake. "Please, Rachel, please! Hide in the hamper, quick, before he comes!"

Rachel looked at her brother. "Why'd you make Daddy so mad?" she whined.

Tom whined in response, glancing from the steps to his little sister. "Please," he pleaded again, tears streaming.

After a brief hesitation, Rachel threw her arms around Tom's neck and squeezed. "Don't cry, Tommy. I'll hide like a mouse."

Kris pried Rachel's arms from Tom's neck and deposited her trembling little body into the hamper.

Rachel looked up at Kris with wide, tear-filled eyes. "Hide Tommy real good, too."

Kris kissed the top of her head. "I will. Stay down and be still like you're sleeping. Don't come out till me or Mommy come get you, okay?"

Rachel raised her tiny thumb in reply. Kris returned the gesture with a wan smile.

"I won't let anything happen to you, punkin'. I promise," Kris whispered.

Rachel bobbed her little head and sank down into the hamper. Kris's eyes filled with tears as she placed towels on top of Rachel and closed the lid.

Tom tugged at her hand, and they raced back into the hallway. They passed the sewing room without stopping, but paused when they reached Kris's room. Peeling Tom off her, she reached around the inside of her bedroom door and turned the lock, then closed it again and wiggled the knob to make sure it had locked.

"What are you doing?" Tom whispered.

"Never mind," Kris said, grabbing his hand. "Come on."

They continued down the hall to Tom's bedroom and slipped inside. Kris closed the door as quietly as possible and locked it. She put her forehead against the door and said the prayer her mother had taught her years ago. "Angel of God, my Guardian dear, to whom God's love commits me here; Ever this day, be at my side, to light and guard, to rule and guide." Finishing the prayer, she turned to find Tom staring at her, horrified.

"We're gonna die. You're praying 'cuz we're gonna die!"

Kris blanched at the terror on his face. His eyes were wide with too much white showing. She had seen a scared horse look like that once on a TV show. The horse's eyes were wild and almost completely white, its nostrils flaring. It had kicked and bucked, trying to escape the three cowboys who were trying to capture it. The horse had been so scared; it bolted and ran itself off a nearby cliff. The memory made her shudder.

She grabbed Tom by the shoulders and gave him a shake. "We are not going to die! Stop it. Stop it right now. You hear me?"

His eyes found hers, and he nodded.

"Good," she said. "Now, help me find a hiding spot for you."

Tom's bedroom was typical of any boy's bedroom. An unmade twin-sized bed with a Power Ranger poster hanging above it. Toys and miscellaneous stuffed animals littered the room. A heap of dirty clothes piled next to a laundry basket filled with bats, balls, and miscellaneous sporting equipment. On one wall, French doors led onto a small balcony. A large cardboard refrigerator box was lying on its side, near the doors. They had used the box as their clubhouse. "Private!" and "Stay Out!" were written in black magic marker on the side, near a flap cut out for a window. A stuffed dog stood guard at the entrance.

Kris ran to Tom's closet and looked inside. Old toys, clothes, and small to medium-sized storage boxes filled the space. She shifted the items around, creating a small hiding nook at the back. Once satisfied it would be big enough, she turned to Tom.

He hadn't moved. He stood frozen, focused on the bedroom door.

"I found a place, Tommy. Hurry and get in!" Kris urged. He didn't respond. He didn't even blink.

"Thomas David Stevenson, get in this closet right now," Kris said in her best imitation of their mother.

Tom jerked, blinking several times before focusing his gaze on her. She gestured for him to get in the closet.

"Where will you hide?" he whispered.

"I don't know yet," Kris whispered back. She glanced around the room, her eyes settling on the cardboard box. "In there. I'll hide in the clubhouse. Now, come on. Get in the closet!"

"No, I want to hide with you."

"No, Tommy," Kris cajoled. "I can pile stuff around you and hide you better if you're in there."

He shook his head. "No. I wanna stay with you."

The sound of heavy footsteps on the stairs made them both jump. Kris closed the closet door, and they rushed to the box entrance. She opened the main flap and Tom dropped to his hands and knees, scrambling to get inside. Kris followed close behind. They crawled to the back of the box and huddled together, listening. It sounded like their father passed the bathroom without stopping, and Kris felt a jolt of relief that he hadn't found Rachel. He must be in the storage room. They could hear his muffled cursing. Then they heard a loud thud, and Kris guessed he had knocked the dress dummy onto the floor.

Tom's fingernails bit into her arm. "He's gonna kill me for telling," he whimpered.

"No, he won't. I won't let him. Now, be quiet!" Kris hissed back.

Heavy footsteps sounded in the hall again. They both stiffened and held their breath. Then his footsteps stopped. She heard him rattling the doorknob of her bedroom, and then a loud bang. Their father cursed. A louder bang and the sound of splintering wood. Kris thought the lock would slow him down. Thought he might even leave to go find the key. She hoped it would buy enough time for her mother, or a neighbor, or someone, to call the police. But he hadn't bothered with a key, and they were out of time.

The sounds of his cursing were getting louder as he searched her bedroom. Kris's heart skipped wildly in her chest as she listened. The sound of glass shattering made them both jump. A single tear leaked down Kris's cheek as she realized what the sound must have been. The fishbowl. Finnie, her goldfish, had just become another victim of her father's rage.

Tom clung to her, breath hitching, as he tried to control the terrified sobs wracking his little body. Kris cradled her arms around him. I should have taken them and ran outside! We could have gotten away! She thought, as her heart drummed frantically. Now, it was too late. He was coming—and he'd be in this room next.

• • • •

Neva crept up the stairs, leaning against the wall as she went. Each step sent sharp pains through her ankle, waves of nausea crashing over her, and the damage to her throat made it difficult to breathe. Despite the pain coursing through her body, Neva's only thought was to reach her children and ensure their safety. No matter what, she had to get to them. She paused near the top of the stairs, ducking down as Robert stormed out of Kris's bedroom.

• • • •

Kris steeled herself, fully aware of the desperate measures she might need to take. This was it. Their father would be in Tom's room soon. When he found them, she wouldn't have much time. She knew what she had to do: throw herself at him and beg and plead. Do whatever he wanted her to do. And if that didn't work, she would fight. Fight as long and as hard as she could. Long enough to give Tom and Rachel a chance to run. Tears streamed down her face as she leaned close to Tom, her voice trembling with urgency. "Cover your eyes, Tommy. Don't look. No matter what, don't look. And when I say 'run', you grab Rachel, and you run outside. Run away as fast as you can, okay?"

Tom nodded, sniffling, and curling into an even tighter ball at her side. Just as hope flickered, the knob on Tom's door rattled ominously. Kris peered at the locked door through a small slit in the window flap. A deafening roar erupted from the other side, followed by their father's fist crashing through the door. Kris gasped, instinctively slapping her hand over Tom's mouth, desperate to silence his impending scream.

• • • •

Neva heard her husband's roar of outrage, and a chill of dread washed over her. She had never seen him this angry. She had confronted him, told him she and the kids were leaving, and then... he had tried to murder her. Robert knew Tom had seen, and if he would kill her to keep that secret, she was certain he wouldn't stop there. The sound of splintering wood from Tom's bedroom door jolted her into action. Summoning her courage, she limped and lurched the rest of the way to the top of the stairs.

• • • •

Kris watched in horror as pieces of wood exploded into the room with the force of her father's booted kick. His large, bloody-knuckled hand shoved the door aside, and his wide, six-foot-three-inch frame stepped inside. Deep scratches marred his right cheek, stretching from temple to jawline, and a deranged snarl contorted his face. A torn blue Henley shirt hung open, exposing his muscular chest, which bore more scratch marks and smears of blood.

Kris felt her stomach shrivel and flip. Was that mom's blood? If he looked like that, mom must have fought really hard. Was she still downstairs? Maybe she got away. Maybe he killed her! No, no, no! Please don't be dead, mom. Please don't leave us here with him! Kris bit down hard on her bottom lip to stifle her moan of despair. That can't happen, she thought. No matter what, that can't happen. I can distract him. I can keep him busy, so they can get away. The thought crystallized into resolve, hardening her fear into determination.

• • • •

Neva made slow, focused progress toward the hallway, using the wall for support. She put too much weight on her injured ankle and inhaled sharply. The combined pain of her ankle and throat triggered a wave of nausea that threatened to overwhelm her. She leaned against the bathroom doorway, eyes closed, struggling to quell the rising bile. After a few controlled sips of air, the feeling gradually subsided.

Two small arms shot out of the laundry hamper and reached for her. The unexpected movement startled her so much that she lost her balance and fell to the bathroom floor with a soft thud. When Rachel's small head appeared out of the basket, wide-eyed and frightened, Neva put a shaking finger to her lips, warning her to keep quiet. Tears of relief filled her eyes at the knowledge that her youngest daughter was safe. Neva crawled to her, capturing Rachel's outstretched hands in her own. Kissing her little fingertips, Neva gently pushed her back down into the hamper, rasping words of comfort and promising to come back and get her soon, each whispered word scraping against her damaged throat.

As she staggered back to her feet, Robert's booming voice jolted through Neva like a bolt of hot lightning. "Boy! Get your worthless ass out here now! You can't hide! I will find you!"

• • • •

Tom burrowed deeper into Kris's side, his arms constricting around her waist. The sudden, potent smell of urine permeated the air inside the box, and Kris realized he had wet himself. She squeezed Tom tighter, a silent gesture of comfort, while peering at her father through the slit in the box.

Her father strode to the twin bed and, with one powerful hand, grabbed the frame and flipped it onto its side. Finding only dust bunnies and dirty socks, he growled obscenities under his breath and crossed to the closet. He flung the closet door open with such force that it banged against the wall, embedding the knob in the drywall.

From her hiding place, Kris watched him fumble for the light inside the closet. A moment later, stuffed animals, clothes, and boxes flew from the closet opening in a violent cascade. Several items hit the side of their makeshift clubhouse with a thud, causing Tom to jump and squeeze her even tighter, his small body trembling against hers.

· · · ·

Body shaking, Neva took the final steps to the bedroom door. She peeked around the edge of the frame, desperate to avoid alerting Robert to her presence. The cardboard clubhouse quivered slightly, immediately catching her attention. Her heart lurched painfully in her chest. Oh God, she prayed silently, please help us.

· · · ·

Kris shifted for a better view through the flap. She could only see her father's back as he tore through the closet, but she had a perfect view when he turned around and looked directly at the clubhouse. She watched in horror as his face transformed from hateful fury to a look of pure predatory satisfaction. A violent shudder ran down her spine.

· · · ·

Neva's breath caught as she realized Robert knew Kris and Tom were inside the box. Her eyes darted around the room, frantically searching for a weapon. Damn it! There had to be something she could use! Her gaze fell on the sporting equipment piled in the laundry basket a few feet away. Without hesitation, she stumbled into the room and snatched the metal baseball bat from the basket, her fingers tightening around the grip with newfound determination.

· · · ·

Kris could only see her father from the knees down as he paced, slow and deliberate, in front of the box. She was the big sister. Protecting Tom and Rachel was her job, and this was all her fault. She kissed the top of Tom's head and gently pried his arms from around her waist. "Don't look, Tommy, and when I say 'run', RUN," she whispered frantically in his ear.

Kris edged toward the box opening. Tom snatched at her arm as a loud "thunk", and a pain-filled groan echoed from their father. She peered through the slit and saw her father's legs staggering sideways toward them. He collided hard with the opposite end of the box, falling forward. The cardboard crumpled beneath his weight. Tom screamed, and she scrambled away from the crushed area, their eyes darting around the enclosed space as they clutched each other in panic.

· · · ·

Neva stared in horror as Robert struggled sluggishly back to his feet. He swayed as he touched his fingers to the back of his head. They came away bloody. He glanced from the blood on his fingers to Neva, his expression shifting from utter disbelief to absolute rage. His lips pulled back from his teeth in a feral grimace.

"You fucking bitch," he said in a low, rumbling growl.

Neva blanched. Her hands trembled violently. Afraid she might drop the only weapon she had, she lowered the bat, leaning on it to take the weight off her injured foot and remain upright. "Leave the kids alone," she croaked, her damaged throat barely able to form the words.

Robert held up his hand, smeared with blood, for Neva to see. "You see this?" he hissed, eyes gleaming with crazed intensity. "I'm not gonna break his arm this time. Just for this," he continued, waving his bloody hand at her, "I'm gonna snap his little fucking neck." He held his hands up in front of him and mimicked the motion of snapping a stick.

She raised the bat again and fixed Robert with a steely glare, summoning strength she didn't know she possessed. "Over my dead body," she rasped.

"Done," he whispered with a nod of agreement, and took a menacing step toward her.

Neva swung the bat low this time, connecting hard with his hip. The blow knocked him off balance, his groan of pain transforming into a string of furious obscenities. He regained his footing, though, and sneered at her, his eyes promising retribution.

Neva lifted the bat back to her shoulder with forced calm and balanced her weight on her good foot, her eyes never leaving his.

Robert let out a guttural cry and lunged for her. She didn't hesitate. He tried to catch the bat as she swung, but the first blow had left him uncoordinated and slow. He missed.

She didn't.

The reverberation of the blow to Robert's head traveled down the bat and into Neva's hands, startling her with its violent intensity. Robert staggered sideways for several steps, struggling to maintain his balance. Blood trickled from just above his ear, matting his hair in a crimson stream. He swayed like a willow tree in a thunderstorm but somehow remained upright.

Neva growled, deep and feral, as she raised the bat again and limped toward him. Something primal had awakened within her—the fierce, protective instinct of a mother defending her young. She could see the fear dawning in Robert's eyes as he staggered backward, but she continued her relentless advance.

Robert attempted to sidestep her but tripped over the stuffed dog that had guarded the playhouse. His arms flailed wildly as he fell backward through the French doors, coming up hard against the balcony railing. The rusted metal groaned ominously under his weight. Robert paused a moment, one arm outstretched, as if trying to steady himself. He looked up at Neva, his expression a mixture of rage and disbelief, and pushed off the rail, taking two drunken steps forward before losing his balance and stumbling backward once again, all of his weight crashing against the weakened metal.

The metallic whine of the railing filled the air with its warning. Neva knew she should pull him away from it or warn him, but she couldn't do it. Didn't want to. A cold certainty settled in her chest. The last piece of her that cared for Robert died the minute she learned what he had done. Now, the part of her that hated him, that was desperate to save her children, was in control. And that part didn't give two fucks whether he lived or died, as long as she and her kids were safe.

Robert's disoriented gaze settled on Neva just as the railing gave one final groan. She defiantly raised a bloody middle finger. His eyes widened in sudden comprehension the instant before the balcony railing gave way. Without a sound, he disappeared over the side.

Neva returned the bat to her shoulder, muscles tense and ready, expecting Robert to somehow reappear. The balcony remained empty. She listened intently, expecting to hear his moans of pain from the concrete patio two stories below. There was only silence. A silence that spoke volumes. Still watchful, she hobbled backward into the bedroom.

• • • •

Kris emerged from the box, with Tom still glued to her side. She froze in horror when she saw her mother. A deep gash, glistening with blood, circled her mother's neck, and her face was bloated and bruised. Neva stood motionless in the center of the room, her vacant stare fixed on the balcony, as if in a trance.

Kris followed her mother's gaze to the broken railing. Her eyes snapped back to Neva and the bat she gripped in one hand, the pieces falling into place like a terrible puzzle.

Tom took a tentative step away from Kris. "Mommy?" he squeaked.

Their mother jerked, as if waking from a nightmare, and looked down at Tom. For a moment, Kris didn't think she recognized him. Then she blinked several times before dropping the bat with a hollow clatter and collapsing onto her knees. She threw her arms open, crying out with a strangled sob that made Kris wince.

Tom ran to their mother and wrapped his arms around her, his little body seeming to turn to jelly in his mother's embrace. His shoulders shook with quiet sobs as years of tension released in a single moment.

Kris remained where she was, her arms wrapped around her middle, crying silent tears of relief.

Chapter 1:
Kris Stevenson-Walker

27 years later...

The Walker acreage was small compared to others in the area, but any local would tell you it was one of the best pieces of land within fifty miles. The house sat on a two-acre, cleared tract in the center of the property, with hardwood timber surrounding it. A meandering stream flowed through the backyard, featuring a natural mini waterfall that cascaded just a few feet over river rock and limestone. At the front of the property, a long, rocked, tree-lined drive led to the house.

Kris Stevenson bought the five-acre parcel of land the year she graduated high school, after noticing the for-sale sign on one of her sanity-preserving country drives. Her therapist called those drives a "coping mechanism." For Kris, the car was her safe haven, a place where she felt in control. She could drive away from the drama of her life, with the doors locked and the radio blaring, and no one could stop her.

On the day Kris noticed the for-sale sign, something had made her slow down to get a closer look. She didn't know why the property had piqued her interest, but looking at it had made her feel something. And feeling anything besides obligation was rare for her.

So, she stopped the car, walked up to the fence line, and fell in love. She knew this was where she wanted to build her future home. Far enough away to give her a break from her family, but close enough to be there if they needed her. If she had to stay in Iowa for them, this place would give her the peace and solitude she craved.

Kris had been babysitting since she was thirteen and working as a waitress for twenty-five hours a week from the time she was sixteen until the day she found the property. She had saved that money like a squirrel burying nuts and built up a considerable stash. And now, she knew what she would use it for.

Eleven years later, she had saved enough to put a down payment on the construction of her dream home on that property. She had been married to Carl for five years by then, and Trent was nearly four years old. Carl had earned his degree in finance three months earlier and had just started his new position at Linn Area Bank. The second income was the final milestone they needed to move forward with the build, and Carl had been happy to turn the entire project over to her.

The house was a modern two-story with clean lines, lots of windows, and no balconies. It featured three bedrooms, two-and-a-half baths, a gourmet kitchen, and a beautiful fireplace in the living room. A top-of-the-line security system had also been installed, with a one-button panic alarm in every room.

Kris loved every inch of the place, but what she loved most was how the light filtered through the trees in the morning. The master bedroom faced east on the second floor. Two large windows covered in crystal organza sheers captured the sunlight every morning, casting her bedroom in an almost magical glow. Until eight months ago, Kris loved waking up to that glow each morning.

Now, she kept heavy curtains drawn over those magical sheers, and only the smallest bit of light emanated from around their edges. This sunny morning was no exception.

A stout, black-and-white cat nosed the door to the bedroom open and strode inside. It stopped at the edge of the king-size bed, crouching, tail twitching, in preparation for the leap.

Kris Stevenson-Walker was asleep in the bed, alone. Her tear-stained face twitched as she dreamed. At least a dozen used tissues lay strewn on the night table, the floor, and the flowered duvet cover. One arm draped across her eyes and forehead; another used tissue crumpled in her half-open fist. Her other arm clutched a framed wedding photo to her chest. In that photo, Kris wore a modest, white, knee-length dress. Her hair was long, curly, and adorned with several tiny white daisies. A handsome man in a basic black suit stood beside her, and she beamed with obvious adoration at him.

Kris had been twenty-three and at the end of her second year of law school when she met Carl. She was in the self-help section of the college library, trying—and failing—to reach a book on the top shelf of a bookcase.

Carl wasn't a student but had tagged along with a friend who was picking up study materials. He had noticed Kris struggling and came to her aid. Carl was tall and lean, and as he had risen on his toes to get the book, his Foo Fighters T-shirt rose as well, revealing well-defined abs. Kris had forced herself to look away from them and focused on his face instead. His light brown hair brushed the collar of his T-shirt, cut in layers that made it appear wavy. She had to twist her hands together to keep herself from reaching out to run her fingers through it.

As he handed her the book, he scanned her from head to toe in a way that made heat flood her cheeks before racing south to her more neglected areas. Flustered, she had stammered a "thank you" as she took the book from him and turned to leave.

"Hey, you forgot to pay my fee," he said, crossing his arms over his chest.

Kris had turned; one eyebrow raised. "Your fee? You want me to pay you for getting this down for me?"

He appeared to consider her question, then gave a slow nod. "Well, yeah. I provided a service. You should pay me for that service."

Kris, slipping into lawyer mode, retorted, "You retrieved this book without my requesting or contracting you to do so. There was no agreement made between us and no discussion of compensation. Therefore, you are not owed a fee."

Carl had grinned a dazzling, panty-dropping smile at her and said, "Well then, my mistake. Allow me to make it up to you with dinner tonight."

That smile had been the first strike to her defenses. A direct hit. She still couldn't remember what she had said but had managed something intelligible enough to turn down the invitation.

Kris didn't date. She didn't want to date. Relationships could be dangerous, and sex was something she avoided as well. She had made a promise to herself that relationships and sex were off-limits until she earned her law degree, and she was determined to keep it. She was confident that, despite what her mother kept telling her, she would have plenty of time to "find a man" once she had finished college. Once she felt stable. Once she was sure she could take care of herself, her mother, and her two siblings if the need arose. She had been perfectly content with that plan... until Carl.

He hadn't taken "no" for an answer. Carl returned to the college every day for two weeks to seek her out. She didn't know how he always found her, but she caught herself looking forward to the moments he would. When he did, he asked her out each time. And each time, she refused. The fifteenth day Carl asked her out, he had brought her a rose, smiled that smile, and threatened to continue stalking her until she went out with him.

His consistent attention had flattered Kris. She couldn't believe that someone like Carl would be interested in someone like her. He was so handsome, so charismatic and confident. She wasn't any of those things.

On a good day, Kris considered herself average. Neva constantly lectured her that if she just "tried a little bit," she would be a knockout. But Kris didn't want to try. She was perfectly happy being average. It made her almost invisible to men, and being invisible was peaceful and safe. Until Carl. Against every rule she had made for herself, and despite her internal warning system blaring like a tornado siren, Kris had agreed to go out with him. She believed that once Carl got to know her a bit, he would lose interest, and she could return to her anonymous existence. But it hadn't worked out that way.

The cat's tail twitched once more before it leaped and landed on Kris's stomach. With a grunt, Kris sat straight up in bed, flinging the wedding photo onto the carpeted floor. She blinked, trying to get her swollen, bloodshot eyes to focus. The cat stood on his hind legs and put both paws on her chest, his own wide eyes staring into her blurry ones. She scowled at her four-legged assailant. "Do you have to do that every morning, Alister?" The cat issued an unapologetic meow. "Yeah, I thought so, you little demon," she grumbled, scooping him up and scratching him lovingly under his chin.

She glanced at the alarm clock and sighed. 6:45 a.m. Time to get another day started—alone. She dropped Alistair onto the carpet and climbed out of bed, accidentally kicking the wedding photo. She picked it up and examined it for damage. Satisfied it was still intact, she ran one finger lovingly over Carl's image. The memories of that time felt like a million years ago. A million mistakes, and a million regrets ago.

On the six-month anniversary of their first date, in the self-help section of the college library where they had met, Carl asked Kris to marry him. This had seemed incredibly romantic to Kris, but she had been nervous about getting married before completing her law degree. Carl had brushed her concerns aside, assuring her he would provide for them until she landed a job after graduation. So, though still reluctant, Kris had agreed. They were married three months later in a small ceremony at the local courthouse.

It wasn't the wedding Kris had always dreamed of, but Carl had convinced her that a traditional wedding would be a waste of their meager income. She had chided herself for feeling disappointed. To want him to spend his money to meet her childish wedding expectations was selfish. She should feel lucky that someone like Carl wanted to marry her at all.

On their wedding day, Carl's parents, brother, and sister had attended their brief ceremony, but Kris had only invited her brother, Tom. She had wanted her mother there, but Neva was not a fan of Carl's. She had been very clear to Kris about what she thought of their union. Kris didn't want Neva broadcasting that view to everyone in the courthouse, which was sure to happen if Neva was drinking whiskey that day. And, of course, Neva would have been drinking whiskey. Kris's mother drank whiskey whenever she felt upset, angry, excited, tired, or disappointed in her children. Kris's wedding would have hit at least three of her mother's whiskey hot buttons.

Kris's little sister, Rachel, who had given birth to a baby girl just a few short weeks before her sixteenth birthday, was also absent from the ceremony. Rachel's venom for her family was at an all-time high, and there was no telling what she might have said or done to ruin Kris's special day. Rachel was also a little ashamed of her situation with the baby, which she would never admit, but didn't need to for Kris to know the truth of it. Regardless, inviting Rachel would have triggered drama that Kris did not want or need. Coupling that with the added drama that came from getting two or more of her family members together in one room would have been even worse. It was stressful enough on a normal day. For it to occur at the county courthouse on her wedding day would have been more than she could bear.

So, Kris had only invited Tom. He had shown up on time, in a nice suit, and had been respectful and silent during the ceremony. Afterward, he made polite small talk with Carl's family and congratulated her and Carl. Kris had been so proud of Tom. He couldn't have given her a better wedding gift. There had been no reception. Just a simple dinner with Carl's family before the two of them were driven to the airport to catch a honeymoon flight to the Bahamas. They'd had five blissful days of sun, sand, and lovemaking before they returned to Iowa, and the reality of their new life together. Six months later, the threads of their new union had begun to fray.

Kris placed the wedding photo back on the nightstand. "I can do this, I can do this," she mumbled to herself as she scrambled to pick up the dirty tissues scattered around the room. She made the bed hastily, pulled her pantsuit from the closet, and shooed Alistair from the room before marching into the adjoining bathroom.

Twenty minutes later, she was showered and standing in front of the full-length mirror. She had the features, skin, and bone structure to be a beautiful woman, but her choice in hairstyle and lack of makeup made Kris look a decade older than her thirty-eight years. Her eyes were a stunning shade of hazel blue that changed color with her mood. Sometimes they looked the same gorgeous aquamarine as her mother's. Other times, if she was upset or had been crying, they turned a deep lilac. Lately, her eyes had been lilac more often than not. She rarely wore makeup that would draw attention to them, except on special occasions when she would add a little mascara. Today was not one of those occasions. Today, she had to pull herself together enough to get through the normal motions of work and the reality of being alone.

Examining the puffy areas under her eyes, she sighed. Makeup would have been pointless, anyway. She was prone to bouts of crying these days, and the mascara wouldn't have made it past her lunch break. Tears gathered at the reminder. She blinked hard to keep them away, snatching her brush from the vanity drawer and pulling it hard through her hair. Her light brown hair was naturally wavy and long enough to hang to her bra line when she wore it down, which she almost never did. Wearing it down made her feel uncomfortable and a little vulnerable. So, most days, she kept it wrapped up tight in a plain hairstyle her mother referred to as a "bitch bun."

Kris kept her clothing just as plain. Today, she would wear a baggy, gray pantsuit which she referred to as "pantsuit number two." She had three identical suits in gray, the only difference being the color of the shell top that peeked out between the lapels of the jacket. Today's shell choice was pale blue. She also had two beige pantsuits, a navy pantsuit, and two identical black pantsuits. All equally baggy, all equally boring, and they all made her look equally frumpy.

Kris sighed at her reflection and pushed "Play" on her old CD player, positioned on the back of the toilet. A soothing voice providing self-esteem mantras emanated from its speakers. Kris spoke in unison with it as she placed the last pin in her bun. "I am a good person. I am perfect and whole. I am beautiful inside and out."

She stepped back and looked at herself in the mirror, smoothing her suit jacket and attempting to smile. Her lower lip quivered. She slapped her hand hard over her reflection and closed her eyes. "Pull it together, Kris. You cannot fall apart. You. Can't. Fall. Apart." She took a deep breath and counted to eight before releasing it slowly. With another breath, she ejected the CD from the player and hustled out of the bathroom into the hall.

Kris knocked once on the door closest to the stairs and then entered. Her fourteen-year-old son, Trent, lay sprawled on his back in bed, still fully dressed in the clothes he had worn the day before, and, as usual these days, every stitch was black. Trent was thin, with straight, glossy, dyed-black hair that almost touched his shoulders. Earbuds, which seemed to be permanently affixed inside his ears for the last six months, were plugged into an iPhone hidden in the front pocket of his jeans. Kris pulled the earbuds from her son's ears and shook him gently. "Trent. Trent. Come on, buddy, it's time to get ready for school. We're running late."

Trent moaned and opened one eye, focusing it on her. "I'm up. I'm up," he said, his voice still heavy with sleep.

She ruffled his hair and hurried out of the room, calling over her shoulder, "Fifteen minutes, Trent. Fifteen minutes or I leave without you!"

Twenty minutes later, Trent loped into the kitchen, a backpack thrown over one shoulder. Kris pulled a hot breakfast burrito from the microwave and covertly scanned her son's appearance. No matter how often she saw him looking like this, she just couldn't get used to it. What happened to the blue-eyed, joyful little guy who used to follow her around like a shadow? Where was the version of Trent that seemed to glow from the inside out with happiness? At least he isn't doing the ear gauge thing, she reassured herself.

She handed him the burrito, still scanning. No tattoos yet. None I can see, at least. Thank God, Kris thought. "All set, buddy?" she asked in the perky tone she had been practicing for weeks.

With a grunt and a nod, the alter ego of her son headed for the back door.

A few minutes later, with Trent riding shotgun, Kris pulled her silver Chevy Impala out of the garage and left the peace of the Walker acreage behind to begin the three-mile trek into town.

In the 1980s, Marion, Iowa, had been nothing more than a bloated small town with a population nearing twenty thousand. The only thing it really had going for it was its location as a bedroom community of the larger city of Cedar Rapids. Since then, Marion had sprawled outward in every direction, more than doubling its population. Today, it was difficult to tell where Marion ended, and Cedar Rapids began.

When she was a child, Kris would dream of the day when she would move as far away from Marion as she could get. Somewhere where no one knew her. Somewhere that was always warm, like Florida or California. With tons of opportunity and large populations to disappear into. It had sounded like heaven, and she promised herself she would do it. But, thanks to her family and her own poor decisions, that promise was another in a long list of promises to herself that she hadn't kept.

Instead, she had enrolled in the law program at the University of Iowa. This allowed her a bit of distance from her family, while staying close enough that she was available if they needed her. Which they frequently did. But the biggest, stupidest reason for not leaving Iowa had been marrying Carl.

Four months after their wedding, Carl had stopped having sex with her. Three weeks after that, he informed her he was unhappy in their marriage. He was no longer okay with his wife earning a law degree and continuing on to a cushy job as a lawyer, while he slaved away as a factory worker. It was a "turnoff," Carl had admitted with a sigh, and immediately followed that revelation with, "I think we should split up."

Kris had panicked. She had wept and begged him to stay, but he had been unmoved. She begged him to go to counseling with her. He refused. Finally, he held her face in his hands, looked into her eyes, and informed her the only way he would stay was if she quit school and worked to support them both while he earned his own degree.

"I've worked really hard for this, Carl. I can't quit school now. I only have one year left," she had tried to reason.

He had closed his eyes for a moment, shaking his head. When he opened them again, they were cold as they stared into hers. "I don't plan to be celibate for two more days. I sure as hell won't do it for another year."

Kris had pushed away from him and paced the room. "You're being unfair. What about all my hard work? It'll all be for nothing."

"Go back to school after I get my degree. You can pick up right where you left off."

Kris stopped pacing and faced him. "It's not that easy. They may not even take me back."

Carl flopped down on their sofa, tossing an arm casually across the back of it, and sighed. "Come on, Krissy girl, don't make me leave you over this," he chided her softly. "Who else will you find to love you like I do?"

The little strength Kris had been gathering drained away. He was right. She was lucky to have a man like Carl. Lucky to have a relationship and a future that would be normal. Her odds of finding that again, of finding any man who would love her, were slim. She was being selfish. If Carl needed to get his own degree to feel good about himself and their relationship, to feel attracted to her again, how could she deny him that? Wasn't it her job to make sure he felt loved and appreciated? They were married, and in a marriage, there should be compromise. There should be give and take. That's what all the books about marriage said. Was she being a "taker" by not being willing to give up her degree?

A bit more coaxing from Carl was all it took. She had agreed to quit school for the sake of their marriage, and they had conceived Trent that evening.

Kris's hands tightened on the steering wheel, and she suppressed a groan of anguish. If she had only known then what she knew now, things would have turned out differently. She wouldn't have Trent, though, and that thought was unbearable. Trent made everything she had endured with Carl seem worth it.

Never, in the fifteen years of their marriage, had the thought of leaving Carl ever occurred to her. No matter how neglected and unloved he made her feel. She didn't want Trent to suffer, or grow up without a father, because she didn't try hard enough. Kris believed that being a good parent meant putting your child's needs ahead of your own, and she thought that belief was something she and Carl shared. She had been very wrong. Ugh, she silently moaned to herself. How had I not known that about him?

Kris stole a worried glance at her son, startled to find him studying her.

He plucked one earbud from his ear. "What's wrong?"

Kris blinked innocently, turning her full attention back to the road. "What? Nothing's wrong." She could feel Trent's scrutiny deepen.

"Well, you look like something's wrong, and you were silently talking to yourself again," he said.

Kris tried to give a casual chuckle, but it stuck in her throat. She coughed to cover the failed attempt. "Nothing's wrong. I was just—I was just thinking about tonight. Grandma's party."

Trent threw his head back, expelling a deep, anguished groan.

Kris scowled at him. "Don't be like that, Trent. Be ready when I get home tonight. I don't want your grandma riding me for us being late."

"Who cares!? Why do you even put up with her shit?"

Kris shot him a warning glance. "She means well. She's just...different."

"Uncle Tom and Aunt Rachel don't jump through hoops every time she barks."

Kris took a deep breath and pushed the air back out with a sigh. "Yeah, well, Uncle Tom avoids conflict like the plague and Aunt Rachel has no patience for your grandma or anyone else. So, that just leaves me-"

"To put up with everybody's shit," Trent finished.

Kris pulled up to the high school, a long procession of cars pulling in behind her. "They're family, Trent."

"They're crazy, Mom," he fired back. "You should tell them all to go fu—"

Kris clapped a hand over his mouth. "Trenton David Walker! Don't even think about dropping an F-bomb in my car." She could feel Trent's smile under her palm and yanked her hand away, hoping to catch a glimpse before it disappeared. Too late. "You know, someday you'll have your own crazy family and—"

"No, I won't," Trent bristled.

Startled by the vehemence in his tone, Kris turned to face him. "What? Why not?"

Trent shrugged. "What's the point?"

Kris reached out to smooth the back of his hair. "Where's this coming from?"

Behind her, a man in a shiny Lexus sounded two quick beeps of his horn, signaling her to get moving.

Trent grabbed the door handle. "I better go," he said, opening the door.

Kris grabbed his backpack, holding him in place. "I want to talk about this later," she informed him in her best worried-mom tone.

The impatient man in the Lexus honked again, louder and longer, making her flinch. She looked over her shoulder nervously and back at Trent. "I'm sorry. I need to get out of this guy's way."

Trent rolled his eyes. "Whatever," he said, shaking his head as he got out of the car.

"Have a good day, honey!" she called after him.

Without a backward glance, he trudged across the front lawn of the high school. Kris watched him go, worried lines creasing her face. The Lexus honked again, making her jump. She waved apologetically at the owner and pushed her self-help CD into the car stereo as she pulled away from the school.

Within five blocks, she was feeling pretty good. "I am intelligent. I am beautiful. I am whole," she chanted, in sync with the soothing voice emanating from her car speakers. At the next stoplight, she looked at herself in the rear-view mirror and managed a smile that was almost real.

Glancing back at the road, she noticed a man and a shapely young woman coming out of a coffee shop on the opposite side of the street. Something about the man captured her attention. She squinted her eyes, trying to get a better look. The man stopped near the curb and pulled the woman in for a quick kiss. When he pulled away, he turned his head and Kris's worst nightmares took a giant, devastating leap into her reality. The hysterical screams of her inner voice instantly drowned the reassuring mantras emanating from her car stereo. He's kissing her in public! We're not even divorced yet, and he's, he's...

Every muscle in Kris's body seized, and her foot slammed the accelerator. Tires shrieked as the Impala roared through the red light, the image of Carl and that woman searing into her brain while she raced through traffic to escape the horror reflected in her rear-view mirror. Tears stung her eyes, smearing the world into streaks of color as she wrestled the tidal wave of rage and grief building in her throat. She had to pull over. She could feel herself spinning out of control, and she couldn't afford to let that happen. There was too much going on. Too many people depended on her. She had to keep it together. Flicking on her hazards, she veered onto a side street, gravel crunching under the tires as she jerked the car to the shoulder. Her hands trembled so violently she fumbled the gearshift twice before grinding it into park.

She sat there, rigid, fingers locked around the steering wheel like it was the only thing tethering her to sanity. She sucked in a breath—then another—praying for calm but it only seemed to expand the tornado in her chest. Kris let out a guttural scream, rattling the windows as her self-control shredded. Her palms pounded the steering wheel as she shrieked obscenities she had never used before. Her fist shot up, punching the roof of the car so hard it left a large dent. The sight of it made her even angrier, and she cursed Carl with every foul name she could think of.

This wasn't her. Kris didn't scream. She didn't curse or punch things. Keeping an even keel and appearing normal, even when she was angry or upset, was a skill she had spent decades honing into a thick shield that let her glide through life unruffled. That protection was gone now, destroyed by Carl's betrayal, the wreckage of her dreams, and the years she'd poured down the drain.

She knew she should calm down. If she kept this up, she would have to walk into work looking like a train wreck, but the torrent of emotion pouring out of her wouldn't cease. "That lowlife son-of-a-bitch!" she wailed, voice cracking into a sob. "After everything I gave up for him!" Snot and tears smeared her face, dripping onto her pantsuit, but she didn't notice. She didn't notice the patrol car as it pulled up behind her and parked, either.

She was banging her head repeatedly on the steering wheel as she berated herself for being weak and not taking her mother's advice of telling Carl to "go fuck himself," when a police officer approached the car and tapped cautiously on her window.

She screamed, a horror-movie shriek, one hand flying to her mouth, the other clutching her chest as Officer Miller's face loomed outside.

He waved awkwardly and stepped back, lips twitching as if fighting a smile.

Kris glanced in her rear-view mirror, mortified to see his police car parked behind her, lights flashing.

He motioned for her to roll down her window. She complied, jerkily cranking the window down, as she hastily wiped tears and snot from her face with the sleeve of her pantsuit.

The officer studied Kris for a moment, then glanced around inside the car before his eyes returned to hers. "Ma'am, are you okay?" he asked.

Kris wiped away another stream of free-flowing snot and forced a smile that was more of a grimace. "Yes, I'm fine," she lied, voice hoarse. "Just... just needed a minute, Officer... Miller," she said, squinting at his name tag.

He offered her a handkerchief, which she took with shaking fingers.

"Are you having car trouble?"

Kris shook her head.

"Are you hurt?" he asked.

Kris stared at him, her mind blank.

"Ma'am are you hurt?" he repeated.

"Hurt?" she echoed, tasting the word. "Am I hurt? Yeah..." she said, nodding her head. "Yes. I guess you could say that."

He bent forward, peering closely at her.

Her face twisted, fury crashing over her like a wave she couldn't hold back. "No. On second thought, 'hurt' doesn't even begin to cut it. Not even close. If I was being accurate, I'd say I was fucking robbed!" Her voice lurched from a growl to a shriek.

Officer Miller flinched, eyebrows shooting up as he edged back from the window, fingers twitching toward his holster.

Kris didn't stop—couldn't stop. "That son-of-a-bitch robbed me! He stole sixteen years—my youth, my law degree, my goddamn sanity—gone!" Her words cracked, splintering into a sob before snapping back to a snarl. "But he didn't stop there. Oh no, that wasn't enough. Nothing is ever enough for Carl Winston Walker! He had to go and rip my heart out of my 'not nearly large enough' chest too!" She threw up air quotes, mimicking Carl's smug drawl with a wild, mocking lilt.

Officer Miller's brows climbed higher. So did Kris's voice, shrill and unhinged. "I want to report a robbery. I want him arrested! I mean, if not robbery, it must count as some kind of assault, right? Can you throw his ass in jail for that?" Her nostrils flared, breaths heaving like a bull ready to charge. When he didn't answer, her eyes bulged wide, voice climbing another octave. "Well!? Can you?!"

He studied her face for a long moment, his look of concern melting into one of barely contained mirth. "Ma'am," he said, steady as a stone, "have you been drinking?"

• • • •

Forty-five minutes later, Kris pulled her car into a parking spot at Newburg and Grimes Law Office, her police escort close behind her. The adrenaline rush from her meltdown had long since dissipated and was replaced with mortification. Ducking down as far as she could in her seat, she glanced around the parking lot, praying no one had seen her pull in.

After establishing that she wasn't drunk, or physically hurt, Officer Miller had asked to see her license and retreated to his car. A few minutes later, he returned and asked her to step back to the police cruiser with him.

Kris had done this reluctantly, still vacillating between anger and heartbreak. Once in the police car, Miller offered her a box of Kleenex and gently extracted the story of how she arrived at the side of the road. His kind tone had calmed her. Within minutes, she had told him the sordid details of her failed marriage and the scene that had pushed her over the edge. He was sympathetic and joined her in chastising Carl's behavior. He even called Carl a "witless man-child," which made Kris snort with laughter.

But now, the extent of her revelations horrified her. She'd spilled her guts to a complete stranger! It was a wonder he hadn't thrown her in jail, or the nuthouse. She was a walking basket case and had acted like a complete lunatic. And now there would be a report somewhere in the annals of the police department that proved it. Dear God, could this day get any worse!?

Kris watched Officer Miller in her side mirror as he walked with a slow, deliberate swagger toward her car. For the first time since they met, she took notice of his physical appearance. He was tall, maybe six-one or six-two, and his olive complexion coupled with his dark hair hinted at Italian, Spanish, or maybe even Greek descent. He looked to be in his early forties, and she could tell he knew his way around a gym. Miller tapped on the car roof as he stepped up to her door. For the love of Pete, Kris thought to herself, what does he want now? To her utter horror, he opened the car door for her.

"Ms. Walker," he said, offering his hand.

Kris felt the blood rush to her face as she took his hand and stepped from the car. "Thank you, Officer. I should be fine now," she whispered, fumbling with her keys so she didn't have to look at him.

He bent his head, attempting to make eye contact. "Are you sure?" he asked.

"Yes, I'm sure. I'm sorry for the inconvenience and for—everything else," she offered with a wave of her hand, finally meeting his gaze.

Kris saw genuine concern in his eyes, and her chest tightened in response. How long had it been since someone looked at her like that? Had someone ever looked at her like that? She felt a shiver run up her spine and shook off the thought. She didn't want to think about it. Everything was still too raw and her control still too tenuous. "Thank you," she said with a curt nod, before hurrying toward the building.

Robin Johnson was sitting at her desk, speaking to a client on her headset, when Kris entered the office. Determined not to make eye contact with Robin, Kris kept her head down, making a beeline for the women's restroom. Robin snapped her fingers at Kris as she passed, attempting to get her attention but Kris pretended not to notice, quickening her pace.

Kris loved her friend, but the last thing she wanted to do was explain why she had gotten a police escort to work while the entire office eavesdropped.

Robin was an attractive black woman in her late thirties and one of Kris's only friends. Kris had joined Newburg and Grimes as a paralegal fifteen years ago, and Robin had started on the same day. They bonded instantly as newbies, and their relationship had deepened over the years to one of close friends.

Robin was outgoing and fun, with wit and a sense of humor that never failed to make Kris laugh. She was beautiful, confident, outspoken, and had a vulgar streak that usually left Kris appalled and awed in equal measure. Robin's tales of her wild weekends were the highlight of Kris's Mondays, sparking daydreams about what it would be like if she was a free spirit like Robin—but those daydreams never lingered, snuffed out by the grim weight of her reality.

Once in the bathroom, Kris had only managed one session of dry heaving into the toilet and two deep breaths before Robin knocked on the door. Kris snatched tissues from the box on the counter and dabbed at her puffy, red-rimmed eyes as she tried to calm down.

Robin knocked again. "Kris, it's me. Let me in," Robin whispered.

Kris unlocked the door and opened it just far enough to pull Robin inside before locking it again. Arms wrapped tightly around her middle; she turned to face her friend.

Robin studied Kris's face for a moment. "Carl?" she asked.

Kris dropped her arms to her sides as if exhausted and nodded.

"Oh, honey, I'm sorry," Robin said, pulling Kris into a hug.

"I feel like such an idiot." Kris groaned. "I saw Carl with her this morning and had a meltdown in my car. I was almost arrested."

Robin pulled away, abruptly. "Arrested? What exactly did you do? How'd the cops get involved?"

"He thought my car broke down, or I needed help," Kris sighed. "Then I freaked out on him and demanded he go arrest Carl. Or something like that. I don't know. Honestly, it's all a blur. But the next thing I knew, I was spilling my life story to the guy."

Robin barked out a laugh. "Are you shittin' me?"

"Not shitting. Then he gave me a police escort to work," Kris said, rolling her eyes.

Robin cocked her hip and rested a hand on it. "What? Why—to make sure you made it here without another meltdown?"

"I guess." Kris shrugged. "It was so humiliating."

Robin grinned. "Was he hot?"

"Who? Officer Miller?"

"Ooo, Officer Miller. Even his name sounds hot," Robin said, waggling her eyebrows.

"I wasn't paying attention to that. I was too upset about Carl."

Robin captured Kris's face in her hands, not allowing her to break eye contact. "You've got to get that man out of your mind."

"I don't know how to do that," Kris whined.

"Yeah, well, I do. You need to get another man into your panties."

Kris snorted. "There isn't a man within fifty miles who'd want in my panties."

Robin released Kris's face and leaned back, looking Kris up and down. "Not looking like that, they won't. You have to let me hook you up with some style! You are too young to be dressing like somebody's grandma. Before you know it, you'll actually be a grandma, and you'll regret all this." Robin said, with a gesture encompassing Kris's whole body.

Kris let out a sob, covering her face with her hands.

"What's wrong? What did I say?" Robin asked, alarmed.

"Carl said I dress like a grandma, too!" Kris howled.

Robin grimaced, pulling Kris into another hug and letting her cry it out.

Chapter 2:
Neva Stevenson

Neva Stevenson grabbed a Texas Fifth of Maker's Mark whiskey off the grocery shelf and deposited it carefully into her cart. She glanced up and down the aisle, checking to see if anyone was watching, before hastily snatching another. It was April thirtieth, and to Neva, that was the best excuse for an extra bottle of whiskey she could think of. If anyone had a problem with a woman buying herself a little comfort on her birthday, they could just go to hell.

She turned fifty-eight today, but you'd never guess it. Soft worry lines and crow's feet framed her striking aqua-green eyes, yet she could still pass for a woman in her early forties. Her flawless makeup highlighted her elegant bone structure, while her wavy, shoulder-length hair, blonde threaded with silver, shimmered under the grocery store's harsh fluorescents. Tall and long-legged, she clicked along the tiled floors in two-inch heels, her curves filling out a turtleneck sweater and black slacks like a sex symbol from a bygone era. At fifty-eight, she still turned heads—and she damn well knew it.

Neva spotted an empty checkout lane and rushed her cart into it. With quick movements, she unloaded its contents- bending over the side of the cart to grab the last few items. As she straightened, she noticed the man in line behind her had his eyes firmly fastened on her ass. Neva's gaze narrowed pointedly at him, but he didn't seem to notice. She smirked, amused by his shameless fixation. At least he had focus—so many men didn't these days.

Enough was enough, though. She wasn't a sideshow. She cleared her throat, snapping her fingers between his gaze and her ass. His focus jerked to her face. Lifting her chin, she glared down her nose at him. "You can't afford it," she said, voice flat as a slammed door.

The man reddened, shifting his focus to the array of candy bars on the aisle display.

The cashier giggled and offered Neva a fist bump. Reluctantly, Neva bumped fists with her.

The young woman looked to be in her early twenties, with a round pixie-like face and a black ponytail streaked with purple and hot pink that sat high on her head. A white name tag, pinned to her smock, identified her as Roxxy—with two x's. Roxxy's makeup was thick and outrageously colorful, making her look like she belonged either in the circus or on a street corner. Neva couldn't decide which.

She studied Roxxy with a mix of frustration and fascination as the woman chewed gum with nervous ferocity while scanning Neva's grocery items at a snail's pace. The time between each scanner beep dragged out like a taunt, needling her patience to the breaking point.

Roxxy scanned the two bottles of whiskey and paused, eyebrows arching. "That's a lot of booze. You having a party?" she asked, grinning. Her large, red-rimmed mouth made her look like an addled clown, lipstick bleeding into the fine lines around her lips.

"Yes," Neva said, silently deciding the circus was where Roxxy would fit best.

"Coool," Roxxy breathed and continued scanning, her long acrylic nails clicking against each item. When she had finally scanned the last item, she looked up with practiced cheerfulness. "Your total is two hundred eighty-three dollars and nine cents. Would you like to purchase a lottery ticket?"

"No, thank you."

"Are you sure?" Roxxy prodded. "I'm reminding everyone to get their tickets for the big drawing tomorrow! It's a record state jackpot. Forty-five million dollars! The store that sells the lucky ticket gets a million, and our store manager said he'll split it up between all the employees if it's us!"

Neva fumbled for the credit card in her wallet. "Wow. Well, good luck with that."

"So? You want one, then? It's for a good cause, too. If our store wins, I'm gonna use the money to get my boobs done, 'cause my boyfriend, Rob, he thinks they should be more like this—" Roxxy grabbed her breasts and, pushing them together, hoisted them high on her chest in demonstration. With her breasts bulging out of the top of her smock, she leaned forward for Neva to get a better look. "What do you think?" she asked. "Much better, right?"

Startled, Neva glanced at the other customers waiting in line behind her and noticed the eyes of the same man riveted on Roxxy's chest. Embarrassed for the girl, Neva grabbed a dollar from her wallet, stabbing it into the air between his eyes and Roxxy's display. "You've convinced me. I'll take a ticket."

Roxxy beamed with delight, and to Neva's relief, and the man's disappointment, Roxxy's breasts resumed their natural position.

With the groceries and whiskey safely stored in the trunk of her Chrysler 300, Neva began the short drive home with her windows down and the radio blaring. It was a gorgeous day, with the temperature hovering near seventy degrees. Neva had always loved springtime in Iowa. The smell of rain and fresh-turned earth in the air, along with the vibrant colors of the trees and flowers, was how she always imagined heaven.

It always feels like anything is possible in the spring. Like you can put the past behind you and get a clean slate, she thought, smiling to herself. The perfect time of year for a birthday.

As she waited for the stoplight to change, she admired the freshly planted flowers outside Marion Square Park. A couple was walking their dog, and a few young children were playing on the park equipment, their mothers standing nearby or watching from benches that lined the play area. A group of teenagers milled around near the fountain at the park entrance. One of them, who Neva thought looked no older than fourteen, was smoking a cigarette. Neva watched as he took a long drag, and her fingers itched to walk over and snatch it out of his hand.

A girl in the group was sitting on the edge of the fountain, making out with a scruffy-looking teen who had his hand up the girl's shirt. Neva winced. Young girls these days seemed to have no respect for themselves. She wondered what the girl's mother would say if she saw her daughter doing that. The grabby boy she was tangling tongues with could have been homeless. His faded jeans looked like they hadn't been washed in some time. His stretched-out t-shirt, which at one time must have been black, had faded to a dirty gray. Neva couldn't see most of his face, as it was busy devouring the girl, but she could tell that his hair was a greasy black and in obvious need of a good cut. She couldn't tell what the girl looked like or how old she was with the boy adhered to her face, but guessed she couldn't have been much older than fourteen or fifteen.

Neva shook her head as the light turned green and the car in front of her started across the intersection. Just as she let off the brake, the girl pulled away from the greasy boy and threw back her hair with a practiced flip. Neva's stomach dropped. She craned her neck to get a better look; her knuckles whitening on the steering wheel. Was that her granddaughter?! No, surely it wasn't Kim, was it? The girl stood up and turned in Neva's direction, the familiar profile confirming her worst suspicions.

Heedless of traffic, Neva jerked the wheel to the left and tromped the gas. The car's tires squealed in protest as the back end completed an abrupt U-turn and she sped toward the offending teens. The Chrysler jumped the curb with a bone-jarring thud and came to a stop within five feet of her granddaughter and the dirty groper she was with, sending pigeons scattering in panic.

The boy stared, his mouth hanging open, one hand frozen mid-air where it had been reaching for Kim, as Neva exited the car and advanced on them with thunderous purpose. Kim's eyes widened in fear when she realized who the crazy woman driving the car was. She scanned her surroundings, calculating escape routes, as if she would make a run for it.

Neva fixed her with a steely glare. "Don't even think about it."

Kim froze and swallowed hard as Neva came to a halt in front of them.

"You," Neva said, pointing at Kim. "Don't move."

Then she turned her full attention to the scruffy boy. "If you so much as think about coming near my granddaughter again, I will hunt you down and make sure those hands and that penis lose all feeling and function," she hissed, stabbing the air near his anatomy with her index finger.

The boy's eyes widened, and he took a step back.

Neva moved closer to him, her face within inches of his. "You understand me?"

The boy nodded. Neva spun on her heel, grabbing Kim by the arm and walking her toward the car.

"Let go of me. I'm not going with you!" Kim declared, trying to jerk her arm away.

Neva's grip tightened, and Kim yelped in protest. Reaching the passenger door, Neva pulled it open with her free hand and pushed Kim toward it. Kim looked from the open car door to her grandmother in steely defiance.

"You can get in the car yourself or I can put you in it," Neva said, eyes squinted.

Kim squinted her own eyes, staring daggers, and didn't move.

Kim's appearance—long, messy, sandy blonde hair partially hiding her heavily made-up face, full lips, and curvy figure—reminded Neva of her youngest daughter Rachel, fifteen years ago.

How many times had she seen that same look on Rachel's face? Too many to count. It seems, Neva thought with a heavy internal sigh, the apple isn't falling far from the tree. Great. Just great. She would be damned if she stood by and let the train wreck that had derailed her youngest child happen all over again with her granddaughter.

Neva pointed at the car. "In! Now!"

Kim threw herself down into the passenger seat and slammed the door so hard the window rattled.

Neva turned to shoot one last poisonous glare at the teen boy before walking around the car and climbing in.

Once back on the road, she stole a glance at Kim, who was staring straight ahead, pouting and silent. Unable to stay silent herself, Neva confronted the situation head-on. "Just what in hell do you think you were doing back there?"

"Nothing," Kim huffed.

"Nothing? That boy had his hands all over you. Why would you let him do that? And in a public place, for God's sake!"

"I like him, Grandma! That's what you do when you like somebody, and you want them to like you back."

Neva blinked rapidly, stunned by the stupidity of Kim's statement. "Kim, you don't get a boy to like you by letting him feel you up! If that's all it took, every prostitute in America would be a happy housewife."

Kim let out a frustrated moan. "Whatever. You made me look like a complete freak."

"Honey, you accomplished that all by yourself," Neva said, reaching out to brush Kim's hair away from her face.

Kim jerked away, accidentally banging her head against the passenger window.

Neva focused her attention back on the road. "Does your mother know you're wearing so much makeup?"

Kim rolled her eyes, rubbing her head and pulling down the mirrored visor to look at herself. "She doesn't care what I do, as long as I stay out of her way. Besides, I look hot like this."

"Is that what your pimp tells you?"

Kim slammed the visor back in place. "I'm so glad you're not my mother. I don't know how Mom could stand growing up with you."

"Well, in a few minutes, you'll get the chance to ask her," Neva replied sweetly.

Kim sat up straighter in the seat. "Why? Where're we going?"

"To talk to your mother."

"So, what? You're just going to nark me off?"

Neva smiled at Kim, batting her eyelashes wildly. "Absolutely."

"God! I hate you!"

"Most people do, dear," Neva said, patting Kim's leg.

Kim folded her arms over her chest and glared straight ahead.

A few minutes later, they arrived in downtown Cedar Rapids. Neva parked in front of an old red brick building with a large green door. A neon sign displayed a large green shamrock and the words 'Lucky's Bar' above it. Neva opened the door for Kim and ushered her inside.

Only a handful of patrons occupied the seats surrounding the long mahogany bar, and two couples sat in booths at the opposite end of the room. Unlike most bars in the area, Lucky's was clean and tastefully decorated. Tiffany-style pendant lighting hung over the bar and booths, reflecting light through their emerald and ivory-tinted glass. The walls were all a dark green, except for the one behind the bar, which was off white. A large shelf hung at the center of the white wall between two large rectangular mirrors. Pictures of Neva's dead husband, Robert, along with a few trinkets that belonged to him, adorned the shelves.

Among the photos was a framed newspaper article from 1986. The article announced the grand opening of Lucky's on the front page and featured a picture of Robert standing, arms crossed and serious, in front of the bar. A much younger version of Neva smiled and posed, as if pouring a drink, just behind him. Seeing it sent a chill up Neva's spine. She cleared her throat and stood straighter, shaking it off.

"Sit right there while I talk to your mother," she said, pointing at the nearest booth.

Kim huffed in reply but threw herself down into the booth.

Lois, Neva's closest and dearest friend, looked up from the beer cooler. "Hey, Neevie! Happy birthday!!" she exclaimed, beaming.

Lois Evans was a buxom woman in her early sixties with bleach blonde hair that seemed to always display about an inch of salt and pepper regrowth at the roots. The deep lines on her face were evidence of the hard lifestyle she had lived, but the adventurous glint in her brown eyes declared it had been a wild and exciting ride that put them there.

Lois had been the first employee Neva and Robert hired when they opened the bar, and it didn't take long before the two women became close friends.

Lois had been a godsend during the time after Robert's death. Neva didn't have any other friends—Robert had made damn sure of that. She had no siblings she could rely on and hadn't been in contact with her parents since she married Robert. She had no intention of seeking help from them after being estranged for so long. Her pride and her shame just wouldn't allow it.

On the night of Robert's death, the police had deposited Neva's kids on Lois's doorstep with nothing but the clothes on their backs. Lois had taken them all in without a question or complaint. She had been there for Neva through the seesaw of anger and depression, the horrible nightmares...and the debilitating guilt.

Those first few years, Neva had fought to keep her sanity like the captain of a ship sailing through a storm. In the back of her mind, she knew if she fell completely apart, the state would take her kids. She couldn't let that happen. The three of them had already been through too much. Neva couldn't bear to think about the additional damage the foster system would inflict on them. She had wanted to help them. Wanted to "fix" the damage she knew had already been done, but she was still so broken herself, it seemed a task too monumental to tackle.

So, she handled it in the only way she knew how. She ignored it. Ignored the problems with the kids, the past, her future, their future—all of it. For four years, she pretended none of it had ever happened and she was someone else. A sexy, tough, confident, single woman, who had three kids and her shit together. "Fake it till you make it" was the only mantra she cared to live by. Unfortunately, keeping up that façade was no simple task, and almost always required the assistance of booze. A lot of booze. There were also a lot of men. She couldn't seem to get enough of the men. Never for more than a few nights, and never around the kids, but she had her fill. And this time, she was the one in control.

In those lost years, Lois had been right there in the trenches of debauchery with her, but she had also kept Neva from going too far. Later, Neva came to realize it had been a full-time job for Lois.

Those were the darkest years of Neva's life, and she wasn't proud of her behavior from back then, but she had needed it. Without it, she wasn't sure if she would have been able to cope and put herself back together again. Her biggest regret was that, while she was fighting so hard to keep herself together, she hadn't been the mother her kids had needed.

Every time she had looked at Kris back then, waves of guilt threatened to pull her under. The girl had gone quiet, retreating somewhere deep inside herself. Neva didn't know how to reach her, and no amount of therapy seemed to help. Tom had been just the opposite, crying at the slightest amount of stress, wanting to be near Neva all the time, and constantly needing hugs. Every one of those hugs reminded her of what a terrible mother she had been, and how damaged her kids were because of it. Rachel had been the worst of all. She cried at night, wanting her daddy, and she became relentlessly stubborn. No matter what Neva had asked Rachel to do, Rachel refused. She didn't want Neva to tuck her in, didn't want to sit on her lap, didn't want her hugs. Kris was the only person Rachel wanted or would listen to.

Lois had also been there for Neva on the days when she couldn't ignore everything and was too weak to pretend. And the nights when Neva was deep in the whiskey and wracked with guilt about the kids, or sobbing and suicidal. Somehow, Lois would always convince her to keep moving forward, calming her down and helping to scrape together what little sense and sanity Neva had left. Lois had been her rock, her confidante, her therapist, and a second mother to the kids. Neva didn't know how she could ever repay her friend for that.

"Hi, Lo!" Neva replied, stepping up to the bar.

"What can I get ya, birthday girl? Jim and Coke?"

"No, thanks. I need to talk to Rachel. Is she still here?"

Lois winked at her before turning to yell over her shoulder, "HEY RACH! YOUR MOM NEEDS YA!"

"Well, I could have done that," Neva chided.

Lois shrugged. "So why didn't ya?"

Rachel popped her head out from the stockroom and held up one finger.

Early afternoon was the best time to take inventory and place any orders the bar needed. Neva realized she must have caught Rachel in the middle of it. She waved Rachel back into the storeroom and turned her attention to Lois. "So, how's it going today? Seems slow."

Lois made a motion as if brushing away Neva's comments and began cleaning bar glasses in the sink. "Nah. About normal for this time. Everything's good. Sucks that I can't do dinner with you and the kids, but the new girl flaked out on us, and Rach needs somebody here to keep an eye on things." Lois turned off the sink brushes and leaned in conspiratorially. "Next weekend, though, it's you and me and a bottle of thirty-year-old scotch I finagled off our delivery driver," she said, waggling her eyebrows.

"Finagled, huh? What did that entail?"

"Just you never mind. It's for your birthday, and there is no length I won't go to help you celebrate that divine day," she said, smiling beatifically while creating a halo above her head with her hands.

Neva threw a bar towel at her friend, chuckling. "Oh, I'm well aware of the lengths you'll go. I'm just worried about the poor delivery driver."

Lois snapped the towel at Neva and leaned over the bar, her eyes glinting with wicked delight. "Speaking of birthdays... do you remember your thirty-fifth? Those Marines that stopped in after their flight was canceled, remember?"

Neva nodded, giving a soft cat-call whistle.

"I know, right?" Lois mused. "Those boys were hotter than a Louisiana crab boil! And those muscles! You were convinced they were strippers I hired for your birthday," she chuckled, giving Neva's arm a squeeze. "and you got that big one to take his—"

Neva spotted Rachel approaching out of the corner of her eye. "Shhh," she warned, tilting her head slightly in Rachel's direction.

Lois went silent, pulling her lips in and making her eyes go round.

Rachel looked back and forth between the two women. "What's up with you two?"

"Nothin', honey. Me and your mom were just chattin'," Lois said. "Have a great birthday dinner, Neeves. Call me tomorrow," she said, blowing Neva a kiss and slapping Rachel's ass before hustling to the other end of the bar.

Rachel was a beautiful woman and Neva's obvious genetic offspring. She had passed the same striking aqua-blue eyes, strong cheekbones, and statuesque frame to her daughter. And, although Rachel's blonde, wavy, hair was longer, it was nearly identical to how Neva's had looked twenty years ago. Rachel was stylish, too, and carried herself in the same confident way that Neva did. The only difference being the sizeable chip on Rachel's shoulder.

Rachel regarded Neva warily. "Mom, what are you doing here?"

"That's what I'm doing here." Neva said, jerking her thumb over her shoulder at Kim, who sat in the booth staring at one of the wall-mounted TVs.

"What happened? Is she alright?" Rachel asked, alarmed.

"No, she is most definitely not alright. I found her outside the park, attached by the tongue to some dirty-looking boy. He had his hands all over her."

Rachel's shoulders dropped and she gave a sigh of relief. "Christ, Mom. I thought it was something serious."

At this, Neva's eyebrows shot up to her hairline.

Rachel rolled her eyes. "Calm down. Kim is a fifteen-year-old girl who recently discovered boys. It's perfectly natural for a teenager to do that kind of stuff."

Neva leaned over the bar so she could speak without being overheard. "Is that how you're bringing her up?" she hissed. "News flash! Your daughter hasn't 'recently discovered' anything. And just so you know, there is nothing natural about letting a boy molest you in public!"

Rachel jerked her hands off the bar and folded her arms across her chest, glaring at Neva with squinted eyes.

And there it was. The same look Kim had given Neva just thirty minutes prior. The "it's all your fault and I hate you for it" look. She knew what was coming next, too.

"I'm not sure you should be lecturing me on the finer points of parenting," Rachel snapped.

And there was part two. The defensive, snarky comment. Neva rolled her eyes. "For heaven's sake, Rachel, grow up before Kim ends up making the same mistakes you did."

Rachel's jaw tightened. "Thank you for picking her up. I'll take it from here," she snapped, then spun on her heel and stormed toward the other end of the bar. Lois was there, balancing a large tray of empty beer bottles as Rachel closed the distance.

Lois sidestepped Rachel to avoid the collision, struggling to keep her balance. The beer bottles wobbled and clinked in ominous protest, but remained upright. Lois watched Rachel's angry retreat for a moment before setting the tray down and turning to scowl at Neva. "What in the world did you say to that girl, now!?"

Chapter 3:
Tom Stevenson

In a small, two-bedroom house on the edge of Marion, Tom Stevenson was getting his two young daughters ready for his mother's birthday party. Toys and stuffed animals littered the floor and overflowed from a large Disney princess-themed toy box that sat in one corner of their bedroom. Dress-up clothes and costumes covered the two twin-size beds. A small table with four chairs sat in the middle of the room, adorned with a miniature tea set and a small plate of cookies.

Ashlea Stevenson, age six, and her four-year-old sister, Megan, were taking turns admiring themselves in the full-length mirror. Tom had decked the little girls out in lacy pink dresses, hot pink ballerina slippers, and purple feather boas. Beaming with pride, Ashlea bounced up and down next to him. "Thank you, daddy! Thank you, daddy! Thank you, daddy!" Each exclamation punctuated with another hop.

Tom patted his bouncing daughter on the head, her silky hair sliding beneath his palm, and scooped up her little sister with practiced ease. Megan planted a wet kiss on his cheek, her small arms wrapping around his neck with fierce affection.

Tom, wearing only a clean white T-shirt and blue jeans, was underdressed compared to his party-ready daughters. His hazel eyes sparkled with mirth, crinkling at the corners, and the dimple in his left cheek was making a rare appearance—a small crater of joy that only emerged in moments of genuine happiness.

He glanced at his own reflection in the mirror, and his smile faltered. He had already combed his hair, but as usual, the dark brown mass had a mind of its own. No matter what he did to tame it or how he had it cut, it always looked like he had just climbed out of bed. In his early twenties, when he was still dating, his hair was the feature women seemed to like most. That benefit made him like it, too—then. But he hated it now. At thirty-three years old, the shaggy mane still made him look like an unkempt teenager. Once, he had considered shaving it all off and starting over, but his mother had put the kibosh on that idea with one of her "life alerts."

"There will come a day when that beautiful mop is gone, and you'll feel like a giant ass for not appreciating it when you had the chance," she warned.

His mother was full of what he and his sisters called "life alerts". Her little pieces of advice about everything from picking your nose to child-rearing, that always seemed more like threats or harbingers of doom than actual helpful advice. Behind her back, they would poke fun at her attempts to guide them, but Tom rarely went against his mother's advice. This was a fact that drove his youngest sister crazy. Rachel had made it her life's goal to never take their mother's advice, and then usually paid for it by suffering the exact repercussions Neva had warned her about. And that fact drove him crazy.

Watching Rachel fall on her face always stirred up his anxiety and only reinforced his resolve to listen to his mother. Tom had always had what his mother referred to as "a nervous demeanor" which, she told him on numerous occasions, was a "blessing in disguise". Swearing that it would keep him thin and make him the envy of everyone he knew by the time he was forty-five. When he was a kid, that explanation had soothed him. However, by the time he was sixteen, he had learned that his "nervous demeanor" was actually moderate anxiety that would sometimes trigger debilitating anxiety attacks—just one more item on his list of personality traits that made him feel ridiculous and weak.

When he was seventeen, Tom learned that working out helped vent his nervous energy, which lessened the attacks. So, he started spending four days a week in the gym, building endurance and toning his muscles. His height and lanky frame didn't allow for Schwarzenegger-style bulk, but he looked fit, and it helped him function, so the workouts had remained part of his daily routine ever since.

Tom ran his hand through his messy hair and grinned at his daughters in the mirror. "I'm so lucky to be escorted to a party by a perfect pair of princesses!" he said, placing Megan back on her feet and bowing low to each one of them.

"That's a tongue twister, Daddy!" Ashlea declared.

Tom froze as if hit by a stun gun. "Holy moley. You're right, you clever girl. Quick! Say it three times fast. Perfect pair of princesses, perfect pair of princesses, perfect pair of princesses."

The little girls made the attempt, but their tongues tangled immediately, and they erupted into a fit of giggles.

Tom laughed with them, spinning Megan in a circle like a ballerina as he repeated the tongue twister.

"Now me! Spin me, Daddy!" Ashlea squealed.

He was spinning both girls when Patty appeared in the bedroom doorway.

Tom had been twenty-four when he first met Patty. He hadn't been looking for a relationship; his focus had been on his goal of leaving Iowa to attend Colorado University. Tom hadn't made the decision to attend college out of state until a year after high school graduation, eager to go, but wrestling with the guilt of wanting to leave his mom and sisters behind. He settled for completing his general credits at a local community college and saving up for the move to Colorado U. He wanted to attend school and explore Colorado without worrying about money. On the meager wage he had been earning, it would mean waiting at least three years before he could save enough, but that was okay. A fair compromise that would give his family time to get used to the idea of him leaving, while allowing him to save money for the experience.

By the time he met Patty, Tom had saved close to thirty thousand dollars and was just three months shy of his goal.

Patty had been so different back then—so confident, fun, and full of life. It hadn't taken long for Tom to fall hard. He tried to convince her to come with him to Colorado, but she wanted no part of it. Patty's parents had money and a chain of successful car dealerships. They required nothing of her, and she was more than content to live up to their minimal expectations. As the time for Tom to leave drew closer, she worked harder to convince him to stay, ultimately persuading him to hold off on college for one more year.

That one year turned into two. By the middle of their second year together, Patty was drinking a lot and nagging Tom to join her at nightclubs. He grew tired of her partying lifestyle and, by the end of their second year, he knew he needed to make the break. He enrolled at Colorado University for the fall semester and planned to leave the first week of August. When he broke the news to Patty, she went crazy. She screamed obscenities in his face as she pushed and shoved him in a fit of rage. She had even thrown a beer bottle at his head, which he dodged at the cost of his car's windshield. It was a side of her he had never seen, and it only made him more determined to go.

Several days later, she issued a tear-filled apology and snuggled up to him as if nothing had ever happened. She swore she understood his choice and promised to make the time they had left together wonderful. And it was.

Then, two weeks before Tom was scheduled to leave, Patty informed him she was pregnant. They had been using protection, so he was stunned by the news, but once the realization of the situation sank in, every thought of himself and the plans he had for college evaporated. He was going to be a father. So, he did what he thought was the right thing and asked Patty to marry him.

When Tom told his mother, Neva had thrown a fit to rival one of Patty's, crying and begging Tom not to go through with it. He had never seen his mother cry when she was sober, and it had frightened him a little. Neva had never liked Patty, and the revelation that Tom was planning to marry her, out of obligation, was too much. She even offered him money. He refused to listen. Patty was having his child, and he saw it as an opportunity to be the type of father his own father had never been.

They were married two months later, in a lavish, hastily organized wedding that Patty's parents insisted on. Then, Tom used his college savings to rent them a small house and outfit a nursery for the baby. When Ashlea was born, he thought he would explode from the joy of holding her in his arms. It completely and irrevocably altered something inside of him, and from that moment, he threw himself into being a husband and father with the single-mindedness of a devoted monk.

When Megan came along, not quite two years later, he felt it all over again. Nothing was more important than his daughters. Nothing. But Patty, it seemed, hadn't felt the same way. By the time Megan began crawling, their lives had settled into a vicious cycle of dysfunction.

Patty frequently stayed out all night at the bars. And when she wasn't drinking, she was flying into violent rages that usually left Tom scratched and bruised. She seemed to resent her daughters and would sometimes refuse to care for them during the day, even if Tom needed to work.

Patty would often call Tom at work, threatening to leave him and demanding he come home. When he did, he would arrive to find her in a rage, passed out, or gone, and the children left home alone. Sometimes Patty would disappear for days, and he would have to rely on his mother and Kris for help while he tried to continue working.

Just when he would reach the end of his rope, Patty would calm down and become 'normal' again. She would apologize, smother him with love, and swear to be a good mother to their daughters. Things would get better for a while. Then, without warning, it would all fall apart again.

He found it all exhausting and humiliating. Tom's employers would eventually tire of his excuses and frequent absences, and he would lose his job. At last count, he had lost nine jobs because of Patty. Two days ago, that number became an even ten.

Tom watched Patty lean against the doorframe, holding a beer in one hand and a lit cigarette in the other. Despite her expertly applied makeup, she looked pale and haggard underneath. She had been an attractive woman in her twenties, but the sun was already setting on Patty's youth. Her naturally auburn hair was now a bright shade of red, which she claimed made her look younger and feel sexier. Tom secretly thought it was more orange than red and made her look like 'Flo' from the old Mel's Diner sitcom. Today, she had the red mass piled atop her head in a messy bun, and she stared out at him from under the fringe of her bangs.

"Aren't you three ready yet?" Patty said before taking a long drag from her cigarette. She tilted her head back, blowing the smoke toward the ceiling.

Tom spun both girls in a circle. "Princess Ashlea and Princess Megan are ready and awaiting their carriage, Queen Patty," he said.

Both girls curtsied for their mother.

Without a hint of interest, Patty held out her empty beer can to Ashlea. "Great. Go get Mommy a new beer."

Ashlea's smile faltered, but she took the empty can obediently and, with Megan hot on her heels, dashed out of the bedroom.

Tom grabbed Patty around the waist, pulling her to him. "Remember that time we did it in the back of that bedding store I worked at on King Street?" he said, nuzzling her neck.

Patty pushed away from him. "Don't start. This isn't gonna help."

"Patty, it's just a couple of hours."

She flicked her cigarette ash onto the floor between them. "I said I'd go. I didn't say I wanted to."

"I know you don't want to, but it's her birthday and it'll make her happy."

Patty rolled her eyes and took another drag of her cigarette.

Tom rubbed one hand over the back of his neck, feeling an unpleasant tingle at the thought of what he needed to say next. "And, just for tonight...please don't drink. Please. I don't want her to see us fighting again."

Patty backed up a step, an angry set to her jaw.

His stomach flipped. He had to defuse this situation—and fast. He lifted his hands toward her, palms up. "It's just one night. That's all I ask, just—"

Patty slapped his hands out of the air between them. "If you expect me to spend the night around your family, drinking is part of the deal."

Tom dropped his arms to his sides and took a deep, defeated breath.

Ashlea and Megan danced back into the room, and Ashlea curtsied again for her mother before handing her the beer. Patty took it from her without acknowledgment and held it a few inches from Tom's face as she popped the top.

Chapter 4:
The Party

Kris and Trent were late. She'd hoped to arrive before at least one of her siblings, but both their cars were already sitting in her mom's driveway. Dang it. Neva had warned her not to be late, smirking over her coffee as Kris promised she'd make it on time. "We'll see," she had said, in a tone dripping with doubt. Kris had been determined to prove her wrong this time, and now here she was, pulling up twenty minutes late.

As she stepped out of the car, Kris studied the house and felt her heart swell with nostalgia, each familiar detail igniting cherished memories. Light from the living and dining-room windows spilled onto the porch that spanned the front of the home. Though nestled in the heart of the Midwest, the house felt as if it had been plucked from the South and dropped here against its will. There were similar Queen Anne-style houses sprinkled around Linn County, but she had always felt this one was unique. With its wide wraparound porch, sunburst scrollwork on the front door, and enormous white pillars standing on each side of the steps, it had looked both welcoming and safe from her twelve-year-old perspective. She could remember the day they had all moved into the house as if it was yesterday.

When her grandfather had purchased this home for them, Neva had refused to accept it at first. Kris remembered secretly watching through a crack in Lois's kitchen door as her mother paced the room, ranting about her parents and the gift of the house. Sitting on the kitchen table, legs dangling, Lois had listened patiently to Neva while smoking a Kool cigarette. Once Kris's mother had fumed herself hoarse, Lois had said, "Neevie, you and the kids need a new place. I love having you here, but it's too small, and it's not their home. Until you all get into a place of your own and make some new memories, the ghost of that bastard is going to keep haunting all of you. What they're offering is a blessing, and you're acting like a spiteful teenager. Make up with your damn parents. Take that house and live in peace, without his ghost in every god-damn room."

When Kris heard those words, her blood had turned to ice. They were all being haunted by her father's ghost? Terrified at the thought, she hadn't slept a minute that night, sure the ghost would materialize at her bedside at any moment. Kris pulled the covers over her head, leaving a small opening to breathe, and prayed for dawn. Once she saw the first rays of light coming through her window, she got dressed and woke Tom and Rachel. Grabbing three bananas from the counter, she ushered them out of the house as quickly as she could. She refused to go back inside, even when Tom and Rachel needed to use the bathroom, making them pee behind the evergreen tree instead. They stayed outside until their mother called them in for dinner.

Once back inside, Kris jumped at every noise and peered around every corner, expecting to see her father's ghost. That night, as she lay in bed with her covers pulled up to her chin and her eyes wide with terror, the closet door slowly creaked open on its own. This had happened before, many times. It was an old house, and many of the doors wouldn't stay closed. She knew that, but now the reason every door creaked open seemed more sinister. It must be her father doing it. Haunting them. Torturing them with fear from beyond the grave. Kris leapt out of bed in a blind panic and ran as fast as she could to her mother's bedroom, heart pounding in her chest.

With tears streaming down her cheeks, Kris pleaded for her mother to protect her from the ghost of their father. She begged her, through hysterical sobs, to take the house her grandparents had offered so he could never find them again. Her mother tried to explain that Robert's ghost wasn't in the house and couldn't hurt them, but Kris would not accept it. She insisted on sleeping with Lois, or her mother, every night for twenty-one nights following her plea. On the twenty-second night, she slept in her own bed, in her new bedroom, in the new house.

Kris could still remember how safe and at peace she felt that first night. Now, as a grown woman, she knew she had misinterpreted what Lois had said, but it didn't change the feeling of safety she still got whenever she came here.

Kris pulled the earbud out of Trent's left ear. "Grab Grandma's gift out of the back for me, please."

Trent's sigh was almost identical to hers, and she smiled to herself. Any similarities she noticed between her and her son always surprised and pleased her, but she doubted Trent would feel the same way, so she kept those happy little observations to herself.

They hustled up the tulip and hyacinth-lined front steps without saying a word to each other. At the door, Kris paused, smoothing her oversized blouse and adjusting the belt on her baggy jeans before turning to Trent. "How do I look?"

Her son flashed her a rare smile. "You look great, Mom."

She gave him a quick squeeze and rang the doorbell.

Trent looked at her sideways. "Why'd you ring the bell?"

Kris grimaced. "I don't know. Come on." Just as she reached for the knob, the door was jerked open and Neva stood before them, whiskey hi-ball in hand and a child's handmade crown on her head.

"Why are you ringing the bell?" Neva asked, amused.

Trent handed the wrapped birthday gift to Neva. "Happy birthday, Gramma," he mumbled before pushing past her into the house.

Neva watched him go for a moment before turning a disapproving gaze back on her daughter. "You're late."

Kris beamed at her. "Happy birthday, Mom! Nice crown!"

A smile transformed Neva's face. "Isn't it beautiful? Ashlea and Megan made it for me."

Kris glanced pointedly at the hi-ball in her mother's hand. "Can't you wait until after dinner to start that?"

"Well, I hadn't really thought about it, Mother Hen. But since it's my goddamned birthday, I think I'll do whatever I please!" Neva said, pulling Kris into the house. She pointed toward the kitchen. "Your sister's in there, and she's in a mood. Patty's in the living room, and she's already half-crocked," Neva said with an annoyed grimace. "You got a preference?"

Kris winced. "Oh, jeez. I'm sorry, Mom."

Neva held up her glass, shaking it to make the ice rattle.

Kris patted her mother's shoulder reassuringly. "I'll take Rachel. Maybe I can smooth her out."

Neva harrumphed but gave her the peace sign before they parted ways.

Well, that was hopeful. At least Mom is in a good mood, Kris mused.

Ten years ago, her mother's kitchen had been remodeled into a modern masterpiece with Rachel's help. It rivaled Kris's own kitchen with its top-of-the-line appliances, quartz countertops, and beautiful white custom cabinets. Although magnificent dinners could be prepared in this room, Kris found its best use was as a refuge from family conflicts occurring in other parts of the house. Rachel was not a talented cook, so her presence in the kitchen meant she was either hiding or attempting to stay calm by removing herself from everyone else.

Kris found her sister standing at the center island, transferring a large ham onto a platter. "Hey, Rach!" Kris said, giving her a peck on the cheek.

"Welcome, sister, to another episode of Family from Hell!" Rachel announced.

Kris chuckled, picking up the carving knife from the counter and handing it to her.

"Is this for my wrists or yours?" Rachel deadpanned.

Kris snorted. "I see Tom and Patty made it. Mom said she's already half-drunk," she whispered, stealing a small piece of ham.

Rachel raised her eyebrows in an almost perfect imitation of their mother. Kris wasn't surprised to see so much of their mother in the gesture. Over the years, Rachel had become more and more like Neva, both in looks and demeanor. So much so, it had become a private topic of discussion for Kris and Tom. Neither had the courage nor the level of stupidity necessary to discuss it in front of Rachel. The result, they imagined, would be something tantamount to throwing a match into a vat of gasoline encircled by sticks of dynamite.

Rachel leaned closer to Kris and lowered her voice. "Get this...I walk in, and Patty goes, 'Rachel, I love your outfit!' Then she says to Kim, 'Doesn't it make you feel weird that your mom tries to dress like she's your age?'"

"What the heck?" Kris said, affronted on her sister's behalf.

"Yah! That's what I thought, too! Seriously. Just once I'd like to knock that drunken bitch on her ass." Rachel said, throwing the oven mitts to Kris. "Grab the carrots out of the oven for me, will ya?"

"I wish Tommy would just leave her," Kris whispered, donning the mitts.

"We both know that'll never happen."

Kris set the serving dish, brimming with honey-glazed carrots, on the island. Keeping her head down, she said, "I saw Carl yesterday on my way to work. He was standing right out in public, kissing my replacement."

Rachel stopped working on the ham and focused on her sister. "Were you driving?" she asked sympathetically.

Kris looked up at her, tears brimming, and nodded.

Rachel's expression changed from sympathy to one of pure malice. "Then you should've run his dumb ass over."

Kris snorted a laugh. She picked up a carrot dripping with honey and threw it at her sister. Rachel caught it and whipped it back at her, laughing.

Neva entered the kitchen and looked from one sister to the other, her interest piqued. "Should have run whose ass over?" she asked.

Kris shot Rachel a look, pleading for her to keep quiet. Rachel answered with a look of silent unity and moved to the bowl of cooked potatoes, further away from their mother.

Neva put her hands on her hips and waited.

Kris knew what that gesture meant. It was over. Her mother would have it out of them in less than a minute.

Rachel knew it too but attempted to stonewall. Picking up the potato masher and refusing to meet her mother's eyes, she said, "Nobody important. We were just talking."

Neva stepped closer to them. "You're a terrible liar, Rachel Stevenson. You were talking about Carl. I can tell by the look on your sister's face." Neva shifted her focus to Kris. "Have you signed the divorce papers yet?"

Kris flinched.

Rachel slammed the masher into the potato bowl hard enough to distract their mother for an instant. "Mom, that is her business. You need to stay out of it."

Neva waved Rachel off as if shooing a fly and turned her full attention back to Kris. "It's been six months. Sign the damn papers and move on!" Neva threw her hands up as if pleading with the gods. "Why can't you kids just make decent lives for yourselves?"

Rachel dropped the masher, shaking her head. "Here we go..."

Kris knew what was coming next, too. The speech their mother gave every time one of them did something she didn't approve of. It was classic Neva, and they all knew it by heart. So much so that Rachel mouthed the words in sync with Neva as she spoke them.

"I worked my ass off to give you a good home and bring you up right—by myself!" Neva scolded. "I swear you all act like you have shit for brains." She noticed Rachel mimicking and stopped speaking, glaring at her.

Rachel, never one to back down from a fight with Neva, straightened her shoulders and replied, "I'm sure that's a trait we inherited from you."

Neva sucked in a quick breath and slowly, purposefully, started around the island toward her youngest daughter.

Kris grimaced as Rachel's bravado took another stab at their mother. "For example, who the hell wears turtlenecks in April? If we have the shit-for-brains gene, then it must've come from you!"

That was it. Neva picked up the serving fork from the ham platter and made for Rachel like a demon from hell. Rachel grasped the carving knife and hustled around to the other side of the island, bouncing back and forth on her feet, and pointing the knife at Neva. Kris stepped between them as Neva came around the counter, the serving fork pointed at Rachel like a sword. The two of them were squaring off like deranged fencers. Kris couldn't help laughing as she held her arms up between them.

"You've got shit for brains from all that booze you drink!" Neva hissed at Rachel.

Rachel smirked. "Again, mother, a trait that must have come from you!"

Neva lurched for Rachel. Kris grabbed for the serving fork in Neva's hand, attempting to wrestle it away from her as Rachel scooted past them and around the island. At that moment, Tom stepped into the kitchen.

Seeming oblivious to the drama, he approached Neva and Kris as they struggled. "Here you are, Mom!" he said, planting a kiss on her cheek. "The girls have been trying to find you. They drew you a special birthday picture and want you to come see it."

Neva's hostility melted away in an instant. She ceased struggling with Kris and beamed at Tom. "They did!? Oh, how cute. Where are they?"

Tom pointed at the kitchen door. "In the spare bedroom. Come see."

Neva pointed the fork at Rachel one last time as if to say, "This ain't over," before placing the utensil back onto the counter and sweeping from the kitchen.

Tom let the door close behind her before whispering, "I could hear her through the door. Thought I'd distract her before she really got going."

Kris grinned at him. "Thanks, Tommy."

Rachel threw the carving knife onto the island with a clatter. "Why does she always have to start that shit? How would she like to be reminded of all her faults? We'd be here all damn night!"

Tom stepped closer, putting a finger to his lips. Kris gave Rachel a stern look and shook her head in warning.

But Rachel's adrenaline was still racing, and she couldn't help herself. "What!? You both know I'm right. She's like the devil at the pulpit! At least we haven't—"

"Don't even start with that crap on her birthday. Leave it alone," Kris warned.

Tom picked up a carrot from the serving dish and tried to stick it in Rachel's ear. "Come on, Rach. Don't be such a party poop."

Rachel turned on him, ready to unload, but one look at his big dopey grin instantly deflated her outrage. She half-heartedly punched him in the shoulder instead. "Yeah, yeah, whatever. You two always take her side," she said grudgingly before resuming her position with the potato masher.

Kris winked at Tom as he exited the kitchen. Grabbing a hot roll from the basket, she threw it playfully at her sister before picking up the dish of carrots and following Tom out. Rachel pummeled the potatoes extra hard in response.

The Stevenson family dining room was festooned with happy birthday banners and balloons in Neva's favorite colors of purple and silver. The antique dining table was passed down to Neva after her parents died, which had only been a few years after reuniting with their daughter. Tonight, it was covered in a linen tablecloth. The table had two leaves that could be added to make room for ten people, and both were currently in use. Neva polished the table weekly, and it had been the center of every family occasion since the day the movers delivered it.

Neva flitted around the table, making sure each place setting was perfect and lighting the candles that rose out of the floral centerpiece. Ashlea and Megan were running in circles around the room, giggling and singing "Pop Goes the Weasel."

Neva snagged them both as they ran by. "Hey, little weasels, go find Kim and Trent and tell them it's time for dinner, okay?"

The girls giggled even more at being called weasels, but nodded enthusiastically and ran out of the dining room in search of their cousins.

Patty came into the room, beer in hand, and surveyed the table. "Jeezus, is this a birthday party or a wake?"

Tom entered with the ham and noticed the look he and his sisters referred to as Neva's "death glare" directed at his wife. He moved quickly to intervene. "Mom, look how amazing the ham turned out. Try a piece and tell me what you think."

* * * *

With their orders from Grandma, Ashlea and Megan split up. Megan was looking downstairs, so Ashlea headed upstairs, searching room to room. She had just left her grandmother's bedroom and was about to give up when she heard a noise coming from the adjoining bathroom. Ashlea crept to the bathroom door on tiptoe and pressed her ear to it, listening. Her face lit up as she realized she had finally found Kim.

Inside, Kim leaned against the vanity, talking on her cell phone. "And then I'm gonna give you the best blow job you've ever had," she crooned into the phone.

On the other side of the door, Ashlea frowned, her forehead crinkling in confusion about what she had just heard. She was tired of searching for Kim and Trent. She wanted to get back to the excitement going on downstairs, the promise of cake and presents calling to her. She pushed open the door without knocking. "Kimmie, gramma says it's time to eat," she announced loudly.

Kim startled, her phone fumbling out of her hands and bouncing off the toilet seat before hitting the floor with a clatter. "Shit!" Kim exclaimed as she scrambled to retrieve it. "I gotta go," she said into the phone, hastily ending the call and clutching the device to her chest.

"Time to eat, time to eat," Ashlea sang, oblivious to Kim's distress, as she swung the door open and shut to the rhythm of her chant.

"Get out of here, you little brat!" Kim said, her voice sharp with anger as she pushed Ashlea out of the bathroom and slammed the door in her face.

Ashlea stuck her tongue out at the door before running out of the bedroom and back down the stairs.

A few minutes later, the entire Stevenson family had settled into their places at the table. Neva was seated at one end, with Rachel on her left and Kris on her right. Kim sat next to Rachel, and on Kim's other side, Megan sat in a booster seat, her attention focused on the basket of rolls at the center of the table. Trent, with eyes closed and music blaring through his earbuds, sat next to his mother. On his other side was Ashlea, who was too big for a booster seat but not big enough to sit at the table without assistance. To remedy this, they had stacked two old phone books on her seat. Patty, her eyes glassy from the alcoholic stupor she had been working on all evening, sat on the other side of Ashlea. Tom was at the other end of the table, opposite his mother. Everyone, except Megan and Trent, was looking expectantly at Neva.

She smiled at them and, picking up the ham fork, said, "Well, what are you waiting for? Dig in!"

Dinnerware clanked and platters were passed as everyone began filling their plates, chattering back and forth.

Kris jostled Trent with her elbow, and he removed an earbud. "No music at the table, Trent. Please put your earbuds away."

He immediately did as his mother asked.

Neva eyed them both critically. "Trent, please explain to me why you've been dressing up like a girl," she said, forking ham onto her plate.

Across the table, Kim scoffed. "He's not, Grandma. It's Emo."

"Emo?"

"Yeah. It's a fashion trend."

Neva raised an eyebrow at her granddaughter. "Dressing like a transvestite vampire is a fashion trend?"

Kim nodded, laughing.

Neva focused her attention back on Trent. "Why do you want to look—"

"Mom, what Trent wants to wear is his business," Kris said, annoyed. "We all went through crazy fashion phases when we were growing up, remember? He's just expressing himself."

"None of you ever ran around looking like that."

"Mom! Enough already. Drop it," Rachel said.

Neva took a deep breath, watching her oldest daughter. Kris and Trent continued dishing food onto their plates, heads down, pretending not to notice. The rest of the table had fallen silent except for the sound of clinking silverware and the soft, satisfied humming Megan was making as she chewed her roll.

"You need to get a man back in that house." Neva said, pointing her fork at Kris. "Trent needs a positive male role model to look up to."

Kris angrily spooned carrots onto her plate, attempting to ignore the comment.

Rachel laughed. "That's funny. I don't remember any male role models around here after Dad died. Is that what's wrong with Tom?"

She was immediately hit with a roll from Tom's end of the table.

Trent glanced around the table nervously before putting his earbuds back in. Head down, he began eating as quickly as possible.

Neva ignored Rachel; her attention still focused on Kris. "When are you going to start dating again? You need to pick yourself up and get back on the horse." She paused, looking Kris up and down. "Which would be a lot easier if you didn't insist on looking like the damn horse."

Kris dropped her fork onto her plate and closed her eyes, breathing deeply.

Sensing his sister's distress, Tom waded into the fray. "Mom, please. Let's just eat."

Neva ignored him, keeping her focus on Kris. "I'm just saying, you could take some lessons from your sister on fashion."

Rachel sat up straighter, giving Patty an evil grin as she said, "Oh, I'm not so sure about that, Mom. Some people think I dress too young."

"Whoever thinks that is an idiot," Neva said.

"Amen!" Rachel said, smiling smugly at Patty.

Upset at being the focus of her mother's ire, Kris said, "Well, Rachel's appearance hasn't seemed to help her in the man department."

Rachel's fork stopped mid-air. "I don't have time to date. I'm too busy with the bar."

Neva's attention swiveled to Rachel. "You should be at home in the afternoons, spending time with Kim."

"Maybe she's gay," Patty interjected with a sneer.

"I'm not gay!" Kim said indignantly.

Patty stuffed a bite of mashed potatoes into her mouth and continued talking. "Not you. Your mom."

"That's ridiculous," Rachel said, rolling her eyes. "I'm just busy. Can't a woman be single without everybody thinking she's gay?"

Patty shrugged. "Just sayin'. I've never seen you with a man or even talking about men. I'm sure nobody would judge you if you owned up to it."

Kim nodded. "There's nothing wrong with being gay, Mom. Lots of people at my school are gay. It's really in fashion right now."

Neva threw her hands up in exasperation. "Being gay isn't the same as choosing whether you wear bellbottoms or miniskirts!"

"It is now," Kim said with a shrug. "Jessica Johnson, who thinks she's the most popular girl in school, decided she was a lesbian last week and convinced her whole group of friends to be lesbians, too. Even Kara, who's been dating Mike Carlson for a year. You could tell Kara didn't want to be gay, but Jessica would have called her a bigot or a fascist or some other crazy crap, so I guess she just went along with it. Come to find out, a few days later, Kara finds Jessica in the backseat with Mike at the basketball game!" Kim explained with glee.

Neva didn't laugh, too busy scrutinizing Rachel. "Have you decided to bat for the other team?"

"No! For fuck's sake, I'm not gay! I have a job that leaves me no time for anything else!" Rachel said, throwing her hands up in the same way her mother had a few moments ago.

"Well, gay or not, at least Rachel has a job. Tom lost his job again a few days ago," Patty said.

Tom hung his head, the tips of his ears turning a bright red.

"I don't know why he can't hold down a job," Patty continued, unconcerned with his discomfort. "I mean, how hard is it to just go to work? It's no wonder my parents don't like him. I keep telling him, if he wants Daddy to like him, then he needs to make more money."

Neva glared at Patty, her knuckles turning white as she gripped her utensils.

Rachel and Kris locked eyes, silently acknowledging their shared hatred of their sister-in-law.

Tom glanced up and saw the storm brewing at the other end of the table. "Honey, my family doesn't want to hear our business. Let's just eat and have a good time," he said.

Kris understood her brother's intentions, but couldn't allow Patty's accusations to pass without defending him. "Maybe Tom hasn't found the kind of work he likes," she said.

Tom jumped on the opportunity to redirect the subject. "I'd really love to find a job working with kids."

Neva softened a bit, interested in this new revelation.

"You mean, like social work?" Kris asked.

Tom nodded. "Yeah, or maybe a child counselor or therapist. At a minimum, I'd need a bachelor's degree though, so I've been thinking about—"

"Last time I checked, working as a babysitter doesn't pay much," Patty interrupted. "You need to be doing something that will provide a better lifestyle for me and the girls."

Tom's smile faded. He nodded at Patty before dropping his eyes back down to his plate.

Rachel and Neva began rising from their chairs in unison, identical death glares focused on Patty.

Kris moved to preempt her mother and sister. She stretched across the table, making a clumsy grab for the basket of rolls. As she reached, she intentionally knocked over Patty's beer. The cold liquid ran across the table and into Patty's lap. "Oh, shoot! I'm sorry, Patty!" Kris said in feigned apology, grabbing a handful of napkins from the center of the table and shoving them at her.

"Oopsie!" Megan called out.

Neva and Rachel slowly lowered back into their seats.

"If you're so concerned about your lifestyle, Patty, why don't you get a job?" Neva said, as cold as ice. "Or at the very least, stop bothering Tom at work when he has one."

"So, Rachel, how are things going at the bar, then? Business been good?" Tom blurted before Patty could react.

Rachel shifted her gaze to Tom, and he mouthed "please" at her. She narrowed her eyes at him, shaking her head.

Neva noticed the exchange and took a long drink from her whiskey glass.

Ashlea, who had been silently watching the scene unfold, decided to add her two cents on the subject. "Daddy, if you need a job, maybe you can ask Kimmie for one."

Tom smiled at his daughter indulgently. "Kimmie? How would Kimmie be able to get me a job?" he asked.

"Well," Ashlea said, dragging the word out. "Kimmie was on the phone and told her friend that she would give them a blow job. The best one ever. So, maybe she can give you a job, too."

Neva choked on her whiskey. Kris jumped up to help her, pounding on her mother's back as she coughed and sputtered. Patty laughed out loud, raising her empty beer can in a salute to Rachel.

The rest of the table was silent as Kim and Rachel's faces went deep shades of red.

Chapter 5:
The Lotto

Exhausted from the debacle that had been her birthday dinner, Neva shuffled into the living room wearing the furry blue bathrobe and memory foam slippers Kris and Trent had gifted her.

She moved the notepad and pen Ashlea and Megan had been scribbling with and placed her glass of whiskey on the end table. Once she was sure the glass would be within reach, she sat down in the recliner and closed her eyes, attempting to shed the stress from the day.

She had told herself not to start trouble with her kids but had been so disappointed in the choices they were making; she just couldn't keep her mouth shut. Neva hadn't been a perfect mother, but she had gone through a lot and made many sacrifices to provide a decent home and keep them all together. She had tried to teach them right from wrong and steer them in a good direction. At least, she thought she had. So, how in the hell had they turned out like this? It would be understandable if one of them had made shitty choices and screwed up their life, but all three? Yes, there had been trauma, but how damn long was it going to keep affecting them? Wasn't there some kind of statute of limitations on that kind of thing? They weren't kids anymore, for Pete's sake. It was time for them to cowboy up before they missed the whole damn rodeo.

As Neva contemplated each one of her grown children, she unconsciously touched the thin red scar that stretched across her neck. Just as unconsciously, she picked up the whiskey and took a generous swig. What she wouldn't give to be their age again. To have the choices they still had and the opportunities that had never been available to her twenty-five years ago. She was certainly no stranger to mistakes. Hell, she could write a book on how to make the wrong choices in life, but she had wanted something better for her children. She believed her losses would be their gain. That the lessons of her own bloodied heart and banged-up life would help steer them away from the same fate. Now, it seemed, all three of them were set to repeat her mistakes or do even worse.

Why hadn't she seen this coming? Deep down, she knew why. She just didn't want to admit it to herself. She hadn't been paying attention. Had been too focused on herself and her own pain. Her own issues. First Robert, and all the guilt, anger, and pain that came along with that complete nightmare. Then, the wild out-of-control years that came after, followed by the grief and regret after her parents' deaths. All those long hours at the bar, working to keep the business healthy and alive, instead of paying attention to the health and lives of her children. How many events had she missed? How many nights did they have to feed themselves because she was working? She had convinced herself that it was good for them. Learning to be tough and take care of themselves would strengthen and prepare them for adulthood. She damn sure didn't want to raise a pack of sissies. But had those absences made things worse?

"Oh, hell!" Neva said, slapping her hand down hard on one thigh. Frustrated with her line of thinking and too exhausted to analyze it all, she gave up and snatched the remote off the end table. She tuned in to the news, settled deeper into the recliner, and reached for her glass.

Half an hour later, the whiskey was doing its job of loosening the muscles in her shoulders, while the news distracted her mind. *I may get some sleep tonight, after all,* she thought.

Just before signing off, the anchorman announced, "Stay tuned for the record lottery jackpot drawing coming up after the commercial break, and goodnight from all of us at WJC News."

Neva perked up at the mention of the lottery drawing. "Oh yeah, the lottery for the boob cause. I can't miss this," she chuckled, putting her glass down and shuffling out of the room to retrieve the lotto ticket from her purse.

A few moments later, settled once again in her recliner, Neva waited for the drawing to begin. The lotto announcer's spray-tanned face appeared on the screen, with white teeth gleaming and a voice full of false excitement. "Tonight's jackpot drawing is for a record forty-five million dollars! Good luck, everybody!"

Neva watched as the first ball was sucked from the group being tossed around inside the air machine. As the number rolled to its spot in front of the camera, the lotto announcer declared, "Your first number for forty-five million dollars is...thirteen! Lucky number, thirteen!"

Neva glanced down at her ticket, noticing that thirteen was one of her numbers. "Oh boy, we got one," she said in a sardonic tone.

The announcer was ready with the second lotto ball. "Your second number is...one!"

Neva checked her ticket and found the number one there as well. She raised her glass to the TV. "Here's to the good old number one!"

"Your third number is...twelve! Number twelve," the announcer said.

Neva froze, her whiskey glass halfway to her mouth. "Jeezus. I've got that one, too. How many is that—three?" She placed her glass on the end table and inched forward in her chair. She was wide awake now and focused on the announcer.

"Your fourth number is...twenty-seven! Twenty-seven! Okay folks, just two more numbers to go..." he declared.

Neva glanced back and forth from her ticket to the television. This could not be happening. She had all four numbers. How much do you win with four numbers!?

The cameras focused on the fifth number as it rolled into view. "It looks like ball five is number eleven! Eleven! Just one more ball and we may have a new jackpot winner tonight, folks!"

Neva stared down at the ticket in her shaking hand. Holy shit! I've got that one, too. I've got all five.

The announcer's voice interrupted her thoughts as the last ball rolled into place. "And your sixth and final number for forty-five million dollars is...twenty-three! Lucky number, twenty-three. There you have it, folks. Your winning numbers for tonight's record jackpot are 13-1-12-27-11, and 23. Good luck and goodnight from the Iowa lottery!"

The numbers the announcer listed were displayed on the screen. Neva snatched up the pen and notepad, jotting the winning numbers onto the paper. She checked them again and again against the numbers on her ticket. She said each number out loud—first from the lotto numbers she'd copied and then from her own ticket.

"Oh-my-God!" she exclaimed, finally convinced of her ticket's legitimacy. She glanced around the room, as if searching for someone to tell, then back to the ticket clamped in her shaking hand. Putting the notebook down, she reached for her whiskey and tossed the rest of it back.

Neva didn't know how long she sat in the recliner staring at the ticket. Although her hand was still shaking, she could still make out the numbers on her winning ticket. The adrenaline racing through her veins had burned off any effects from the whiskey. My God, she thought to herself. I just won forty-five million dollars. Forty-five million! What in the hell do I do now? She pulled in a deep breath and stood. Her legs wobbled, and her heart was beating so fast she feared she might have a heart attack. She took another deep breath, willing herself to calm down as she made her way into the dining room to retrieve her cell phone.

Who should I call first? Lois? The kids? Neva paced, circling the table once, then twice, thinking. She dropped the phone into the large pocket of her bathrobe and took another deep breath. She was getting ahead of herself. Before she called anyone, she needed to make sure the ticket would be safe and not get damaged.

Neva raced to the windows in the dining room and looked out, scanning the yard and the street. Satisfied that they were empty, she drew the curtains. Next, she checked the lock on the front door before running to the kitchen and locking the side entrance. Finally, she hurried to the living room and closed those curtains, too. She couldn't remember the last time she had closed them. She always kept them open because she felt too isolated and alone in this big house when they were closed. Not tonight, though. Tonight, complete isolation was exactly what she wanted.

Neva marched to her bedroom and pulled her pistol out of the nightstand drawer. With practiced hands, she ejected the magazine, checking that it was loaded. Satisfied, she snapped it back into place and double-checked the safety. Having the weapon in her hand calmed her racing heart and steadied her mind. She was fine. Nobody was waiting outside to rush in and try to take the ticket from her. There was no danger. No rush to do something about the ticket, either. Neva took another deep breath and snapped off the light.

When she emerged again into the dining room, she placed the pistol on the table and went to the antique wooden desk in the corner. She removed several sheets of stationery and a pen from the top drawer. With extreme care, she placed the lottery ticket in the same drawer and closed it. Satisfied that the ticket was safe, for now, she sat down at the table with paper and pen.

She needed to sort out her thoughts. Once she claimed that money, everything was going to change, and she wanted to make certain she could stay in control. She wasn't even sure how much she had won. The jackpot had been forty-five million, but maybe someone else had a ticket with the winning numbers, too. Then there would be taxes taken out, and who knew what else? She needed to talk to someone knowledgeable about these things. She needed to talk to a lawyer.

Neva placed a number one at the top of the first page of paper and next to it, she wrote: Richard Hastings ASAP. What next? The kids. She wrote each of their names at the top of three additional sheets and sat back in her chair, pondering her choices.

For three days, Neva avoided her children and every other human in Marion by sequestering herself in her home. She didn't answer the phone or go outside. One of the Texas fifths of whiskey she had purchased just a few short days ago was gone, and she was halfway into the second. She had gone through a full notebook of paper, two pens, and eaten all her birthday cake as well. Sleeping had been impossible, and her pacing was wearing a path in the hardwood of her dining room floor. Neva wasn't a smoker, but if there'd been a pack of cigarettes in the house, she would have happily smoked all of them.

By the fourth day, Neva had, at last, put the final touches on her plan for the lotto winnings. She was ready to move forward. She placed the lotto ticket on the table and poised her phone above it, getting the entire ticket in the frame. As she tapped the button, the snapshot sound effect seemed to echo through the empty house. She checked the image. It was clear, and the date and lotto numbers were visible. She put the phone in her purse as if storing a priceless artifact.

Next, she retrieved the lotto ticket from the table and placed it face down in the desk drawer under a tablet of paper. She closed the drawer and used a small key to lock it before tucking the key into her bra. Smoothing her shirtfront, she grabbed her purse and the manila envelope off the desktop and walked out the front door, locking it behind her. She needed to make one quick stop before her appointment, and she was already running behind.

Neva had been meticulous about her appearance that morning, choosing to wear one of her favorite spring outfits: a white short-sleeve sweater that showed off her lean, well-muscled arms and attractive bustline, accompanied by a pair of form-hugging navy slacks, navy peep-toe pumps, and a white scarf tied strategically to cover the scar on her throat. Her hair was styled in an elegant twist, and her makeup was as flawless as that of a cover model. This was an important meeting, and she needed to look her best.

She pulled the car into the parking lot of the law firm and checked her makeup in the mirror. "This is it. Let's get the show on the road," she said to her reflection.

Neva approached the reception desk at Hastings Law Firm with her clutch purse and a large manila envelope tucked under her left arm. A tube-shaped gift bag dangled from the hand of the other.

"Neva Stevenson to see Richard Hastings, please," she informed the petite young woman behind the counter.

The woman smiled at Neva and motioned toward the upholstered wingback chairs across the room. "Please have a seat, Ms. Stevenson, and I'll let him know you're here. Can I get you anything? Coffee, juice, or perhaps a soda?" she asked.

Neva declined all three and took a seat in the wingback. She inhaled deeply, willing her hands to stop shaking. This was no time to get cold feet. She had thought this through. Had pondered her options and the repercussions of those options for days. She knew this was the right thing. She had always tried to do what was best for her children, but her judgment hadn't always been spot-on, and she spent the last twenty-five years doubting each choice she had made with them. She wasn't going to doubt herself this time, though. None of those old mistakes mattered now. What did matter was making sure she could straighten her kids out. Get them to "fly right," as her own mother used to say. These lottery winnings were going to help her kids do that, come hell or high water. And she expected both.

The petite young woman returned. "Ms. Stevenson, he's ready for you. Please follow me," she said, smiling.

Neva followed her down a wide hallway with several doors on each side. The receptionist opened the last door on the left and motioned Neva inside. "Please have a seat. He'll be right with you," she directed before pulling the door closed.

A large mahogany desk and plush leather chair took up a sizable amount of space at the center of the room. Two wing-back chairs, duplicates of those in the lobby, sat in front of the desk. Neva placed her clutch, envelope, and gift bag on one of the chairs and studied the upscale office. Large mahogany bookshelves, lined with law books and classic literature, stood floor to ceiling, flanking the large window behind the desk. The leather and mahogany theme was continued with accent furniture tastefully arranged throughout the room, and the faint scent of Scotch and cigars lingered in the air. My, my, he's certainly done well, she thought to herself.

At that moment, Richard Hastings entered through a side door. A wide smile transformed his serious expression when he saw her. He took Neva's outstretched hand in both of his. "Neva Stevenson, you look amazing. It's so good to see you again," he said with obvious sincerity.

"Hello, Richard. It's good to see you, too. It's been a long time," Neva said.

"Twenty years or more, isn't it?" he asked.

"Twenty-seven. You were fresh out of law school then," Neva replied. "It looks like you've done very well for yourself."

He motioned toward the chairs. "Please, have a seat so we can catch up."

"I brought you something," she said, claiming the gift bag from the chair and handing it to him.

He took it from her reluctantly. "Brought me something? What is it?" he asked, holding it as if it were a bomb.

Neva chuckled. "It isn't going to bite you, Richard. Just open it."

Embarrassed, he quickly removed the tissue paper and reached into the bag. His eyes fixed on the label of the twenty-five-year-old Glenohumeral Scotch as he pulled the bottle free. He let out a low whistle.

"You approve?" Neva asked.

"Approve!? This is a rare batch. It must run at least seven hundred dollars a bottle," he said. His eyes snapped from the bottle to Neva. "I was surprised to get your call. Now, frankly, you've got me more than a little worried. It can't be good if you're plying me with this," he said, brandishing the bottle. "What's happened?"

Neva barked a laugh. "Don't worry. This meeting won't be nearly as dramatic as our last encounter," she promised. "It's just that—well, some money has come my way, and I need you to help me sort it out."

"Money? I'm a defense attorney. You know that. I can give you the name of another attorney that might be able to..."

"No, Richard. I need you," Neva interrupted. "This is going to be a bit dicey and you're the only person I would trust with this." She pulled her cell phone from her purse and tapped the image of the lotto ticket. When it filled the screen, she handed the phone to Richard.

He studied the screen for a moment, then his eyes widened and he looked back at Neva. "Is this—"

She nodded.

Richard pushed the intercom button on his desk phone. "Emily, please reschedule my afternoon appointments. I'm no longer available today."

Two and a half hours later, Richard leaned back in his chair, gazing at Neva in silence. She met his stare and waited. She could see the wheels turning behind his eyes, but he just sat, studying her.

No longer able to bear it, she said, "If you've got something to say, just say it."

His gaze fell to the paperwork they had been working on. "You have to know that your kids won't like the demands you're placing on them. They're not children you can simply tell what to do," he said.

"They're not demands; they're...conditions," she replied.

"Call it whatever you want, but it's still tantamount to blackmail, Neva."

"I love my kids, Richard. They need to make these changes."

"This may drive a permanent wedge between you," he warned.

Neva folded her arms over her chest. "It might. That's just a chance I'll have to take."

"Big chance," Richard said.

Neva adjusted her scarf. "You'd be surprised what people will do for the sake of their children."

Richard's expression softened as he leaned forward in his seat, his eyes still locked with hers. "No, I wouldn't," he said.

Neva cleared her throat, tearing her gaze from his. "Are you sure Patty and Carl won't be able to get their hands on the money if we set it up this way?"

"They won't see a dime," Richard said with a smug smile.

She smiled back, grateful for his unspoken agreement to do as she asked, despite his concerns. "Good. Make sure of that and keep my name out of the media. That's all I'm asking," Neva said, standing to leave.

Richard stood as well and extended a hand. "This is going to be an interesting ride, Ms. Stevenson."

Taking his hand, Neva grinned. "It always is, Richard. It always is."

· · · ·

Lois was on her front porch smoking a cigarette when Neva arrived at the farm. She had phoned ahead two hours ago, letting Lois know she needed to share some important news. She had planned on arriving sooner, but packing for her trip proved more challenging than she thought. *Lois is going to kill me for keeping her in suspense for so long,* she thought, her own excitement growing. *She's probably on her second pack of smokes and her last nerve by now,* Neva mused as she made her way to the house.

Lois threw her cigarette onto the wood decking and stomped it out with the toe of her shoe. "You better move your ass, Neva Stevenson! Two hours I've been waiting. You've got my nerves in a knot."

Neva had agonized over the right timing to tell Lois about the lottery win. There was never a doubt that she would share part of the winnings with Lois. She couldn't wait to tell her that part. But the part about the kids would be harder to explain, and one of the biggest reasons she had waited to share the news. That, and the fact that there were questions Neva needed answers to first. Now that Richard had answered those questions, she couldn't wait to blow Lois's mind with the news.

Neva reached the porch and did a little tap dance, finishing with a bow.

Lois placed her hands on her hips and studied her. "Now you're just scaring me."

Neva beamed at her. "What I'm about to tell you will be life changing."

"A coffee kind of life-changing, or a whiskey kind of life-changing?" Lois said, opening her front door.

"Maybe both!" Neva said as she slipped by her into the house.

Forty minutes later, they were seated at Lois's table, two half-empty cups of coffee, a bottle of Johnny Walker Red, and two whiskey glasses between them.

Neva had explained everything about the lottery winnings, the lawyer, the kids...everything. Through it all, Lois had sat in shocked silence, with wide eyes and her mouth hanging half-open. Whether it hung open in awe or shock, Neva couldn't tell, but she was beginning to worry. She had finished her explanations a full minute ago, and Lois's expression still hadn't changed. Neva snapped her fingers a few times in front of her friend's face. "Hellloo? Anybody in there? You still breathing, Lo?"

Lois blinked as if coming out of a trance. She snapped her mouth closed, raising one hand to her heart and the other to her forehead. "You. won. forty-five. million. dollars?" she whisper-yelled.

"All of that and you're still stuck on the first thing I said. Come on, I know it's a lot, but try to keep up," Neva teased. "Did you hear the best part? I'm giving you two million of my share!"

"I heard it all. I just can't believe it," Lois said, picking up her whiskey glass with a shaking hand and taking a loud gulp.

"I know. Took me three days to wrap my own head around it," Neva said, taking a drink from her own glass.

They sat in silence for a few moments. Neva watched Lois's face as her friend processed it all. She had to give Lois credit. She was absorbing it much better than Neva thought she would. There were no hysterics, no denial or disbelief, no fainting. Thank God there was no fainting. She didn't think Lois was a fainter, but when someone gets news this big, there's no telling what they'll do. Just surprise and acceptance, Neva thought, bemused. But I suppose she's used to crazy shit happening with me.

Lois took Neva's hand in hers. "Listen, Neeves, what you're doing with the kids...I get it. I do. But are you sure you wanna light that fire?"

Neva sighed. "One hundred percent. You know better than anybody how messed up we all are. It's too late for me, but they still have time to change course. If I have to be the 'bad guy' that makes them do it—so be it. Tough love and all that jazz," she said, dismissing Lois's concerns with a wave of her free hand.

"Who says it's too late for you? You've got plenty of time to fix things in your life, too. You want a list of shit to fix? 'Cause I can whip one up for ya real quick. I mean, what's good for the goose is good for the mother goose, right?" Lois teased.

"Okay, smartass. You go ahead and make that list while I'm relaxing in my beach cabana," Neva shot back.

Lois feigned disgust, throwing Neva's hand away from her theatrically. "I can't believe you're leaving me here to work side by side with the one person who will absolutely, one hundred percent, lose her mind when she finds out."

Neva winced. "Yeah, I'm really sorry about that part," she admitted, pouring them another whiskey. "I would have taken you with me, but it would leave her short-handed, and I need you to be here for them in case anything bad happens."

"They're not babies. You know that, right? They're full-grown adults," Lois said.

"I know!" Neva said, kicking Lois under the table. "I've never been away from them before, though. Let alone being two thousand miles away," she confessed. "I know it's necessary, and I'm the one that planned this whole damn thing, but the being away part is giving me anxiety."

Lois snorted. "That's the part giving you anxiety?"

Neva crossed her arms over her chest and glared. Lois pulled in her lips, struggling not to laugh. Neva raised a perturbed eyebrow, and Lois let out a choked guffaw that quickly gained steam into a full-on laughing fit.

Neva sipped her whiskey and waited for Lois to settle.

"Are you about done, chuckles?" she chided. "That's the last time I tell you anything personal."

"You're a good mom, Neva Ruth. Crazy as a fucking loon, but a good mom," Lois said, sniffing and dabbing at her nose.

Neva huffed in response.

Lois raised her whiskey glass between them. "I'll make you a deal. I'll stay and make sure the kids are okay if you promise that you and I will take a girls' trip to a tropical beach somewhere when this is all over."

Neva raised her own glass to seal the deal, but Lois pulled hers back, holding it to her chest. "Annnd..." she added, "you also have to promise to think about what I said. About you making some changes, too. You've let the last twenty-five years jerk you around just as much as your kids have. Maybe it's time for all of you to make some changes."

Neva opened her mouth to argue, but Lois put a hand up to stop her. "Nope. No excuses. You don't do it; I'm not helping you or taking the money."

"You're taking the money."

"No, I won't. If this cash is going to be such a life changer, then let it be a life changer for all of us. You included. If you don't, I want nothing to do with it."

Neva eyed her. "You realize making changes for all of us includes you too, right?"

"Of course," Lois said.

"What are you planning to change, then?"

"Just you never mind about me. You've got bigger fish to fry. Do we have a deal, or what?" Lois said, extending her glass.

Neva pursed her lips, fixing her scariest glare on her friend. The corners of Lois's mouth quivered.

For the love of Pete! The idiot is about to start laughing again, Neva thought, irritated. She had a plane to catch in three hours, and she needed Lois's help. She was also determined that Lois take a share of the winnings. "Ugh!" Neva moaned. "Alright. It's a deal, you despicable hyena," she said, raising her own glass.

Lois winked and kissed the air in Neva's direction before clinking glasses to seal the deal.

Chapter 6:
Ultimatums

It was a cloudy, chilly Saturday afternoon, and Kris was enjoying her day off by reclining on the sofa with a hot cup of tea. Trent, as usual, had isolated himself inside his bedroom after breakfast. She was sure she wouldn't see him again until dinner. Things had been strained between them since the night of her mother's party. She thought he might just get over it, but it had been two weeks, and he was still acting sullen. Kris wasn't sure what she could do or say to fix it.

Neva was like a dog with a bone when she had a point to make or was doling out her particular brand of advice. Usually, that advice came disguised as a series of insults, coupled with demands and delivered in her not-so-passive, passive-aggressive style. Kris was used to it. She'd grown up with it and usually let it go in one ear and out the other. She was emotionally immune. But Trent was not.

Kris had raised her son differently than she had been raised—a fact she was proud of. Trent had her support and her ear, without judgment. She talked with him, hugged him often, and the words "I love you" were said, and meant, every day. Because of this, she was sure his grandmother's attack seemed even more vicious to him, and her lack of outrage over it must have felt like a betrayal. Kris didn't know how to explain that she wasn't comfortable talking to Neva in the way he expected. Her relationship with her mother was complicated in ways she couldn't put into words. Throw Kris's relationship with her two siblings into that mix, and there was no hope of ever making sense of it. She was grateful, however, that this was the problem she needed to solve with Trent and not the kind Rachel was facing with Kim.

The revelations about Kim's sexual exploits, which had been spotlighted at the birthday dinner, surprised everyone—especially Rachel. Kris feared Kim would make the same mistakes Rachel did as a teen, and though Rachel was a lot like Neva, Kris doubted Rachel could handle a pregnant teenage daughter as well as Neva had. Raising a girl in today's morally crippled society was a nightmare filled with landmines. And Rachel's hot temper wouldn't make that any easier. A chill ran down Kris's spine. *Thank God I never had a girl,* she thought.

The ring of the doorbell drew her out of her reverie. She picked up her phone and checked the security feed. The camera showed a young man standing on the doorstep, holding two envelopes.

By the second ring, Kris had reached the door. She opened it a few inches and peered out. "Yes?" she said.

The young man craned his neck to see her face through the small opening. "Delivery, ma'am," he said, waving the pair of envelopes.

One envelope was white and the size of an invitation or greeting card. The larger envelope looked like the legal envelopes she used at work.

"Are you Kris Walker?" he asked.

"Yes..."

"Sign here," he said, thrusting a clipboard and pen toward the crack.

Kris opened the door wider and took the clipboard. "Who are they from?" she asked suspiciously.

He shrugged. "No idea. I just deliver 'em."

Kris hesitated for a moment, thinking. *What is this? It can't be divorce papers. Carl sent those a month ago. What else could he want?* She sighed, signing her name on the line marked 'recipient' before handing the clipboard back.

"Here ya go. Have a nice day," he said, handing her the envelopes.

"Thank you!" Kris called as he hurried away.

She closed the door and examined the envelopes in her hands. The white one bore her name and address in her mother's familiar, sweeping script. Curiosity surged, tempered by alarm bells ringing like a four-alarm fire in her mind as she hurried to the living room and sank onto the couch. Allister hopped up beside her, purring under her absent strokes while she studied the envelopes. She hadn't spoken to her mother since the party. Maybe an apology note? Kris dismissed the thought. Neva wasn't the type. Besides, the second envelope, with its stark, legal appearance, suggested something far less personal.

She opened the white envelope first. Inside was a folded note and a photo of her mother sitting on a beach in a lounge chair. In the photo, Neva was wearing a large-brimmed beach hat, a pale pink sleeveless blouse, black shorts, and a pink scarf tied around her neck. In her hand, she held some kind of tropical drink in a tall glass with a wedge of pineapple on the rim. Neva was smiling, holding the drink up for the camera as if to say, "Cheers!" to the photographer.

Kris stared at the photo, dumbfounded. Where had this been taken? When had this been taken? She placed the photo on the coffee table and unfolded the note.

My Dears,

What you are about to read may upset you at first but, once you've had time to think about it, I know you'll see the opportunity in front of you and will do the right thing. See you in three weeks!

Love, Mom

P.S. Leave Lo alone. She knows about this but has signed a legal NDA to keep from discussing ANY of it with ANY of you.

Kris tossed the note aside and picked up the large manila envelope. She turned it over in her hands, noticing the weight of it. It was heavy and about half an inch thick. Putting it back down, she picked up the note again. Neva had addressed it to "My Dears." Had she sent the same package to Rachel and Tom? Whatever was inside the other envelope was going to make them "upset at first"? Holding her breath, Kris tore the large envelope open and pulled out the contents.

• • • •

Less than half an hour later, the same courier delivered a duplicate of those envelopes to Rachel at Lucky's bar. She immediately took them to a corner booth and extracted the contents. A few minutes later, she sat in stunned disbelief as she read through the information in the manila envelope.

• • • •

Across town, Tom had been indulging Ashlea and Megan in a dress-up game when the courier arrived. Now, perched at their tiny bedroom table, decked out in fairy wings and a crown, with children's makeup finger-painted on his face, his expression was solemn as he poured over the delivered pages. Nearby, his daughters twirled in matching costumes, their laughter a stark contrast to his growing dismay.

· · · ·

After reading the document for the third time, Kris tossed it onto the coffee table and raked her fingers through her hair in frustration. She had no doubt her mother had sent the same details to Rachel and Tom. Her phone should've been buzzing nonstop by now, and the silence could only mean one thing. Soon they would be banging on her door instead. A bomb like this would send both her siblings into orbit. A simple phone call would not be an adequate response from either of them. She slapped her hand down hard on the paperwork, scaring Allister and sending him running out of the room. Kris wished she could run away with him. "Never a dull moment, Mother. I'll give you that," she said to the empty room.

· · · ·

Four thousand miles away, Neva situated herself on the beach under an enormous umbrella for her fifth full day of rest and relaxation. She was adjusting to beach life at a rapid pace and came prepared today with a wide-brimmed hat, sunscreen, and a book. The phone number for the resort bar was on her speed dial, which kept her supply of Rum Runners constantly replenished. She had splurged this morning, buying a two-piece bathing suit and sarong made of a polyester blend she would have sworn was silk. To her chagrin, she also felt compelled to purchase a matching scarf, which she tied expertly around her neck, hiding the scar. As she had stood in the checkout line, she decided it would be the last scarf she ever purchased.

Neva had promised Lois that she would give some thought to making changes of her own, and she planned to make good on that promise. In fact, she hadn't slept the first night at the resort, her mind too busy sorting through her choices for change to relax enough for sleep. Sometime around 4 a.m. Neva chose what the first change would be: her scar. When she returned home, she would schedule an appointment with a plastic surgeon to remove the damn thing. It wasn't a huge change, but it was a start. She would add more to her list later. Until then, she had every intention of thoroughly enjoying herself.

As Neva sipped her rum and pretended to read her book, her eyes wandered the beach. People-watching was her new favorite pastime, especially watching the men. It had been far too long since she had seen a man naked, and although the men on the beach were wearing swimwear, she had an excellent imagination.

A muscled, darkly tanned specimen in his mid-forties made his way across her line of vision. Neva sucked in her breath and let out a low whistle as she lowered her sunglasses to get a better look. "Oh, yes. I'll take two, please," she purred.

The guy glanced up, caught her staring, and flashed a grin. Neva returned it, lashes dipping as she gave a playful little wave. He hesitated, ready to approach, when the shrill ring of her cell phone shattered the moment. He waved once more and strolled off down the beach. Neva cursed under her breath and retrieved the phone without taking her eyes off his retreating backside. "Hello?"

"Neva, it's Richard Hastings. How's your sabbatical going?"

"It is positively divine," she said with a little sigh of contentment. "Did the kids get their contracts?"

"That's why I'm calling. All three packets were delivered this morning. The lottery winnings have been secured and deposited into the accounts we discussed. Everything is on track," he said.

"Here we go, then! Thanks for letting me know, Richard."

"My pleasure. Enjoy your time away and let me know if there is anything you need on my end."

Neva ended the call and tossed the phone into her bag. Well, that was it, then. She was sure the shit had officially hit the fan back home. She was equally sure that she didn't care. It didn't matter how much they kicked and screamed or fought her on this. She would stick to her guns, and that was all there was to it. It was time all the Stevensons made some changes in their lives, even if it meant they did it kicking and screaming.

. . . .

Removing a beer from the fridge, Kris placed it on the small tray next to a cup of coffee, a bottle of Dr. Pepper, and a small plate of cookies. She gathered the assortment and left the kitchen, heading to the entry table by the front door, where she set the tray down. She drew a deep breath. It wouldn't be long now—five minutes at most. She inhaled again, but before she could exhale, headlights swept across the dining-room windows. A quick check of the security feed on her phone revealed Tom's car rolling up the drive. She'd expected Rachel to be the first one here.

Kris took another deep breath and held it for a few seconds before exhaling. She heard footsteps on the porch and opened the door before he could ring the bell. Tom's face startled her. Bright blue and purple eyeshadow circled his eyes like a bruise, and red lipstick outlined his mouth. A bedazzled fairy crown sat atop his head between two short pigtails. Kris bit her bottom lip hard, trying not to laugh.

Tom didn't notice. Waving the legal document in front of her, he said, "Did you get one of these, too?"

Kris nodded and gestured for them to come in. In her calmest voice, she said, "Let me get the girls settled upstairs, and when Rachel gets here, we can sort everything."

"Rachel's coming?"

"What do you think?" Kris replied, a teasing lilt in her voice. She handed Tom the Dr. Pepper and took the plate of cookies off the tray. "Come on, baby girls," she said, leading her nieces toward the stairs.

Ashlea tugged on Kris's hand. "Are we spending the night again, Aunt Kris?"

"Yay! Spend the night, spend the night!" Megan chimed.

Kris glanced back at Tom for confirmation; he shrugged, indifferent. "Where's Patty?" she asked.

Tom studied his shoes. "Out. Having a spa day and a girl's night with some friends."

Kris had to bite her tongue. She looked down at Ashlea and smiled. "I'm not sure, honey. Let's wait and see, okay?"

Both girls gave a happy nod and followed her up the stairs.

Kris knocked on Trent's bedroom door. When he opened it, he glanced from his mother's pained expression to his small cousins and back again. "What happened? What's going on?" he asked.

Kris grimaced. "Family stuff. I need to talk to Tom and Rachel. Can you watch the girls for a bit?"

Trent hesitated for only a moment before nodding and opening his door wide for the girls to come in. Kris handed the plate of cookies to Ashlea. "Do you want Trent to read you your favorite story?"

The girls bobbed their heads with excitement.

"Again? I read it to them every time they stay over. Like a billion times!" Trent said, making a tortured face as the girls grabbed his hands.

Kris laughed and gave him a quick kiss on the forehead. "One more won't kill you," she said.

Trent rolled his eyes and allowed the girls to drag him toward the beanbag chairs. Kris blew him a kiss before closing the door.

• • • •

Tom drank his Dr. Pepper as he peered out the entry window, watching Rachel's Jeep careen onto Kris's driveway, kicking up gravel and dust as it barreled toward the house. He felt Kris come up behind him as the Jeep skidded to a halt, pinging rocks off the garage doors and his car. He swore under his breath. "Rachel's here," he announced flatly, moving to position himself slightly behind his sister.

The door was thrown wide before Kris could reach it, and Rachel burst inside, her hair wild and eyes blazing. "What the fuck is going on!? Did you two get one of these!?" Rachel shouted, waving her documents at them.

Nodding, Kris handed Rachel the beer from the tray. Snatching it from Kris's hand, Rachel took a long pull from the bottle and wiped her mouth. "She's lost her goddamn mind! Sell the bar? Who the hell does she think she is!?"

Kris motioned for Rachel to keep her voice down and pointed at the ceiling to signal that their nieces were upstairs. "Calm down. We'll figure this out," she said. "Come in and sit down so we can talk about it."

Without another word, they followed Kris into the living room. Rachel perched on the sofa arm, as if ready to jump up at any moment. Tom flopped onto the sofa, spreading his arms across the back. Rachel glanced at Tom and did a double take. "Wow. Nice ensemble, Princess Tom."

Tom shot a confused look at Kris, who pointed at the tiara on his head and then made a circle around her own face with the same finger. Chagrined, Tom removed the tiara and rubber bands from his pigtails, leaving two horn-like clumps of hair. He rubbed his face with both hands, which only smeared the makeup further. Kris had to avert her gaze to keep from laughing.

"That's so much better. Good job, dork." Rachel sneered.

Tom flipped her off.

Rachel returned the gesture, then focused a gimlet eye on Kris. "Well? Talk."

Kris sat down in the recliner, trying to project an air of calm nonchalance. "Okay. So, apparently, Mom is trying to coax us into making some changes and—"

"Coax, my ass! She's trying to force us into doing what she wants, or she won't give us any money. It's blackmail." Rachel said, throwing her document onto the coffee table with a disgusted huff.

Tom nodded in agreement. "Is that legal? Can Mom do that?"

"It's her money and our choice. Hastings is a really talented attorney, so I'm pretty sure she can," Kris said, nodding slowly.

Rachel emitted a low, guttural growl, frustration simmering just beneath the surface.

Kris turned to her. "You said Mom wants you to sell the bar? Why?"

Rachel shot off the couch, her frustration bubbling over as she began pacing. "She doesn't think I'm being a decent mother! She thinks I need to be at home more until Kim graduates. Get her 'under control,'" she seethed. "Where in the hell was she when we were growing up? Working at the same bar she wants me to sell, or at the bottom of a bottle!" She halted her pacing, searching her siblings' faces for agreement and support.

Tom averted his gaze.

Kris sat forward in her chair, elbows on her knees. "I don't know, Rach. Maybe it's not such a bad idea. You've been wanting to cut back on your hours anyway, and if you get the money, you wouldn't even need the bar. This could be really good for you and Kim."

Rachel stared at Kris, incredulous. "Are you kidding me? I love that bar! It's all I have left of Dad."

Tom and Kris exchanged a quick glance as Rachel raged on.

"I'm not selling it. And therapy? Therapy for what? She's the one that needs therapy!"

"She didn't say why she wants you to get therapy, or what kind?" Kris asked.

"Hell no. She's just pulling demands out of her ass," Rachel said, kicking the sofa angrily.

"Well, my money's on anger management." Tom sniggered.

Rachel lunged toward him, but he threw himself over the back of the sofa, popping up at the other end, grinning at her like a crazed clown.

Before Rachel could make another move, Kris stood, her arms outstretched as if to keep them apart. "Okay! Okay! Stop. This isn't helping. Tommy, what did Mom instruct you to do?"

Tom's smile fell. Coming around the sofa, he sat down heavily in Kris's recliner and looked up at them both as if in pain.

"Jeezus. You look like she wants you to commit suicide. Just spit it out," Rachel demanded.

Tom hung his head. "She wants me to divorce Patty—and enroll in college."

Kris didn't blink. She had already assumed her mother would require something to be done about Patty, but Neva's demand that Tom enroll in college intrigued her. "Really? What courses?"

Tom shrugged. "Whatever I want, I guess."

Kris grinned at him and sat down on the couch, motioning for Rachel to do the same. "That's not so bad!" she said.

Tom looked at Kris, dumbfounded.

Rachel perched on the arm of the couch, pointing at Tom with her beer. "Mom's doing you a favor. Take her up on it and divorce that bitch," she said.

"I can't do that. Patty would go crazy."

"Tom, that's no reason to just throw—" Kris started.

"I shared mine. What about you?" Tom interrupted. "What does she want you to change?"

Kris looked at each sibling for a moment and then took a deep breath.

"Stop doing your breathing thing and just say it," Rachel growled.

"She wants me to sign my divorce papers, buy some new clothes, go out with my girlfriends, and—" Kris paused, glancing toward the stairs to ensure Trent wasn't there, listening. Satisfied but still wary, she whispered the last requirement. "And she wants me to clean up Trent's appearance."

She waited, expecting to hear her siblings berate their mother on her behalf. But they both just looked at her, mouths slightly agape.

After a minute, Rachel took a swig of her beer and sat back, shaking her head. "You always were her favorite," she said.

Tom nodded in agreement.

Kris felt like they had punched her in the stomach. "What!? How can you even say that? I have four things to change. You guys only have two!" she yelped.

"Two really hard things!" Tom countered.

"Boohoo, I have to go shopping. Boohoo, I have to go out with my friends. Big damn deal!" Rachel sneered.

Kris folded her arms over her chest and glared at them both. "I can't believe you two," she said.

Rachel pointed at Tom with her beer. "Are you gonna do it, Princess?"

"I can't divorce Patty just because Mom tells me to."

"Well, going to college is a great idea. You should check into it," Kris encouraged.

"Maybe," Tom said.

The three were silent for a few moments, and then Rachel spoke up. "Well, we'll all outlive her," she said matter-of-factly.

"Outlive who? Mom?" Kris asked.

"Yeah. She's gotta die sometime, right? I say we live our lives like we want and wait for her to kick off. Then we collect our winnings through our inheritance, and we—"

"We can't do that," Kris interrupted.

"Why not?" Rachel asked. "It happens every day."

"Did you read the entire contract?" Kris said.

"My head almost popped off by the fourth page! There was no way I was gonna read the rest."

"I didn't read it all either," Tom admitted.

Kris sighed. She picked up her own contract off the coffee table and turned to page eight, pointing to a paragraph in the middle of the page. "We have a time limit of three months to make all the changes and—"

"Three months!?" Rachel and Tom exclaimed in unison.

"Yes, three months. If, at the end of that time, the conditions in the contract haven't been met, then our unclaimed shares go to charity," Kris finished.

"Is she serious?" Tom asked.

"Fine. Let's just kill her then, before the three months is up," Rachel said, fully embracing her rebellious side.

Kris and Tom stared at their younger sister as if she had two heads.

"What?" Rachel said, looking back and forth at them. "Don't tell me you haven't thought of it. Full bank accounts and no more pain-in-the-ass Neva. It's a win-win."

Kris rolled her eyes at Rachel, but Tom stared at her in disgust.

Rachel held her serious demeanor for a few more seconds before breaking into a smile aimed at Tom. "I'm kidding, Tooth Fairy!" she chuckled, tossing a pillow from the sofa in his direction. "It would serve her right, though. What comes around goes around."

"Jeezus, Rachel," Tom said, throwing the pillow back at her. "You can be such a bitch."

"Jeezus, Tom, you can be such a spineless wuss," Rachel shot back.

"Hey!" Kris said, throwing up her hands again. "It doesn't matter anyway. Death is covered too. The money would still go to charity."

Rachel mulled this information over before offering a third alternative. "What if we make the changes, get the money, and then change back? She can't do anything about that, can she? The money would be ours at that point."

Tom looked hopeful. "You mean divorce Patty, get the money, and then remarry her?"

"Yeah!" Rachel said, nodding enthusiastically. "I'll sell the bar and then buy it back. Bet there's nothing in the contract about that."

Kris pushed her own contract away and picked up Rachel's. She flipped through a few pages, running her finger down the text. Rachel and Tom looked on, hopeful they had found the loophole they needed. Kris stopped on page ten and began to read.

"In the event that Rachel Stevenson enters back into ownership of the previously owned establishment, all monies, and property, including Lucky's Bar, will immediately revert to Neva Stevenson, plus interest, at eight percent per annum. Neva Stevenson retains the right to garnish wages."

Rachel's face had gone a shade of deep pink as she listened. Her eyes bulged, and a vein on her temple stuck out as if about to burst. "What. The. Actual. Fuck? That meddling, controlling—"

"Yep, but she knows you like a book," Kris said, tossing the contract back onto the table.

"No shit," Tom said in awe.

Rachel slammed her beer down on the coffee table.

"I've got a similar clause in my contract. I'm sure Tom does too," Kris offered in a conciliatory tone. "So now that we know where we stand with Mom, what are we going to do?"

Tom ran his hands through his mess of hair. "The money would be great. I could finally go to school and not worry about trying to work while I get my degree—but Mom telling me I have to divorce my wife is too much. What about the girls? That's their mother."

"It takes more than biology to make somebody a good parent," Kris said gently.

Rachel pointed her beer at Kris. "Exactly! That's what I've been telling you about Neva for twenty years. Now look what she's doing," Rachel said, gesturing to the contracts. "That's a Mother of the Year move right there," she added with disgust.

Kris sighed, suddenly weary to her bones. "Well, bad move or not, this is the hand she's dealt us. There's a lot to consider."

Tom rubbed the back of his neck in agitation. "I guess so. We've got a little time, so—"

Rachel jumped to her feet. "Are you kidding me!? You're both actually thinking about caving to her demands?"

Tom shrugged, not meeting her gaze.

"We should all try to look at this as—" Kris started.

"We? There is no 'we.' You two can do whatever you want, but my fucking life is not for sale!" Rachel growled before stomping out of the room.

A moment later, they heard the front door slam.

Chapter 7:
If the Shoe Fits...

On Monday, Kris found it hard to concentrate at work. She was preparing two cases for her boss, Michael Newburg, and was behind on both. Kris and Robin usually ate lunch together, and twice a week they would dine at one of the restaurants on their block. Today, however, Kris was not allowing herself that break.

She needed to stop thinking about the bomb her mother dropped and focus on work. No matter what she did, though, her mother's ultimatum continued to plague her. She didn't agree with her siblings that the things Neva demanded of her were "easy things." After all, Tom didn't want to divorce Patty, so why did he think divorcing Carl would be any easier? The other things—buying new clothes and going out with her friends—might sound easy, but Kris knew Neva really meant that she should buy clothes she wasn't comfortable wearing and go out with her girlfriends to hunt for a man. Neither of those things would be easy, and she didn't want to do them. Kris didn't need to change herself for her mother or anyone else, and she resented Neva for always making her feel worse about herself than she already did.

Kris felt Neva's fourth demand, cleaning up Trent's appearance, was just plain mean. It was bad enough that Neva made her feel inadequate. Kris would not allow her mother to do the same thing to Trent. Neva could shove that money where the sun didn't shine if she thought Kris would do that to her own child.

Robin entered her office, carrying a bag of food and a drink. She handed them to Kris and pulled a chair up to the desk. "It's Yellow Submarine today. I picked up your usual."

"Thank you," Kris said as she unwrapped her sandwich. "I can't take much of a lunch break, but I seriously need the energy boost." She took the first bite of the turkey, cheddar, lettuce, and tomato sandwich and moaned her approval.

Robin watched, wrinkling her nose. "How can you eat the same sandwich every single time?"

Kris swallowed and took a sip of her iced tea. "I like this lunch. It's comforting and keeps me slim."

"Keeps you boring," Robin snorted, pulling a box of fries from the bag for herself. "Everybody needs a change now and then."

Kris wiped her mouth on a napkin. "You think so?" she asked.

"Absawootly," Robin said through a mouthful of fries.

"Okay, what if someone offered you five million dollars, but to get it, you had to change something about yourself to meet their specifications? Would you do it?"

Robin swallowed the fries and took a sip of her drink before answering. "Change something about myself for five mil? Are you serious!? As long as they didn't want me to become deformed or somethin', hell yes I'd do it!"

"Really? Just like that?" Kris asked.

"Uh, yeah! Wouldn't you?"

Kris picked up her sandwich again but didn't take a bite. "What if it was your mom who told you to change something?"

"My mom tells me that on the daily," Robin said, rolling her eyes. She picked up one of her French fries and pointed it at Kris. "But I tell you what—if my momma's got five million dollars, she better fork some over no matter what."

Kris snatched the fry from her. "You think she would?"

"She loves me! Of course she would. She damn well better," Robin said.

Kris pulled back, intrigued. "Oh, yeah? Why's that?" she asked, sipping her tea.

"'Cause I'm the one picking out her nursing home," Robin said with a wicked grin.

Tea spilled down Kris's chin and suit jacket as she guffawed. Chuckling, Robin dabbed at Kris's face and jacket with a napkin as Kris swatted at her, still laughing.

A few minutes later, Robin put the chair back and leaned against the side of Kris's desk. "Hey... I was thinking about hittin' the club Saturday night. A little dancin', a little hottie watchin'," she said, doing a pop-and-lock dance move. "You're basically single now. Why don't you come with me?"

Kris chuckled at her friend's dance attempt. "No, thanks."

"Why not?"

Kris shrugged. "I'm too old for that stuff. You know it's not my thing."

"Well, what is your thing, then?" Robin asked.

"Do I need to have a thing?"

"Oh yeah, girlfriend. You definitely need to have a thing. I try to have my thing at least three times a week," Robin said with a wink.

Kris snorted, causing tea to rush up her nose. She coughed and sputtered while Robin giggled.

"Leave my office, you weirdo, before I drown in my tea," Kris said, throwing her wet napkin at her.

Robin shot Kris with finger guns as she sauntered backward out of the office. "Think about it!" she called from the hallway.

· · · ·

Rachel wove the Jeep through traffic, trying to get home. She had never been as angry as she was at her mother right now. So angry, in fact, that she couldn't even think straight. As a direct result, she had driven all the way to work today before realizing she had left the bar's accounting books at home. This wouldn't have been a big deal any other day, but today she had deliveries coming and needed those books to receive them. Now she was on her way back home to pick them up during one of the busiest parts of the day, which only fueled her anger.

Rachel couldn't believe her mother had just dropped a bomb like that and then disappeared. Who did Neva think she was, trying to dictate how Rachel should live her life? She had no right to demand anything from her or from Tom and Kris. It felt like Neva was holding their damn lives for ransom. Rachel revved the engine as the light turned green, squealing the tires.

She had tried to call Neva several times but had gotten a message saying her number had been disconnected. Disconnected! Neva had dumped this shit on them and then ran off to hide, living it up on a beach somewhere while they all stewed in their pissed-off juices. The woman was a walking nightmare.

Rachel's home was in a well-kept, older neighborhood in Marion. The houses had been built between 1950 and 1968, and most of them were ranch-style homes. Rachel's house was a white, two-bedroom ranch with smoky blue shutters, a one-stall garage, and a short cement driveway. Finally reaching that driveway, she slammed the Jeep into park and jumped out.

As she pushed open the front door, Rachel saw that the accounting books were still on the sofa table where she had left them the night before. Scooping them up, she heard a noise that stopped her in her tracks. She didn't know what had caused it or which room it had come from; she just knew it was a sound that was out of place in an empty house. The hair on the back of her neck stood on end. Holding her breath, she strained to listen over the pounding of her heart. Her eyes went wide as she heard a muffled scuffling noise, followed by a soft thump. It sounded like it was coming from one of the bedrooms.

She placed the books on the sofa and scanned the room for something to use as a weapon. Her eyes fell on the architecture and home design books that lined a nearby shelf. They were large and heavy, but wielding them would be difficult. Maybe one of the lamps? No. They were too bulky, and she didn't have time to mess with removing the lampshades. She should call the police. Step outside and call them to come deal with whoever or whatever was in her house. That would be the smart thing to do, but being forced to deal with this on top of everything else made her see red. She would handle this herself. Whoever or whatever was in her house had picked the wrong day and the wrong woman to piss off.

Her eyes flitted to the entertainment center. The large statuette of a mother holding an infant caught her eye. Crossing the room as quietly as she could, Rachel picked it up. The statue was about eighteen inches tall and carved from a solid chunk of wood. It had a hefty weight to it. She swung it like a bat to get a feel for it. It wasn't ideal as weapons go, but it would work as long as the intruder didn't have a gun. Stealthily, she made her way down the hall, stopping to hold her breath and listen every few feet.

She heard the noise again and was sure it was coming from her own bedroom. Tiptoeing to the door, she pressed an ear to it. Yes, the intruder was in there. She could hear them moving around inside the room. Gathering her courage, Rachel took a deep breath and silently counted to three, bouncing slightly on her heels with each number. On three, she raised the statue above her head and kicked open the door. Screaming like a banshee, she charged inside.

Rachel froze, staring in disbelief and horror at the scene in front of her.

Kim was in her bed, naked. A guy who appeared to be in his early twenties was also naked—and in bed with her daughter. He rolled off Kim and scrambled to cover himself with the sheet. The volcanic rage inside Rachel rose several notches, threatening to consume her.

"Mom!" Kim said indignantly. "What are you doing home so early!?"

Her daughter's tone snapped Rachel back into action, and the volcano erupted. Dropping the statuette, she lunged for the guy, intending to commit violence with her bare hands. "She's a minor, you son of a bitch!" she bellowed, hands outstretched as she went for his throat.

"Mom! Stop it!" Kim screamed, clambering to a sitting position on the bed.

Rachel was deaf to her daughter's protests. She had lost herself to her inner berserker. The naked guy was fast. He lurched backward, away from Rachel, but fell off the bed in his hasty retreat. Kim grabbed at her mother's waist and legs, trying to keep her on the bed. Rachel's eyes stayed trained on the guy as she worked to pry Kim's hands loose. He stared back at her from the floor, eyes wide with shock.

Rachel kicked out, and Kim's grip loosened. In an instant, Rachel rolled off the bed and was on her feet. She glared with murderous intent at the guy. "I am going to rip your fucking dick off."

The guy was off the floor like a jackrabbit, racing toward the door. He stopped for only a second to scoop up his clothes before fleeing the room in a naked panic.

"Leave him alone! Mom! Leave him alone!" Kim screamed.

Rachel turned to stare in disbelief at her daughter.

Kim stared back, chest heaving and panicked.

Rachel huffed in disgust and rocketed out of the room in pursuit of her prey.

She made it to the front door just in time to see him sprinting across her front lawn. His bare ass and bobbing balls were visible to any of her elderly neighbors who might be outside or looking out their windows. This made Rachel even more furious. Not only was her daughter the harlot of the neighborhood, but the whole damn town would know about it before the end of the day. The mere thought made Rachel want to beat this guy to a bloody pulp and dance on his entrails. She shot out of the house, intent on doing just that.

The guy made it across the street to his car and began fumbling through his clothes for the keys. Rachel ran toward him at a sprint, her face promising absolute violence. He saw it and abandoned the car, sprinting down the sidewalk with his clothes clutched tight against his chest.

He was fast. Rachel knew she could never catch him, but she chased him another fifteen yards anyway before stopping and yelling after him, "If you ever come near my daughter again, I'll castrate you with a pair of rusty scissors!"

As the guy glanced over his shoulder, he tripped on a raised piece of the sidewalk, sending him sprawling onto the lawn of Rachel's seventy-five-year-old neighbor, Mrs. Collins. He scrambled back to his feet and ran a few more steps before stumbling again. This time, he fell and rolled onto his back at the feet of Mrs. Collins herself, who had been watching the fiasco from her mailbox at the curb. She stood, mouth open and eyes glued to the groin of the naked man in her front yard. He stared back just long enough to catch his breath before snatching his clothes from the grass and continuing his escape from the neighborhood.

Rachel bent over, hands on her knees, trying to get her wind back. Glancing up, she noticed several neighbors watching from windows and lawns nearby. She closed her eyes and cursed under her breath. Jesus Christ! When her mother heard about this, she was never, ever going to hear the end of it!

"See?" Neva would proclaim. "What did I tell you? You're a terrible mother, and your daughter is now a fifteen-year-old whore."

I am going to kill Kim! I will kill her and bury her fucking body in the backyard, Rachel thought to herself. Standing back up, she lifted her chin and tucked her hair behind her ears before striding purposefully back to the house.

By the time she got there, Kim had covered herself with a bathrobe and stood in the living room, arms crossed over her chest, glaring at Rachel. "Way to go, Mom!" she spat in disgust.

The look Rachel gave her daughter would have made the Devil cringe. Kim's eyes widened, and she instinctively took a step back.

Rachel advanced, grabbing the front of Kim's bathrobe and shaking her. "Is this what you do when I'm at work? Skip school and have sex in my house? In my goddamn bed!?"

Kim's anger reignited. "Why not? Someone should be."

The slap landed hard on Kim's cheek, sending her staggering sideways. For a moment, they stood staring at each other, both stunned. Rachel recovered first. She took a deep, shaky breath and placed both hands on her hips. She stared down at her feet, blinking back her own tears. "I'm sorry—I shouldn't have done that. This is just—"

"You are such a hypocrite!" Kim bawled, raising a hand to cover the angry patch of red on her cheek. "You weren't a virgin when you were my age!"

Rachel's eyes snapped back to her daughter.

"I know all about it! I heard you and Grandma fighting about it when I was twelve. You were quite the little slut, weren't you, Mom? Drinking and—how did Grandma put it? Whoring around!"

Rachel raised her hand to slap Kim again, but immediately dropped it when she saw her daughter flinch.

This seemed to intensify Kim's anger. "I'm proof of it! I was just an accident!" she screamed. "Just a by-product of your whoring years."

"Kim," Rachel said through gritted teeth. "That is not true, I—"

"Yes, it is! Just admit it!" Kim sobbed. "You're only sixteen years older than me, Mom. Do the math!"

Rachel's jaw tightened. "That's beside the point. I was not whoring around when I got pregnant with you. We've discussed this. And it doesn't matter, anyway. I don't want you to make the same mistakes I made."

Too late, Rachel saw the impact of those words in her daughter's eyes. She reached out for her, but Kim pulled away. "That's not what I meant," Rachel said flatly. "Listen, I was really messed up and confused when I was young. There are things you don't know about—that you couldn't possibly understand—"

"Oh, I understand perfectly. I'm just a mistake you've been trying to get away from since the day you had me," Kim snarled, before bolting from the room.

"That's not true! I've worked my ass off to give you a good home and provide for you—by myself!" Rachel called after her.

"Whatever you say—NEVA!" Kim shouted back before slamming her own bedroom door.

Rachel staggered backward as if Kim had just slapped her. Neva!? She was not like her mother. Not at all! She replayed the last few minutes in her mind and cringed. Holy shit, she thought to herself, did I just repeat my mother's mantra to my own daughter? She had said it word for word and unfortunately, it was as true for her and Kim as it was for her and Neva. Damn it! She needed a drink. A very stiff, very cold drink.

Grabbing her stainless-steel travel mug from the cupboard, Rachel poured two jiggers of vodka from the Texas fifth sitting on the counter. To that, she added ice and half a can of Sprite. After swirling the mug in the air for a few seconds, she took a long drink. She let her head fall back and sighed. "Thank God for vodka," she said and took another drink.

A few minutes later, mug in hand, Rachel approached Kim's bedroom door. She heard muffled sounds of crying coming from the other side and raised her hand to knock. She paused, wrestling with what she would say. Her hand dropped back to her side. Without a word, she walked away.

• • • •

In her hotel room, Neva prepared for another day of relaxation. She slipped a colorful sundress, a new purchase from the local gift shop, over her head and smoothed the fabric down over her hips. It was a perfect fit. She ran her hands lovingly over the cloth. She never wore things like this at home. Never exposed so much skin. Doing so now made her feel young again. Young, and vibrant, and beautiful, and sexy. The entire vacation had been making her feel that way. Slowly bringing her back to life.

Lounging on the beach drinking cocktails, reading risqué romance novels, and man-watching had awakened a part of her she thought long dead, and it was just as frightening as it was thrilling. So, today she wanted to try something different. She decided she would start in the hotel lounge with a few drinks and then take one of the boat tours the hotel offered.

Neva loved the ocean and had always wanted to take a vacation like this, but raising her children had been a full-time job layered over the full-time job of managing the bar. There had never been enough time for her to take a vacation and never enough money to take them all on one. That was the reality of being a single parent and trying to raise children with only one income. The closest thing to a vacation the Stevensons had was spending two days at the Adventureland amusement park in Des Moines. She hadn't been as emotionally or mentally present for her kids as she should have been during the first four years after Robert's death, but she had made it a point to take the amusement park trip with them each year.

Every summer, she took two days off from the bar and loaded her children into the car for the two-hour drive to Des Moines. The kids loved the amusement park, and it gave her the rare opportunity to set her daily stresses aside and have fun with them the way she used to. For two days they would laugh, and sing, and race through the park from one ride to the next. All their baggage and troubles forgotten. Then, they would retire to the hotel, and Neva would watch the kids swim in the pool until management forced them back to their room, where they would collapse into bed, happy and exhausted.

After Rachel got pregnant, those trips ended. They hadn't discussed it or come to any conscious decision. They had just stopped. Neva never let it show, but the absence of that time with her kids had been devastating to her.

Where has the time gone? She would give all her winnings to relive just one of those trips with them. In that time before they had grown up and made such terrible choices. Their failures were like a slap in the face after everything she went through to regain her sanity and provide for them. Watching their adult lives become as much of a train wreck as hers had been was Neva's own unique version of purgatory.

She groaned and attempted to push all thoughts of the kids out of her mind. Her children and the promise she had made to Lois felt like invisible companions over the last few days. Neva had been giving her life a lot of thought and found many things about it she would like to change. Things she had given up on or denied herself. Happy times she wanted to have with her kids and grandkids, if they'd let her. New adventures she wanted to have before she became a doddering old lady. She wasn't young woman anymore, but she wasn't dead either. There was still time.

Neva crossed the enormous suite to the full-length mirror and studied her image. She ran a finger lightly over the fine lines around her eyes. She had taken good care of her skin, and it showed. Making her look at least ten years younger than her true age of fifty-eight, but time is a stealthy adversary, and Neva could feel it beginning to creep up on her.

Her eyes drifted to the scar on her neck. She brushed her fingertips across it and swallowed hard. No matter how much time went by, the sight of it always had the same effect on her. Dreadful memories crashed through her mind, causing her heart to squeeze painfully in her chest. Sometimes, she woke in the night, gasping and struggling to breathe, grasping at the ghost of the rope. It didn't happen as often as it used to. Maybe once or twice a year—but it was still too often.

Clearing her throat, she stood up straight and gave herself a stern look in the mirror. "Snap out of it! You've got shit to do." With that, she grabbed the new scarf off the end of her bed and draped it expertly around her neck, covering the scar completely. Satisfied that it was hidden, Neva checked the fit of her dress once more. She had been blessed in the bust department and the cut of the dress made that fact clear. Her stomach was still where it should be. No bulges or bumps and still nearly flat. Her hips, legs, and buttocks had remained lean and tight due to all the miles walked every day when she still managed the bar. After she'd turned it over to Rachel, she'd started power walking five miles every day to maintain her lower half. She was proud to see the results of her efforts in her reflection. When she was younger, Neva feared being on her feet so much would give her varicose veins, but either good genes or pure luck had prevented it. The Almighty had probably decided the scar on her throat was punishment enough. Giving her varicose veins too would have been overkill.

Her eyes traveled back to the scarf, and she caught herself frowning in the mirror. "Enough", she commanded to her reflection. Grabbing her bag and sunglasses from the end of the bed, she pulled her shoulders back, lifted her chin, and left the hotel room, closing the door firmly behind her.

When the elevator doors opened a few moments later, Neva stepped into the lobby with high hopes for the day. The ocean could be seen through the floor-to-ceiling windows, and her stomach gave a small flutter at the thought of the boat tour she had booked. She loved spending time near the water more than she thought she would. Maybe she would buy a house on the water with her part of the lotto winnings and have this view and a beach to enjoy every day. It wouldn't be the same without the sexy male bodies parading by in their shorts and Speedos, though. Chuckling to herself, she pondered how much of her love for the beach was linked to the half-naked man parade. By the time she entered the hotel's private lounge, she decided it must be somewhere in the neighborhood of fifty-five percent. Maybe sixty.

She secured a seat at the end of the bar, where she could sip her morning cocktail and watch the other guests. The bartender was an attractive young woman of about twenty-five. "Relaxation Ambassador" was etched in gold on the name tag pinned to her Hawaiian-style shirt. Underneath, the name Stacy was written in flamingo pink marker. She approached Neva with a beautiful smile, and her opinion of the girl instantly rose a notch. In Neva's opinion, the cleaner your teeth, the better you were as a person. When she was a girl, her mother told her repeatedly, "Soap is cheap and toothbrushes are plentiful. There's no excuse for walking around with a dirty body or a dirty mouth. Anyone who does, is either a shitty human being or a lazy one. Stay away from both types, Neva Ruth."

Neva had discovered from her own experiences that, with very few exceptions, her mother was spot-on with those particular words of wisdom. She couldn't say that about every piece of advice her mother had given her, but that pearl, and the warning about not marrying Robert, had been incredibly accurate. Not heeding her mother's counsel had been a devastating mistake. She was young and naïve back then. Thought she knew everything. She had lashed out at her mother viciously. Neva winced at the memory of how awful she had been. Her mother had only been trying to keep her from making a terrible mistake. If she had realized that, then—if she had listened to her mother—her life would have turned out differently.

"What can I get you this morning?" Stacy asked, placing a coaster on the bar top in front of Neva.

"Jack and Coke," Neva answered automatically. Then, remembering her new goal of breaking out of old habits, she changed course. "No, wait! Let's make that a strawberry margarita instead. Blended please, with a pineapple umbrella."

"You got it," Stacy chirped before stepping a few feet away to construct the drink.

Neva watched her work, impressed with the young woman's skill. She had been nimble behind the bar at Stacy's age, too. Once Neva had made the same drink a few dozen times, it became muscle memory and took almost no thought at all. In a busy place like this, it was a wonder Stacy wasn't making the margarita with her eyes closed.

A man sat down next to Neva, distracting her from her thoughts. He appeared to be in his late fifties, with graying hair cut in a professional style. Even though he was clean-shaven and dressed in expensive beach attire, he gave off a shady car-salesman vibe that made Neva want to scoot her chair away from him. She opted to ignore him instead.

Stacy delivered Neva's drink with another stunning smile. "Would you like me to start a tab for your room?"

Neva grinned back and handed over the room key. "That would be fantastic, Stacy. Thank you." She took a sip of the margarita. "This is divine. You know your stuff," she praised with a wink.

Stacy's smile widened. "Thank you!" She swiped Neva's card and punched a few buttons on the register. "You're all set!" she said, handing the card back and turning her attention to the man. "Good morning, what would you like?"

He flashed a sly smile. "I know what I would like," he said, winking. "But I guess I'll have to settle for a drink. Vodka tonic on the rocks, please, sweet thing."

Stacy's smile faltered at his words. Seeing it, Neva had the urge to knock the sleazy idiot off his chair. Instead, she smiled warmly at Stacy and rolled her eyes. The young woman's smile returned, and she retreated to make the drink.

Neva focused her attention on a couple sitting at a table in the far corner of the lounge. They were sitting close together, snuggling and laughing with each other as they sipped their drinks. Obviously in love. Probably newlyweds, Neva thought. She wondered absently if, at the eight-year mark, they would be counted in the fifty percent of couples that make it, or the fifty percent that don't. After watching them for another minute, she decided she wanted them to fall into the fifty percent that made it.

The man next to Neva leaned toward her and whispered, "Penny for your thoughts?"

"I'm sorry, what was that?" she asked, leaning away from him.

The man turned his chair toward Neva and took a sip of his drink as he studied her. "You look troubled, and that's a rarity around here. Illegal, I think."

"Thanks, I'll keep that in mind."

"John Williams," he said, extending his hand.

Neva hesitated, then took it and gave a weak handshake in return. "Betty Rubble."

John chuckled. "Well, Betty Rubble, it's a pleasure to meet you. You here with Barney or your boyfriend?"

"Neither," she said, self-consciously adjusting her scarf. She didn't look at him as she spoke and turned her body away, hoping he'd take the hint and buzz off.

"Must be my lucky day, then. Can I buy you a drink?" he asked in a smooth tone.

Stacy glanced at her with a wrinkled nose in an expression of disgust. Neva was really starting to like this girl. "Trust me, Mr. Williams, I'm not your type," she said coolly.

"Really? And what type is that?" he asked, amused.

"Easily flattered. The type that thinks money, a smile, and any degree of interest makes you a decent man," she said, turning to look him directly in the eye.

"Ahh—divorcee, then," he said with a nod.

"Widow," Neva said, stirring her drink with the umbrella.

John's smile faded. "I'm so sorry to hear that. Was it an illness or something unexpected?" he asked, with exaggerated kindness.

"Very unexpected," Neva replied, keeping her eyes on her drink.

"Heart attack, huh?"

"No, he was killed," she said, turning to face him once again.

"Killed!? How awful. I can only imagine how hard that must have been for you." Reaching out, he laid his hand over Neva's. "With such a beautiful, vivacious wife, I'm sure his last moments were filled with thoughts of you."

"Oh, I have no doubt about that," Neva said. She leaned toward him, her lips almost touching his ear. "Because I'm the one that killed him," she whispered. "With a baseball bat." She pulled back just enough for him to see her wicked grin.

His mouth dropped open, and his eyes went wide.

"Careful, John," Neva crooned, running an index finger under his chin. "You'll catch flies if you leave that open." She snapped his jaw closed.

John startled at her touch, snatching his hand back and leaning away slightly.

Neva pouted her lower lip, frowning as if he had hurt her feelings.

John turned away, making a point of studying his drink. "Right. Well, nice to meet you."

Neva pulled a hundred-dollar bill and her sunglasses from her bag. She placed the bill under her margarita glass and donned her sunglasses.

"See ya on the beach, Mr. Williams," she cooed, running her fingers lightly down John's arm.

He shivered. "Yeah. Sure. See you on the beach, Betty," he mumbled.

Neva delivered her best maniacal chuckle, feeling immensely satisfied to see his hand shaking as he brought his drink to his mouth. Neva winked over her sunglasses at Stacy and strutted out of the lounge, grinning like a well-fed cheetah.

· · · ·

Tom pushed open the doors of the college administration building and stepped into the brilliant sunlight. Spring term was ending soon. Students were gathered throughout the grounds, reading, talking, and enjoying the beautiful day. Tom watched them for a few moments, feeling happier than he had been in a long time. He glanced down at the pamphlet in his hands and smiled. He could be one of them. If he did what his mother asked, he could attend college here and create a better life for himself and his girls. The meeting he had with Karla, the college guidance counselor, had gone very well. She had taken him on a tour of the school, and he had fallen in love with the smell and feel of the place. It reminded him of the way he felt when he was a kid and visited the library.

Tom had been a voracious reader as a child. He had dreamed of escaping his life and becoming a different person. Someone who was brave, and strong, and went on exciting adventures. The library had provided him temporary access to that life through the countless books he read.

He had been an excellent student, testing above his grade level and earning excellent marks in every subject. By the time high school started, his intellect had grown to that of a college student. His body had done a lot of growing, too. By sophomore year, Tom was six-foot-two and what his mother liked to call "well-put-together." His lean and muscular build, with broad shoulders that tapered to a perfect Y-shape at his waist, together with his dark-lashed hazel eyes and perpetually messy brown hair, had ensured a constant stream of female admirers. He hadn't minded those. It had been the male admirers that bothered him. Specifically, the basketball coach, football coach, and baseball coach, who were all constantly trying to recruit him to their sport. Tom was a decent athlete too, but didn't enjoy contact sports. He couldn't understand the point. Why would people want to fight over a ball, or anything else, for that matter? Fighting off their constant recruiting efforts had been exhausting.

During school registration in his junior year, Coach Phillips tried another tactic and cornered Tom's mom on the subject. Tom would never forget the way his mother had dealt with it. Neva had smiled at the coach in a way that lit up her eyes and pretended to hang on his every word as he bragged about his success as a football coach. Then, he had said, "Ms. Stevenson, surely you understand that playing high school football is a rite of passage for every young man. It just isn't normal for a sturdy guy like your son not to play."

He had emphasized the word "normal" as if to imply Tom was far from it for not wanting to sign up. The coach's implication had wounded him. Tom looked up from his shoes to find his mother's eyes on him. He shrugged slightly, glancing around to see who might have overheard. When his eyes fell on his mother again, her gaze had shifted back to the coach, and a sly grin had replaced her warm smile. The instant Tom saw it, he knew there was going to be trouble.

When the coach had finished his spiel, Neva had lifted her chin and loudly declared, "If you think I want my son to chase around after a goddamn ball while a whole pack of dumbasses tries to kill him, you are sadly mistaken. He's got more brains in his pinky toe than your entire football team put together."

Tom would never forget the look on Coach Phillips' face, or the way his neck had flushed red, surging upward to engulf his entire face as his mother continued speaking.

"Surely you understand, Mr. Phillips, that I want more for my son's future than a concussion, or the career position of head jock strap at a local high school. He will not be playing football, or anything else- and that is my decision, not his."

Then, his mother had turned on her heel and walked out of the gym, leaving Coach Phillips and a handful of parents staring after her, frozen like deer caught in the headlights.

Tom had followed her in complete shock. Besides the parents, there were at least four of his classmates that had overheard his mother. By the first day of school, everyone would know about it.

In the car, he fumed silently most of the way home, angry that she had made his high school life harder than it already was.

"What's wrong with you, Brooding Billy?" Neva chided.

"Nothing," Tom shrugged.

"Don't lie, Thomas. You're horrible at it."

Tom shifted uncomfortably in his seat. "Why did you have to say that to the coach? Everyone's going to know about it by the first day."

"Yes, I'm sure they will," she said, pleased.

Tom stared at her, dumbfounded.

His mother glanced over at him and laughed. "Do I have to spell it out for you?"

At his silence, she sighed and said, "You don't want to play football, right?"

Tom shook his head.

"Well, that shit-for-breath coach may be a fool, but he has a point. Other kids will think it's weird for someone who looks like you, to not play. By the end of the first term, they'll be spreading rumors you're gay or some other crap, if they aren't already." She glanced at him, watching his response. "Am I right?"

He rolled his eyes. He knew she was right, but he was still too angry to admit it.

"Yes, I'm right, and you know it. Only now, you have a different excuse for not being involved in sports. Now, it's because your mom: A. Won't let you, or B. Is just plain crazy. Either way, it's not on you anymore. Now the coaches will back off."

Tom sat in stunned silence the rest of the way home, his head spinning with the revelation of just how brilliant and diabolical his mother truly was. When she pulled into the driveway, he got out of the car, still contemplating what she had done.

She leaned over the passenger seat, raising her voice to be heard out the open window. "I'll be home after the bar closes. There's a casserole in the fridge for dinner. Don't drink my Coke and don't let Rachel drink it either."

She had backed out of the driveway and into the street before Tom snapped out of his reverie.

"Mom!" he yelled after her. She stopped and waited. He rushed over to her open car window and leaned down. "Thanks for making that up," he said, giving her a quick kiss on the cheek.

"I didn't make anything up. You're a smart kid, Tommy," she said, patting his cheek. "Smart enough to do anything you want in this life. Do you think I want some idiot in a helmet to take that away from you?"

That was the day—the exact moment—he had promised himself that he would go to college and do something amazing with his life.

Tom smiled at the memory, but as he settled back into the reality of the present moment, his smile quickly faded. He hadn't gone to college, and "amazing" wasn't even close to how he would describe his life.

He glanced at his watch. It was nearly five o'clock. Cursing under his breath, he jogged across the green lawn of the campus to his car. He threw the college paperwork onto the passenger seat as he climbed into his beat-up Ford Focus. Getting back across town during rush hour traffic meant he'd be home later than expected, and Patty would be upset. If he had a cell phone, he'd call and let her know he was on his way. He really needed a cell phone, but they could only afford one right now, and Patty had decided she needed it more than he did. He hadn't argued with her about it. Now, he wished he had.

Tom wished he could argue with her about a lot of things, but it just wasn't his way. He hated to argue and fight with Patty, with his family, or with anybody, really. It made him feel physically sick and always brought back the nightmares. Then, the nightmares would set off his anxiety attacks, and he would feel like his life was spiraling out of control until his mind and body settled back down. Rachel had always teased him about it. She thought he was a freak for never getting angry about anything. As usual, his sister didn't know half of what she thought she did.

The fact was, Tom was angry about a lot of things almost all the time. He just didn't show it. He kept his anger tucked safely into boxes in his mind, where it couldn't get out and cause trouble for him or anyone else. Arguing with Patty or releasing even a fraction of his anger would put his girls in danger, and he wasn't going to do that to them.

Fifteen minutes later, he tapped the steering wheel nervously as he waited to turn onto his street. Three cars waited ahead of him, none of which seemed to be in any kind of rush. "Come on, come on," he muttered. When Tom was finally able to make the turn, he raced up the street and pulled into his driveway, slamming hard on the brakes to avoid crashing into the garage door. He barely had the car in park before grabbing his paperwork off the passenger seat and getting out.

Loud music emanated from the house—Guns and Roses. "Fuuuck," he moaned to himself. That meant she was angry and drinking. He frowned and leaned against the car, staring at the front door. He didn't want to go in. Didn't want to deal with Patty tonight.

Just an hour ago, he had been feeling good about college and the possibilities it would create for them all. Now he was filled with dread. Leaning back into the car, he put the college brochure in the glove compartment. Maybe tonight wasn't the right time to bring it up. His teeth ground together as his jaw tightened. There was the anger, rattling its box, trying to escape. Tom closed his eyes and took a deep breath, the way Kris had taught him to do. He let it out slowly. Taking another breath, he opened his eyes. Time to get it over with.

The small house was a wreck. Toys were strewn everywhere. Leftover plastic trays from frozen dinners sat on the end tables, and a haze of cigarette smoke hung in the air. The television was muted but tuned to the Nickelodeon channel. Colorful cartoon characters danced across the screen as if choreographed to the tune of "Welcome to the Jungle," which was blaring from the sound system.

Ashlea and Megan danced into the room, oblivious to their father standing in the doorway. They were both still in their pajamas. Megan giggled as she watched her older sister pose with an unlit cigarette in one hand and an empty beer can in the other. Ashlea pretended to take a drag from the cigarette and then a fake gulp of beer.

Tom had seen enough. He pulled the plug on the stereo, startling the girls with the instant silence. He took the cigarette and beer can from Ashlea's hands. "Ashlea, you know these aren't for little girls," he scolded.

Ashlea's eyes filled with tears. "I was pretending to be Mommy," she said in a small voice. Tom took another deep breath and tried for a softer tone. "Mommy shouldn't have these either. Don't do that again, okay?"

"Since when do you decide what I should or shouldn't have?" Patty sneered as she entered the room. Her hair fell in soft waves around her perfectly made-up face. Her gold sequined top was cut in a deep V that extended an inch above her belly button and showed more of her breasts than it covered. It hung over the waistband of her skin-tight, black leather leggings. Black high heels and the beer in her hand completed the outfit.

Tom held up the cigarette and beer can. "When I walked in, she was holding these and pretending to smoke and drink them. I'm trying to explain that she shouldn't do that," he said reasonably.

Patty snorted. "Why? Because you don't?"

"Patty, she's six," he sighed, tossing the empty can and cigarette onto the end table. "Never mind. I don't wanna fight, okay? It's been a long day and—"

Patty took an aggressive step toward him. "You've had a long day? You have!? Why don't you try sitting here all day with these kids?"

Ashlea and Megan joined hands and inched closer together, their mouths drawn into small frowns as they watched their mother.

"You're right, I'm sorry. What can I do to help?" Tom said, reaching out to embrace her.

Patty slapped his hands away and glared at him. "What can you do to help? Seriously? Oh, I don't know, let me think..." she said, tapping her chin as if in thought. "How about you get a job so we can afford a babysitter! Did you manage to do that today?"

"I don't know yet. I had three interviews, and I think they all went well, but..." Tom trailed off, stuffing his hands into his front pockets. "I've been thinking—maybe I should go to school. Get a degree. I'd be able to get a better job and make a lot more money if I had a college background."

Patty stared at him, wide-eyed. "What in the hell are you talking about? How are you gonna support this family if you're in classes all day?"

Tom knew he should give in. Knew he should just apologize and shut up, but he couldn't. He wanted to talk about it. To convince her that his going to college was a better plan. He wanted to enroll.

"I can get student loans that'll help, and my schedule can be flexible so I can work at the same time. They even have a childcare program that—"

"You've already looked into it?" Patty hissed, hands clenching into fists at her sides. "Without talking to me, you've already looked into it?" She shoved Tom hard in the chest, sending him stumbling backward a few steps.

Tom bobbed his head sheepishly. "Well, yeah, I drove by the school today and..."

Patty let out an infuriated howl and punched Tom in the face with all her strength.

He staggered backward, as much from surprise as from the blow itself. Before he had time to recover, she lunged at him, screaming obscenities, and punching wildly.

"Sneaking bastard! Selfish! Lazy! Worthless!" Patty screamed, punctuating each word with blows to his face and torso.

Tom attempted to block her strikes while simultaneously trying to grab her arms.

Megan stood, transfixed, against the sofa as her parents brawled. Ashlea, tears streaming, ran into the fray. She grabbed the tail of her mother's shirt, trying to pull her away from her father. "Mommy, stop it! Stop!"

A loud ripping noise caused them all to freeze. Patty grabbed for the back of her shirt, which was no longer there, and whirled to see it dangling from the hands of her daughter. Sequins glittered on the floor around Ashlea's feet. Patty snatched the ripped fabric out of Ashlea's hands. Tom didn't have time to intervene before Patty slapped their daughter hard across the face, sending her sprawling.

Tom grabbed Megan and hoisted her onto his back, then rushed to Ashlea's side as Patty removed the rest of her shirt, huffing like a speared bull.

"Run to the car," he whispered in Ashlea's ear.

Ashlea shook her head and took Tom's hand.

"GET OUT! GET OUT OF MY HOUSE! ALL OF YOU—GET OUT!" Patty screamed.

Tom scooped Ashlea up by the waist and, with Megan still clinging to his back, they raced out of the house. Patty slammed the front door behind them, shattering the glass.

"Go Daddy! Let's go!" Megan urged as he settled her into the backseat of the car. Ashlea had already climbed in on the other side. Tears streamed down her beautiful little face, which was stained a deep red on one side from her mother's slap.

An hour later, after driving aimlessly around the city, the gas gauge in Tom's car was just as low as his spirits. He pulled into the parking lot of a bank and took the ATM card from his wallet. His left eye throbbed painfully, and it was difficult to see out of it. He looked at his reflection in the rear-view mirror and winced. Shifting his focus to the backseat, he studied his daughters. Ashlea's slap mark was finally beginning to fade, but there was a haunted look in her eyes that he'd never seen before. She had been silent during the drive, and he could tell there was a lot going on behind those eyes. Megan had also been uncharacteristically quiet, staring out the window as if in a trance from the moment they pulled out of the driveway. Tom wasn't sure if her behavior was because of the fight she had witnessed or just plain exhaustion. Regardless, it wasn't good. And he didn't know what to do about any of it. They shouldn't have to live like this. They shouldn't have to see their parents fight. He knew he was failing them. Everything was so complicated. Now, with his mom's demands, he wasn't sure of the best way to handle it all.

He needed help to figure that out, but first, he needed gas.

"I'll be right back," he said to his daughters, and got out of the car.

He inserted his ATM card, punched in the PIN, and selected the twenty-dollar cash withdrawal option. The machine refused his request. Tom stared at the screen in disbelief. Did Patty withdraw all our money? He chose the option to print out his account balance and snatched the paper receipt from the machine. The numbers on the print-out brought tears to his good eye. She had taken it all. Tom was left with two little girls and $6.36. Leaning his head against the ATM, he kicked the bottom, hard. A white-hot flame of pain rushed up his leg, and he cursed vehemently as he hopped around under the lamplight. What else could go wrong? Pulling himself together, he approached the ATM once again and inserted his card. Five dollars would have to do for now. It would provide enough gas to take him and the girls where they needed to go. A minor victory, but he would take it.

• • • •

Neva finished pinning up her mane of blonde hair and checked her appearance in the mirror. She adjusted her fluffy white bathrobe, smiling. She looked good, and she was beginning to feel even better. For the hundredth time, she wondered if her children had taken her up on her offer. Hopefully, they would. She wanted them to feel the same optimism she was feeling. Fishing her cell phone out of the bottom of her beach bag, she clicked number two on her speed dial list and paced the room as she waited for Kris to pick up.

"Hello?"

"Hi, honey!" Neva responded with exaggerated happiness.

It took Kris a beat to respond. "Hello, Mother. Is this your new number?"

"It is, but keep it to yourself. If you give it to Rachel, I'll have to kill you." Neva said with a chuckle. She was met with silence on the other end. She cleared her throat. "So, how are you all doing?"

"Upset. I'm upset. They're upset. How did you think we were going to be?"

"Upset? About what?" Neva asked innocently.

"You," Kris said flatly. "We're upset at you and the latest stunt you pulled."

"Oh, poo," Neva said dismissively. "Have you signed the divorce papers yet?"

"No, and I'm not talking to you about it."

"How about your brother and sister? Has Tom filed for divorce?"

"Mom, I'm not your—"

"Is Rachel selling the bar?"

"You need to ask them yourself."

"You know damn well I can't talk to Rachel without her hissing at me like a drunken alley cat, and Tom just tells me whatever I want to hear. So... spill it."

"You're crazy, you know that? You really are. You can't just bribe us into—"

A loud knock at the door distracted Neva.

"Honey, I have to let you go," Neva interrupted. "My masseuse is here."

"Masseuse?" Kris said, perplexed.

"See you in a few days!" Neva chirped and ended the call, dropping the cell phone into her robe pocket as she strode to the door and opened it.

A chiseled man in his late thirties stood in the hallway. His white shorts showcased long, muscled legs that were a deep tan from the Florida sun. The white polo shirt highlighted his upper body, and Neva noticed his well-muscled biceps and forearms. She felt a flush race from low in her belly to the top of her head. Forearms. It was a mystery why men with thick forearms had this effect on her. Her eyes traveled up his arms to his broad chest and hovered for just a moment, admiring his pecs, before continuing to his face. He was smiling at her with gorgeous, white teeth and... dimples. The man had dimples! Neva's heart gave a flutter, and she willed it still. His eyes were the shade of Blue Curacao over ice and framed with dark lashes. His hair was thick and a dark brown that was nearly black, feathered off to one side. Neva squeezed her hands into fists to prevent herself from reaching out and running them through it.

She had ordered a massage, and they had sent her a Greek God.

The God-turned-masseuse cleared his throat and spoke. "Ms. Stevenson, I'm your masseuse, Garrett."

Neva blinked, trying to recover. "Of course, of course," she said, extending a hand for him to shake. "I'm Neva Stevenson."

He took her hand in his, and the strength and warmth of his touch made her shiver. "Please come in," she said, standing aside so he could pass by.

Garrett adjusted the bag on his shoulder and lifted a large, folded table by its strap, carrying it into the room as if it were a briefcase. Neva watched his arms and chest flex as he began setting it up. When he turned his back and bent over the massage table, she nearly swallowed her tongue. The front view had been stunning, but the back of him was stirring something deep in her core. His ass was muscled and tight, like the haunches of a racehorse. The muscles of his back flexed under the light polo material, and Neva imagined what it would be like to rake her fingers down it while...

Garrett cleared his throat, bringing Neva's daydream to an abrupt halt. He was facing her now, and she had been staring at his ass... which was now his crotch. Flustered, she raised her gaze and met his eyes.

A slow, gleaming grin blossomed on Garrett's face. "I understand you're in need of some special treatment this evening, Ms. Stevenson."

Neva didn't miss the subtle emphasis he had placed on the word "special." Slowly, almost casually, she allowed her gaze to drift from his eyes down to the slight bulge beginning to show promise in his shorts.

She met his eyes again. "I ordered a massage. What other special treatments do you offer?" she asked with a devilish grin.

Garrett fixed Neva with a hooded gaze that made her core boil. He allowed his eyes to wander down the full length of her with the same deliberate casualness she had used on him before meeting her eyes again. "What else do you need, Neva?" he said, with a huskiness in his tone.

Neva felt a thrill at his veiled invitation. Without a second thought, she opened her robe and let it fall to the floor. "Ohhh honey, you have no idea," she purred.

• • • •

Kris pulled her bathrobe closed tighter and opened the front door. Tom stood on the other side, his shoulders slumped, his eye a disgusting shade of purple and blue.

"Oh my God, Tom! What happened? Are you okay?"

Tom wouldn't meet her eyes. "We can't go home tonight," he said.

Ashlea and Megan stood mute next to him. Kris had no trouble deciphering their body language. They were asleep on their feet and filled with a sadness that was both palpable and familiar to Kris. Without another word, she ushered them all inside.

A few minutes later, Kris closed the door to the spare bedroom. Trent was waiting for her in the hallway, and she put a finger to her lips, warning him to keep quiet.

"What's going on?" he whispered.

"Tom and Patty had a fight, so he and the girls are staying over," she whispered back.

Trent rolled his eyes, shaking his head in disbelief. "Again? Jeezus! Why does he put up with her?"

Kris gave him a warning look, and he rolled his eyes again. She chuckled. "You keep rolling your eyes like that, and it's likely to cause a seizure."

"Whatever, Mom," he murmured, shaking his head again.

She kissed his forehead. "Be a help and get me an extra blanket and pillow from your closet."

Without a word, Trent slipped into his room and came back a few moments later with a comforter and a fluffy pillow.

Kris hugged her son tightly for a moment. "Goodnight, kid," she whispered, before taking the pillow and blanket from him.

Trent watched her disappear down the stairs. Not for the first time, he marveled at his mother's patience with her two siblings. She was like the Mother Teresa of the family. If they had a problem, needed money, or advice—it wasn't their own mother they turned to. It was his. He had never understood their strange dynamic. Grandma wasn't a saint, and she definitely possessed a "no-nonsense" mentality that could be a little scary... but she was still their mother. Didn't her help and advice mean more to them than anything their sister could do or say? Trent didn't have a sibling. This had disappointed him when he was younger, but now that he saw what his mother went through with her own siblings, he was glad about it. Even if he'd had siblings who were older than him, he was sure he would have preferred his mother's support and advice over theirs. He was also certain that his aunt and uncle didn't deserve the attention and care his mother gave them.

For as long as he could remember, she was the one who helped them navigate their lives and pick up the pieces whenever something went wrong. She was always there at a moment's notice whenever they needed her. Where had they been when his mom needed them? Where had they been when his dad left, and all his mom could do was cry? Neither of them had come to the house to comfort or help her. They hadn't called, either. When she called them, they rarely picked up the phone and, when they did, the conversations were always short. Yet, the moment they needed something from her, here they were. Like tonight. What had the "infamous Patty" done this time to bring Uncle Tom to their door? Trent crept to the top of the stairs and sat down, then slid down two more steps and strained to hear what was going on.

· · · ·

When Kris entered the living room, Tom was standing near the fireplace, holding a framed photo from the mantle. He stared lovingly at it. In the photo, six-year-old Tom and three-year-old Rachel sat in a wagon. Tom was in the back with his arms wrapped around Rachel. Eleven-year-old Kris stood near the front of the wagon, the handle in her right hand. Her left hand rested on the top of little Rachel's head. She was looking down at her siblings with a small smile as they both beamed brightly at the camera.

Kris laid the pillow and blanket on the couch. "That's a good one, isn't it?" she asked, smiling.

Tom glanced up at her and nodded. He looked back at the photo. "Yeah, it is. It was earlier that same week, wasn't it? A day or two before?" he asked, his voice soft.

Kris's smile faded. "I'll get you an ice pack for that eye," she said.

"Don't bother. It's too late for ice," he answered, putting the photo back on the mantle.

"Sit down then, and I'll get us something to drink," Kris replied and left the room again.

Tom collapsed onto the couch, the weight of the world pressing down on him. He practiced the breathing Kris had taught him, giving his body permission to let go. This was one of the few places where he could truly relax, where it felt safe to be honest about his feelings. He exhaled slowly, feeling his shoulders drop.

Kris returned to the living room with two bottles of Dr. Pepper. Handing one to Tom, she settled next to him, rubbing his back with her free hand as they sat in silence for a long moment.

Finally, Tom took a swig of his soda and turned halfway to face her. "You know what I don't understand?" he said. "You had it the worst out of all of us back then. How is it that you turned out so normal, and me and Rachel are so screwed up?"

Kris shrugged. "I try not to think about it," she said, bumping shoulders with him. "Besides, I'm not normal. I just fake it better than you do."

Tom snorted, the gesture sending a sharp pain into the area under his swollen eye. He winced.

Kris grabbed his hand, her grip firm and grounding. "Want to talk about what happened?"

He was silent for a long moment. "Mom's right. I should divorce Patty and make a better life for me and the girls. But the thought of leaving scares the hell out of me."

"I know," Kris said softly.

"Patty would go nuts if I told her I wanted a divorce."

"Don't tell her, then. Just leave. Take the girls and go, Tom. Let your lawyer handle it."

Tom stood, pacing the room restlessly. "She wasn't always like this. It was never like this in the beginning. Remember?"

"She's like this now. What kind of life is that for you and the girls? You're making excuses, just like Mom did all those years."

Tom halted, spinning to face her.

Kris stood, leveling him with a look, hands on her hips. "You don't want to hear it, but it's the truth. Deep down, you know I'm right."

"Oh, so you're the high and mighty one, and I'm the one making excuses like Mom?" Tom said, his face contorting into a look of derision. "Look at you! Carl has filed for divorce and is living with another woman, but you're refusing to sign the divorce papers. What kind of life is that for you and Trent?"

Kris threw her hands up in retreat. "Fine! Fine! What are you going to do then, let her keep using you for a punching bag?"

"I don't know!" Tom exclaimed, throwing himself back down onto the couch. "I'm sorry. I don't wanna fight with you. Everything is just such a freaking mess. It feels like I'm drowning, and I don't know how to swim."

"I know," Kris sighed, sitting down next to him again on the couch.

Tom grabbed her hand, squeezing it tightly. "What are you going to do? Have you decided?"

"No, I haven't. If I had the money, I wouldn't have to worry so much about everything. I could pay off this house and I could pay for Trent to go to college, but..."

"But what?"

"I don't know. That whole thing about making Trent change his appearance is just...wrong. I don't want to force him to change how he looks if that's what makes him happy. And what if Mom is wrong about Carl? Maybe he'll change his mind and..." Kris trailed off as Tom met her eyes, shaking his head.

"Do you really believe that?" Tom asked softly.

Kris looked away and they both fell silent.

After a few moments, Tom broke the silence again. "I've been thinking about that night a lot lately. About what might have happened if I hadn't told Mom what he was doing."

"Tommy, it wasn't your fault. You know that. The truth would've come out sooner or later." Kris squeezed his hand, her grip a silent promise of solidarity. "I'm glad he's dead. It saved all of us. You saved all of us."

"Rachel doesn't see it that way," he whispered, fighting the lump in his throat.

"She'd feel that way if she knew." Kris said. "Now stop bringing up old ghosts or we'll both have nightmares." She stood and motioned for him to lie down on the sofa.

He kicked off his shoes and settled the pillow behind his head. Kris draped the comforter over him like a protective shield and sat down on the arm of the couch.

"Now try to get some sleep. Things will be easier to figure out in the morning."

Tom closed his eyes obediently, and Kris stroked his hair until the creases in his forehead relaxed and she thought he was asleep. She was tiptoeing out of the room when Tom called out to her.

"Hey, Kris...don't tell Mom about this, okay?"

Kris's lips curled into a soft smile, her eyes sparkling with mischief. "You're lucky mom isn't here to see that eye. She would kill Patty if she knew."

"I know."

Kris's grin widened. "Maybe we should tell her. It'd be an easy way out of that marriage."

Tom's pillow hit the wall beside her, narrowly missing her head. She giggled, scooped it off the floor, and tossed it back to him.

"Smart ass," he said, a hint of a smile breaking through his earlier tension.

"Goodnight, Tommy," Kris said, blowing him a kiss.

• • • •

Trent rose and crept back up the stairs, each step calculated to avoid creaking floorboards. He watched through a crack in the door as his mom went to check on his cousins and then disappeared into her own bedroom.

He closed his door the rest of the way and leaned against it, thinking. What did she mean, "make him change his appearance"? Grandma was going to give her money for that? How much? And why hadn't she told him about it? Did she think he wouldn't do it or didn't care? Well, he did care. If

Grandma was going to take the money issues off his mom's shoulders, he was one hundred percent onboard. Whatever it took to help his mom, he'd do it. He just needed to know how to do it. When Grandma came home, he was going to pay her a visit.

• • • •

Kris leaned her back against her bedroom door and closed her eyes. She didn't know how to get through to her brother. How to make him see that staying with Patty was a terrible idea. Money or no money, the risk was too great. It made her sick to think of the girls going through something like she and Tom had experienced as children. How could he not see that? She clenched her fists, his willful blindness igniting a familiar fire of frustration within her. Or was it her own blindness she was upset about? She was right about Tom, there was no doubt about that—but he had been right about her, too.

Kris rubbed her hands over her face and pushed away from the door. Determined, she snatched the wedding photo of her and Carl off the nightstand and threw it in the tissue-filled trash can beside her bed. It felt good to do it. For a moment, she felt lighter, freer. Stripping off her robe, she climbed into bed and turned off the bedside lamp.

An hour later, she was still tossing and turning, trying to find a comfortable position. With an exasperated groan, she turned on the bedside lamp and fished the photo out of the garbage can.

"Screw you, Carl," she said to his smiling, suit-clad image. "I hate you."

Kris held the photo over the garbage can once again. She wanted to throw it in. She wanted to be done with this pain and regret. Done with him. Her hand hovered over the trash, but she couldn't let go. The memories and fear still had their hooks in her heart, refusing to release their grip. With another groan, she placed the photo on the pillow next to hers and clicked the light back off again.

Chapter 8:
That's Life - Suck It Up

Rachel stood by her living room window, morning light streaming across her face as she marveled at how beautiful the neighborhood looked. Comparing details in architecture and exterior design choices of the homes on her street was one of her favorite things to do. She noticed everything. The trim. The shutters. The way light played across different textures. She wished she could get inside each house and see the choices her neighbors made in color and décor. Her own home may have been a standard ranch of its time, but she had spent months picking out the exterior paint and landscaping features. Even longer in making design choices for inside the home.

It had been a labor of love. Each choice was a reflection of who she was, each detail carefully considered until it felt right.

This passion had grown over time. Books about architecture and interior design lined her bookshelves, and several magazines on the same theme adorned her coffee table. She had fallen in love with interior design and architecture when she had helped Kris design the floor plan and color palette for the Walker home. After that, she had immersed herself in every book she could find on the subjects.

Her second project had been the remodel of her mother's kitchen and bath. They had turned out more beautiful than she or her mother had expected, igniting a spark that had grown into an unquenchable flame. She hadn't kept that passion a secret in her family, but none of them knew Rachel had been secretly taking college classes on the subject for nine years, building a foundation for a dream she hadn't yet dared to speak aloud.

A year after Kim was born, Rachel got her GED, and determined to make it on her own, had moved out of Neva's home. She had been a very young mother, working as a waitress and struggling to survive on the wages and tips she made. The weight of responsibility pressed down on her shoulders each day as she counted pennies and worried about tomorrow. Rachel knew she would struggle to raise Kim on a food server's wage, but had no idea what she could do instead. One night, she had confided her worries to Lois, her voice breaking with exhaustion.

Lois wrapped her arms around Rachel, her embrace warm and steady. "Baby girl, you are a born designer. Just look at what you were able to do with your momma's house. You're a natural, and you love it. Start there. Always start with what you love."

A week later, Rachel signed up for her first class, her hands trembling with both fear and excitement as she filled out the forms. Now she was about to finish her last class.

In three months, she would earn her degree in architecture and design. While she was proud of the accomplishment, a quiet triumph after years of late-night studying, she wasn't sure what she would do with it. Giving up the bar was not an option, no matter what her mother said or did. The bar was the last link she had to her father, each bottle and worn barstool a tenuous link to him that she couldn't bear to lose. The thought of selling it made her feel disloyal. She shook her head at the thought, as if physically rejecting the idea.

No. No matter how design work would fit into her future, it would have to be as a side job. She just didn't know how the bar, design, and her daughter were all going to fit into one schedule. Kim would go off to college in a couple of years and maybe then it would be easier. The thought both relieved and terrified her.

Today was one step closer to that possibility.

Today was the last day of school for Kim, before summer break. Rachel congratulated herself as she sipped her coffee, savoring the small victory. She had gotten Kim through another year of school. Only two more years and then she could relax. Kim would graduate and go to college or find a job somewhere, and Rachel could take one major source of stress off her plate. She couldn't wait. She was tired of driving this damn car, or truck, or train, or whatever the hell being a single mom was. Working full time and raising Kim alone had been so much harder than she ever thought it would be. Her mother had been right.

When Neva found out Rachel was pregnant, she had begged her to consider giving the baby up. Told her that keeping the baby would mean throwing her own future away. Hearing her mother say that had made Rachel wonder if Neva felt that way about raising her and Tom and Kris. The question had lingered between them for years, unspoken but ever-present.

Knowing what she did now, Rachel could understand why her mother might have felt that way. Raising Kim was hard enough. She could not imagine trying to raise three kids alone, each day a marathon of needs and demands. At the time, her mother's words had made Rachel angry. She had been beyond furious when Neva declared the baby would be lucky to graduate high school if Rachel raised her. Until that moment, Rachel had been undecided about what she wanted to do about the pregnancy, but hearing Neva predict her failure as a mother had lit a fire of determination within her.

She would never admit it, but keeping Kim had been a decision made more out of spite toward her mother than out of a desire to be a mother herself. A rebellion wrapped in diapers and midnight feedings. Even so, she had done it. Rachel had raised Kim and worked full time as a waitress until she was old enough to work at the bar. Four years after that, Neva sold her the bar. She had been managing the bar, taking classes, and raising Kim, despite her mother's prophecies of failure, ever since. Two years from now, when Kim walked down the aisle to accept her diploma, Rachel would finally prove her mother wrong. The thought brought a fierce satisfaction that made her feel a little heady.

Rachel heard Kim's bedroom door close. Smiling, she turned to greet her daughter, but her smile morphed into open-mouthed horror when she saw what Kim was wearing.

Kim had teased her blonde hair into two pigtails, which would have been cute if they weren't in such stark contrast to the rest of her outfit. Her make-up was heavy, and dark eyeliner made her eyes look older and wilder than her years. She wore a black, studded choker around her neck like a declaration of rebellion. A white button-up blouse hung open at the chest, displaying a frightening amount of cleavage, despite the white spaghetti strap halter top Kim had on underneath. She had the button-up tied in a knot at the waistline of a Scottish kilt that looked like it was a size more suitable for Ashlea or Megan. Thigh-high white stockings and black army boots completed the outfit, each element carefully chosen to provoke maximum parental distress.

Rachel gripped her coffee cup in both hands, her knuckles whitening as she forced calm into her voice. "Is that what you think you're wearing to school?"

Kim turned like a runway model, pivoting with practiced grace, oblivious to her mother's disdain. "Isn't it hot!? It's the last day, and I want to look extra fabulous going into summer break."

Rachel set her jaw. "It's not fabulous, it's trampy. Go change right now," she said, pointing toward the hallway, her finger as rigid as her resolve.

Kim glared at Rachel, defiance flashing in her eyes, ready to argue, but a motorcycle horn blared outside. Before Rachel could stop her, Kim scooped her bookbag off the couch and raced out the front door, a blur of outrageously dressed teenage rebellion.

At the curb, a guy who looked much older than her daughter waited on a motorcycle, his leather jacket and confident posture screaming trouble. He revved the engine impatiently as Kim ran toward him, her kilt fluttering dangerously in the morning breeze.

Rachel put down her cup and raced to the door, panic rising in her chest. "Kim! Get back here and change those clothes, right now!" she yelled, stamping her foot in frustration. Her demands fell on deaf and determined ears.

Without a backward glance, Kim hopped onto the back of the motorcycle and grabbed the guy tightly around the waist. The motorcyclist pulled a small wheelie and sped off down the street with Kim clinging like a baboon to his back, her pigtails flying behind her like victory flags.

Hands shaking, Rachel picked up her cup from the end table and headed for the kitchen. Her mind was racing, thoughts colliding like bumper cars. Kim did not seem to have a single brain cell programmed for common sense, and it made her want to scream. Rachel imagined herself driving to the high school, finding her daughter, wrapping one of those pigtails around her hand, and dragging Kim out of the school and down the street by it. The fantasy played out in vivid detail, satisfying in its impossibility. If only that was an option, she thought bitterly.

She took a large glass from the cupboard and grabbed the vodka and orange juice from the refrigerator. The bottle felt cool and familiar in her hand, promising relief. Damn it! She had told herself she wasn't going to drink today. She was supposed to be cutting back. Her plan was to be completely sober by the time Kim graduated. Today was supposed to be the first day of that plan, a fresh start that was already crumbling.

"Fuck, fuck, fuck!" she cursed at the bottle of vodka, each word sharper than the last. Pushing away from the counter, she walked out of the kitchen and made it all the way to her bedroom before retracing her steps back to the bottle, drawn by an invisible tether.

"Tomorrow," Rachel told the vodka, as if negotiating with an old friend. "Tomorrow will be a better day to cut back." She poured half a glass, the clear liquid splashing against the sides, topped it off with the orange juice, and stirred the drink with her finger before taking several large gulps. The familiar burn traveled down her throat, spreading warmth through her chest. She would be fine. Kim would be fine. She didn't need to worry about it, or even think about it, today. Right now, she needed to get herself to work. She took another drink and walked out of the kitchen, glass in hand, her resolve to change postponed for another day.

• • • •

Kris handed a cup of coffee to Tom and sat down, taking one of her calming breaths. The morning light filtered through the kitchen window, casting soft shadows across the table between them.

Tom's eyes dropped to the table, unable to meet his sister's gaze. "I know what you're thinking, but she said she's really sorry and wants to change this time. She's talking about going to counseling and AA. I can't just walk out."

"Tom, you can't possibly believe that crap. You know better than that," Kris said, squeezing his arm, her fingers pressing urgently into his flesh.

He looked up at her, and the sadness she saw on his face was more than she could stand. It was the same look he'd worn as a child, trapped and resigned, a prisoner of circumstances beyond his control.

"Please don't stay married to her, Tom. Please!" Her voice dropped to a desperate whisper. "If not for your own sake, think of the girls."

Trent walked into the kitchen with Ashlea and Megan in tow. He noticed their tense body language and froze, his adolescent instincts immediately sensing the undercurrent of conflict. "What's going on?" he asked, eyes narrowing with suspicion.

Tom sat up straight and smiled, the expression not quite reaching his good eye. "I was just telling your mom that me and the girls will be heading home this morning," he said with fake enthusiasm.

Trent looked from his mother to his uncle and back again, reading the truth in their faces. "Seriously?"

Tom nodded, his smile wilting at the look of incredulity on his nephew's face.

"Whatever," Trent said, grabbing a piece of toast from the toaster. "I'll be in the car, Mom," he mumbled, heading out the back door, the screen slamming behind him with punctuated finality.

Ashlea and Megan flanked their father on either side of his chair. Kris looked at each of them and then at Tom, her heart breaking for these children caught in an adult's mess. "Don't go back," she whispered, leaning forward. "Who knows what she'll do next time."

"I have to try. She said she's going to change." He said, the words sounding hollow even to his own ears.

Ashlea laid her small hand over Kris's, the gesture so adult it was heartbreaking. "It's okay, Aunt Kris. I'll take care of him," she said in a tiny, determined voice that carried the weight of promises no child should have to make.

Kris felt her eyes stinging with tears and had to look away, unable to bear the sight of this little girl assuming a role she knew so well herself.

Tom stood from his chair and scooped Megan into his arms, holding her like a shield against the truth. "See? Everything is gonna be fine. You girls are happy to be going home to Mommy, aren't ya?"

• • • •

A few minutes later, Trent watched his mother climb into the car, mumbling to herself. He pretended not to notice as she fastened her seat belt, then banged her head several times on the steering wheel, each thud a punctuation mark to her frustration. It was rare to see his mother get upset like this. She was always so calm and reasonable. Even when his father left.

Trent had wanted her to yell at his father. Wanted her to punch him, or kick him, or call him terrible names. Something. Anything. Instead, she had tried to talk to him. Nicely. Only when that had failed, and his father had left, did his mother finally break down and cry. Not in front of Trent, though. Never in front of him. Only when she was alone, in her bedroom at night, when she thought the walls would keep her secrets. During the day, she put on a good show, but Trent knew she was only keeping it together for his sake. He was angry about that. Angry at her for not being honest about how she felt and angry at his father for making her feel that way.

What he was seeing from his mother today, though, was new. She was talking to herself now, her lips moving rapidly, and if his lip-reading skills were correct, she was cursing like Grandma Neva. Amused and slightly alarmed, he took out his earbuds to listen.

"Skanky, foul, abusive, alcoholic bitch! How in the hell can he want to stay married to that?" Kris hissed, as she fumbled to put the keys in the ignition, her fingers trembling with rage. She fumbled the keys, dropping them onto the floorboard. "Uggh!" She let her head rest on the wheel and took one of her deep breaths, the kind she always encouraged him to take when he was upset, her shoulders rising and falling with the effort.

As she exhaled, he watched her slow transformation back into the calm mom, sister, and daughter that the family depended on. It was like watching a magician's trick—the anger folding itself away, tucked neatly behind a practiced smile. It scared him a little. He knew his mom wore a mask about what was going on with his dad, but he was realizing she had more than one mask, each one carefully crafted for different occasions. "You okay, Mom?" he probed, studying her face.

"Fucking fabulous," she murmured, grabbing the keys off the floor, her voice still carrying an edge of bitterness.

Trent grinned at her, relieved to see a glimpse of honesty. "A little early for an F-bomb, don't you think?"

She gave him the side-eye. "Smart ass." Kris said, starting the car, the ghost of a smile playing at her lips.

Dulcet tones and positive mantras issued by her favorite self-help CD emanated from the car's sound system, the soothing voice promising inner peace and harmony. Kris ejected the CD with a swift, violent motion and threw it out the window, the plastic disc sailing through the air like a frisbee. Trent had to bite down hard on the inside of his cheek to keep from laughing, the unexpected rebellion delighting him.

They discussed the Tom and Patty situation the entire drive to the school, dissecting it from every angle like surgeons over a hopeless case. "He's never gonna leave her. You know that, right?" Trent said, as his mother pulled the car up in front of the high school.

Kris sighed, and Trent noticed how tired she looked. The morning light was unforgiving, revealing the shadows beneath her eyes. "I know," she said with a shrug that carried the weight of resignation. "I just want better for him and the girls."

Trent's tone softened a bit, his teenage bravado giving way to genuine concern. "You can't fix everything, all the time, Mom. Maybe you should work on fixing yourself for once."

She gave a soft snort, surprised by his insight. "Yeah? What part of me do you think I need to fix first?"

A car honked behind them, making Kris wince visibly. She glanced in the rearview mirror at the Lexus behind them, its polished surface gleaming with impatience.

Trent exhaled loudly. "To start, you should stop being everybody's doormat. Say no. Stand up to somebody, for once."

Another honk from the angry Lexus driver made her jump, the sound sharp and demanding. She shot a frustrated glance behind her. "We can talk about this later. I need to move for this guy."

Trent stared at her pointedly, his eyes challenging her, as if to say, "Case in point."

"What?" she asked innocently, though she knew exactly what the look meant.

He shook his head and got out of the car, disappointment evident in every movement. Without a word of goodbye, he stalked off toward the school.

Kris called to him out the open passenger window. "Trent! Have a good day!"

He kept walking, head down, and shoulders slumped.

The car behind Kris honked again. Longer, and more persistent, this time, the sound drilling into her skull. Frowning, Kris looked from her rearview mirror to her son's retreating back and felt something shift inside her. Before she could talk herself out of it, Kris placed her foot firmly on the brake and put the car in reverse. She revved the engine and felt the car straining to lurch backward, like an animal pulling at its leash. Butterflies fluttered in her stomach at the thought of what she was about to do, and she almost changed her mind. Almost.

Glancing in the rearview again, she saw the honking man's furious face. Saw him flailing his hands at her as he ranted, alone, in his car, his mouth moving in what she imagined were colorful expletives. The butterflies stilled, replaced by a calm certainty. She revved the car louder and took her foot off the brake. It launched backward three feet and slammed hard into the front of the honking car, metal crunching against metal in a satisfying collision.

Trent spun around at the sound of the crash, and their eyes locked across the distance. Kris gave him a thumbs-up sign and pulled her car forward ten feet. With her foot on the brake, she put the car in reverse and revved the engine again. With a giggle that bubbled up from some long-dormant place inside her, she released the brake. The car shot backward and slammed even more forcefully into the grill of the Lexus.

This time, she let out a loud, throaty laugh as she pulled her car forward, feeling free and exquisitely naughty. It's like being in the demolition derby, she thought with glee. She had always loved the demo derby. Loved the sound the cars made when they collided, and the raw power and ruthlessness of it all. But being inside the car when it intentionally smashed into another car was infinitely more satisfying than watching it. The vibration of the impact traveled up her arms and through her body, releasing something that had been coiled tight inside her for years. She let out a feral howl and pulled the car forward again.

Trent stared, open-mouthed, as she revved the engine and slammed into the car behind her for the third time, the sound of crunching metal echoing across the school grounds. He dropped his bag onto the lawn and ran to her car, his face a mixture of shock and awe.

"Mom, stop! What are you doing!?" he whisper-yelled, leaning in through the passenger window, his eyes wide with disbelief.

Kris beamed at him with a grin that stretched from ear to ear, her eyes alive with a fire he'd never seen before. "How's that for change?" she quipped, her voice light and carefree.

A slow grin spread across her son's face, recognition dawning. "It's a start!"

• • • •

Half an hour later, Kris stood in front of the school with a police officer and the angry, honking man. To her horror, the policeman that arrived on the scene was Officer Miller. The same Officer Miller who had discovered her having a breakdown in her car a few weeks ago, his kind eyes now filled with professional concern.

He was busy scribbling notes into a small notepad as the angry honking man ranted about how the accident had occurred, his face red with indignation. The man said his name was Bob Schmidt, but Kris preferred "Angry Honking Man" and had referred to him as such in her account of what had transpired. Officer Miller had patiently corrected her with Bob's real name, but Kris had just shrugged and said, "yeah, him" each time, which drew raised eyebrows from Officer Miller and a look that bordered on violence from Bob Schmidt. Both reactions made her want to bust out laughing, but she kept her mirth under control, though it bubbled just beneath the surface.

She stood, rocking back and forth on her heels with a look of utter contentment on her face, as Angry Honking Man continued his rant, his words washing over her without leaving a mark.

"She wasn't moving, so I honked a second time. Then she revved her car and slammed into me on purpose! I was just sitting there, and she smashed in the front of my car! Three times!" His voice rose with each word, hands gesturing wildly at his damaged vehicle.

Officer Miller stopped writing and glanced up at Kris, his pen poised over the notepad. "Ms. Walker? Is that an accurate statement?" he asked patiently, his tone professional.

Kris nodded, standing tall. "Yep, that's pretty much it—except that he honked at me three times, not two. Three times. Three annoying and unnecessary times," she said, holding up three fingers boldly in front of Bob Schmidt's face, unrepentant and oddly liberated.

Schmidt took a wary step closer to Officer Miller, his body angling away from Kris. His voice dropped to a stage whisper, as if she couldn't hear him. "You see this? She's crazy."

Officer Miller cleared his throat and wiped the back of his hand across his mouth. Kris was pretty sure he was trying not to smile, his eyes crinkling at the corners despite his professional demeanor.

• • • •

Tom and his daughters walked back into their home through the broken front door. The shattered glass had been swept up, and the house was spotless. The windows were all open, and the fresh smell of the place gave him hope, a fragile thing that fluttered in his chest. Ashlea and Megan were not as eager to be home as he had thought they would be. Megan had cried when they pulled into the driveway, her small body shaking with sobs, and it had taken him nearly five minutes to convince her to get out of the car and come inside. In the end, she had refused to go in without being carried; her fear palpable. Even now, she clung to his neck and scanned the room with anxious eyes, looking for danger in every corner. Ashlea had walked in with Tom but clung to his side with one arm wrapped around his leg, her fingers digging into the fabric of his jeans.

"Patty?" Tom called out, his voice echoing in the quiet house. "We're home."

A few seconds later, Patty entered the living room looking rested and happy, as if the previous night's violence had never happened. She smiled warmly as she rushed toward him, her movements fluid and graceful.

"Oh man, I'm so sorry, honey," she said, dabbing the area around his black eye with gentle fingers. "I'll be a better wife from now on, I promise," she said, peppering the unbruised area of his face with kisses, her breath smelling of mint and coffee.

Tom nodded and returned one of her kisses, wanting desperately to believe her.

Patty turned her attention to Megan and tried to take her out of Tom's arms, but Megan turned her face away and clung to Tom's neck, her small body going rigid with resistance.

Patty stepped back, her smile faltering for just a moment before she recovered. "I'm sorry girls," she said, sticking her bottom lip out as if pouting, her voice taking on a childlike quality. "Mommy just got so angry—I didn't know what I was doing. I promise I won't get angry like that again, okay?" She looked expectantly from Megan to Ashlea, waiting for their forgiveness, her eyes demanding it.

After a long moment, Ashlea nodded in a mechanical response.

Tom placed Megan on her feet next to her sister. Megan grabbed Ashlea's hand, their fingers intertwining in silent solidarity, and the two backed up a step in unison as Patty knelt in front of them, her perfume permeating the air around them. Megan sneezed.

"I made breakfast. Anybody want some chocolate chip pancakes?" Patty asked, her voice bright with forced cheer.

Both girls looked at their father, their eyes seeking permission, guidance, protection.

"Go ahead, girls," Tom encouraged, his voice gentle but firm.

Megan shook her head, her pigtails swaying with the movement, but Ashlea gave her hand a squeeze and she stilled, understanding the silent message from her older sister.

"Yes, please," Ashlea squeaked, her voice barely audible.

"Let's go then!" Patty grabbed Ashlea's free hand and towed them toward the kitchen, her movements too quick, too eager, like a predator that had successfully lured its prey.

Megan looked over her shoulder at Tom as they went. The look in her eyes nearly froze his heart. He knew that look, and what it meant, all too well. It was the look of a child who had learned that adults couldn't be trusted to protect them. He shook it off. It would be fine. Things were different now. Patty promised she would get help, and things would start getting better.

Tom caught his reflection in the hall mirror as he walked by. He stopped, abruptly. His damaged eye was a gory purple-blue color with tinges of yellow around the edges. It looked awful and felt even worse, but that wasn't what caught his attention. In his undamaged eye, he saw the same haunted look he had just seen in Megan's. Staring at his reflection, flashbacks of his own childhood echoed through his mind and tendrils of anxiety began trickling down his spine like ice water.

Another call from Patty startled him back to the present. One more try, he promised himself. One more chance to make it work. If she didn't change... What would he do? He didn't know. He could figure that out later. For now, Patty was a loving wife and mother again. For now, he could breathe.

. . . .

The last thirty minutes of Neva's flight back to Iowa were very bumpy. The pilot's calm voice had announced that they were experiencing turbulence because of gathering storms in Iowa, but no cause for alarm. She had laughed at that. "Gathering storms in Iowa" was an understatement. Neva sent a silent nod to God. Thanks for the head's up, old man, but I am already well-aware of what I'm coming home to. The metaphor wasn't lost on her.

She hadn't let her kids know she was coming back today. She had no intention of ringing the bell for round one to start before talking with Lois and getting a good night's sleep in her own bed. They would find out soon enough, and the battles would begin.

Forty-five minutes later, she snapped her mirrored compact shut as the cab driver pulled up to the curb next to her. Despite the impending battle, she was glad to be home. Florida had been wonderful, and she looked and felt twenty years younger with her skin bronzed by the tropical sun, but she was ready to face the next phase of her life. That meant dealing with her children...and making some changes of her own. The time for hiding was over.

The cab driver approached with a welcoming grin, his uniform crisp despite the humid air. "Hello, I'm James and I'll be your driver today."

Neva grinned back, feeling lighter than she had in years. "Nice to meet you, James. I'm Neva. Just the two bags," she said, gesturing to her luggage.

He tipped an imaginary hat and placed her bags in the trunk with practiced ease. Neva slid into the backseat of the cab, the leather cool against her sun-warmed skin, and James was behind the wheel a few seconds later. He glanced at her in the rearview mirror, his eyes friendly.

"Which hotel can I drive you to today?"

"No hotel. Home. 1443 Beacon Drive." Then, because she was still feeling so damn good from her trip, she added with a playful lilt, "Home, James, and don't spare the horses!"

James chuckled and met her eyes in the rearview, his face crinkling with amusement. "Yes, ma'am, Miss Scarlet," he drawled, in a poor attempt at a southern accent, before pressing down hard on the accelerator, the cab surging forward into the Iowa afternoon.

• • • •

Robin stepped into Kris's office and struck a vogue pose, one hand on her hip, the other behind her head. Kris didn't notice. All of her attention was focused on the computer screen as her fingers flew across the keyboard, the rapid clicking a testament to her concentration.

Robin clapped her hands above Kris's monitor, the sharp sound cutting through the office. "Hey! Earth to Kris!"

Kris startled, looking up and blinking as if emerging from a trance. "Is it five o'clock already?"

Robin tapped her watch, her red nails bright against her wrist. "Almost! It's afternoon break—thought we'd start the weekend early," she said, pulling two travel-sized Bacardi rum bottles from her blazer pocket and waving them in the air above Kris's computer monitor.

Kris pushed Robin's hands away as she glanced past her friend to make sure no one else was watching. "Are you trying to get us fired? Put those away you lunatic!" she whispered.

Robin giggled but put the bottles back in her pocket. "I'm still going out tomorrow night, and I want you to go with me. It will do you some good to experience the magic of freedom and a night on the town," she said, in a teasing voice.

Kris stretched her arms above her head and yawned, her body protesting the hours of sitting. "Thanks, but I think I'll pass on the magic this time."

Robin picked up Kris's stress ball and threw it at her. "Come on! You don't know what you're missing. Saturday is eighties night," she said, breaking into the robot dance.

Kris caught the stress ball and put it back on her desk. She cleared her throat with a loud "Ahem" to get Robin's attention. "Some people have work to do, you know."

Robin dropped her robot arms. "God, I love the eighties," she confessed, eyes sparkling.

"I don't. Now take your contraband and dance your way out of my office," Kris said, resuming her typing.

"Suit yourself, party pooper," Robin said, sticking out her tongue and moonwalking her way toward the door. She hadn't made it far before she ran into something hard and gasped, her playful demeanor vanishing instantly.

Kris looked up and let out a gasp of her own, the sound catching in her throat.

Carl Walker stood in Kris's doorway, staring at Robin with obvious disdain, his posture rigid and imposing. He wore his best bank manager attire. Black dress slacks, a long-sleeve dress shirt, and a politician's tie—the uniform of respectability. Shiny black shoes and gold cufflinks completed the ensemble, each element carefully chosen to project success. His hair was longer than Kris was used to seeing it. She noticed the feathering of gray that had been there for years was gone. In fact, all of his natural hair color was gone. Replaced with a bizarre, and obviously fake, shade of dark brown that somehow made him look ten years older. Like a middle-aged man trying desperately to recapture his youth, despite only being forty-two.

Robin glared at Carl, her body tensing like a cat preparing to pounce. "What the hell are you doin' here?" She said, her voice sharp with menace.

Carl straightened his tie, a nervous habit he'd always had. "Nice to see you, too, Robin. I need a minute with Kris," he said, stepping around her to stand directly in front of Kris's desk, claiming the space as if he had a right to it.

"It's okay, Robin," Kris reassured, though her racing heart suggested otherwise.

Robin put one hand on her hip and focused a disapproving scowl on her friend. "Are you sure? Cuz, if this lyin', cheatin' man-baby is bothering you, I have no problem bouncing his ass outta here." Her voice carried the promise of action.

Carl made a pfft noise, dismissive and condescending.

"You think I won't?" Robin challenged, taking a half-step forward.

Kris came around the desk and put an arm around her friend's shoulders, whispering into her ear. "It's really okay. I need to talk to him." Her voice was steady, but her fingers pressed into Robin's shoulder with nervous energy.

Robin huffed, but allowed Kris to walk her to the door.

"I'll talk to you later," Kris said, squeezing Robin's arm in silent thanks.

Robin shot one last glare in Carl's direction before walking out of the office, her eyes promising retribution if needed.

Kris closed the door and turned to face her husband, her stomach churning with a sick dread that crawled up her throat.

Carl was leaning on the edge of her desk with his arms crossed over his chest and his face set in a scowl. When Kris's eyes met his, her dread formed itself into a large, hard ball, settling heavily in her gut.

"Have you signed the divorce papers yet?" he asked, his voice clipped and impatient, as if inquiring about a delayed business transaction rather than the end of their marriage.

His tone differed from the last time they had talked. He seemed calmer. Almost nice. Hope bloomed inside of her, a fragile flower pushing through concrete. "No. Why? Are you having second thoughts, because—"

"We've been through this," he said, shoving his hands into his pockets and shaking his head, cutting her off before hope could fully form. "I'm with Diane now." The name fell between them like a stone.

Kris flinched but pressed on, her voice smaller than she intended. "I don't know how you can just end our marriage without at least trying counseling."

Carl groaned, the sound theatrical and exaggerated. "Kris, listen to me. It's over. Over. I don't love you. I need someone fun, and sexy, and exciting in my life. You are not that person." Each word was precisely aimed, a surgeon's knife cutting away at her self-worth.

His words hit their mark. She wrapped her arms around her middle and braced herself, as if preparing for a physical blow as Carl continued, his voice gaining momentum.

"When we were married, I always felt—I don't know—like I was missing out. You never really gave me what I needed. Diane gives me what I need, and I'm not giving her up," he said with an edge of finality, his jaw set in stubborn determination.

Kris felt like she was going to faint, or puke, or both. The room seemed to tilt slightly, the edges of her vision blurring. She swallowed hard instead and gave it another try, clinging to the remnants of their life together.

"Marriage isn't about one person. What about my needs? What about Trent? He needs his father." Her voice cracked on their son's name.

Carl ran his hand through his hair in a way Kris recognized. It was a gesture as familiar to her as her own reflection, the prelude to a storm. He was frustrated and beginning to lose his temper, his carefully maintained facade starting to crack.

"Trent doesn't need me anymore, he's a teenager. And if he ever does need me, he can call me anytime." The casual dismissal of their son hung in the air between them, breathtaking in its callousness.

Kris's pain turned to anger at the speed of a hot flash, heat rising from her core to flush her cheeks. "He can call you!? Are you serious? You're his father, Carl, not his freaking AA sponsor," she hissed, her voice low and dangerous.

Carl pushed off the desk and shouldered past her to the door, his cologne—different from what he used to wear—lingering in his wake. "Goddamnit! I am not arguing this with you." He threw the door open as if to storm out, then stopped, his back to her, shoulders rigid. "Sign the divorce papers, Kris. We are done. I need to move on," he said and walked out the door, his footsteps echoing down the hallway.

Kris stood frozen in place for several seconds, waiting for the tidal wave of devastation to hit her but, to her surprise, it didn't come. The expected collapse, the familiar ache, the desperate need to call him back—none of it materialized. Quietly closing her office door, she returned to her desk chair, her movements measured and calm.

Carl stared at her from a 5x7 framed photo that sat next to the computer monitor, his smile frozen in time from a happier day. She stared back at him, waiting for the tears. They didn't come. The longing she usually felt when she looked at his picture wasn't there, either. She didn't feel sad, or abandoned, or depressed. She wasn't feeling worthless or ugly either, despite his cutting remarks. She sat quietly for a few moments, searching for her emotional footing. What did she feel?

Then it hit her. Relief. It was relief. Like a weight had been lifted from her shoulders. Almost as if she had been waiting for this moment for some reason. But that wasn't all. There was something else stirring inside her...She took a sip of her iced tea as she contemplated this new reaction she was having to her estranged husband. Her hands were shaking as she placed the cup back on her desk. Not from anxiety or distress, which usually accompanied her chats with Carl. No, she realized, this was different. This time they were shaking from anger.

And she was angry. Truly and thoroughly pissed off and sick of putting up with Carl's abuse. Done putting up with it. What a selfish asshole she was married to. His declaration that the time, sacrifice, and love she had put into their fifteen years of marriage wasn't enough for him, was more than she could take. The audacity of it burned in her chest like acid.

She thought about her mother's demand to divorce Carl. Why am I fighting it? Why am I holding on to this, this—? She couldn't think of a description low enough to label him with. Words failed to capture the depth of his ugliness.

Her mother had offered enough money for Kris to provide for herself and Trent. Enough to put Trent through college. And she was refusing it, to hold on to someone who didn't care about her or Trent at all. Good Lord, could she really be that much of a pathetic idiot? Her mother was right. They were all right. It was foolish for her to hang onto something that had passed its expiration date a long time ago. She may not be the best catch on the tuna boat, but she and Trent deserved better than this.

She narrowed her eyes at the photo, Carl's smug smile now seeming like a taunt. "I'm not fun or sexy?" she asked the photo version of Carl, her voice low and dangerous. "Well, you're a selfish, cheating, son-of-a-bitch with a peanut-sized dick and a hairy back." She sneered, the words tasting like freedom on her tongue.

Snatching the photo off the desk, she dropped it in the trash as she stormed out of the office, each step more determined than the last. After a few strides down the hall, she stopped and retraced her steps, a new idea forming. She picked up the potted fern on the shelf near her door and, with a wicked grin, turned the plant upside down, emptying the entire contents on top of the photo. Soil cascaded over Carl's face, burying his smile under the dark earth. Then, she threw the pot in too, for good measure, the ceramic breaking with a satisfying crack. "You know what else?" she said to the trash can, her voice rising with newfound confidence. "Your new hair looks like a bad toupee!"

A few moments later, Kris stomped up to Robin's desk, her steps fueled by fresh determination. "Is that invitation still open for tomorrow night?" Kris asked, in a tone that dared Robin to say it wasn't.

Robin beamed at her like the Cheshire cat, recognition of the transformation dawning on her face. "Hell, yes!"

"Good. What time are you picking me up?" Kris planted her hands on Robin's desk, leaning forward with purpose.

"How 'bout eight?" Robin suggested, barely containing her excitement.

Kris gave her a curt nod, then shrugged out of her beige suit jacket—the uniform of the woman she used to be. She held it in front of her, examining it as if seeing it for the first time, then dropped it on the floor with deliberate carelessness. "I think it's time I bought some new clothes and had my hair done, too. You busy after work?"

There was dead silence between them for a few moments, Robin's mouth hanging open in shock, before she let out a high-pitched squeal that turned heads throughout the office. "Ooo, girl! Now you're talkin'!"

Two hours later, Kris and Robin were in the mall, shopping the racks at Macy's. The bright lights and bustling energy matched Kris's mood as she moved through the store with purpose. She held up a shirt for Robin's approval—a blouse nearly identical to the ones already hanging in her closet. Robin grimaced, making a gagging noise, her entire face contorting with disapproval.

Kris groaned, the sound half-frustrated, half-amused. "What's wrong with this one? I like it!" She clutched the safe, familiar fabric, a last vestige of her comfort zone.

Robin leaned toward her over the rack, her expression incredulous. "You cannot possibly like that shirt. It's so billowy it might as well be a parachute, and it has giant pink roses all over it! Are you looking for clothes or a couch cover!?" She flicked the offending fabric with her fingernail as if it might be contagious.

Kris crammed the shirt back on the rack and threw her hands up. "I give up, then! I can't find anything that looks good." Her voice carried the defeat of someone clearly out of their depth.

Robin pounced, seizing the opportunity she'd been waiting for, her eyes gleaming with anticipation. "Are you ready to let me find something now?"

Kris lifted her shoulders and let them drop dramatically, surrendering to the inevitable. "I guess so. Just don't make me look like a hoochie-momma."

Robin's hand flew to her chest, and her eyes widened in an expression of innocence that fooled no one. "Moi?" The single word dripped with mischief.

Twenty minutes later, Robin was pacing outside Kris's dressing room, her heels clicking impatiently on the tile floor. "Come on! What's taking so long!? I wanna see!" She rapped her knuckles against the door impatiently.

Kris inspected herself in the dressing room mirror, frowning at her reflection. The woman staring back at her was both familiar and foreign, like meeting a version of herself from another life. "I don't know about this one, Robin. It looks a little..." She tugged at the neckline, unused to showing so much skin.

Robin slapped the dressing room door, the sound echoing through the fitting area. "Just get out here and let me see!"

Kris slowly opened the stall door and stepped out, her movements hesitant. She was wearing a black ruffle-front tank top with tiny diamond-like jewels sewn along the edge of its deep V neckline. The hemline of the top hung loosely over the waistline of her slightly faded, form-fitting jeans. Glimpses of skin could be seen between the black laces that ran up the sides of each pant leg. Black two-inch heels, studded with diamonds, completed the outfit, adding height and confidence to her already statuesque appearance.

Robin gaped at her, momentarily speechless—a rare occurrence. Her eyes traveled from Kris's face to her feet and back again, taking in the transformation.

"This one might be a little much," Kris hedged, fighting the urge to cross her arms over her chest, to hide from the scrutiny.

"Nooo, it's definitely just enough. You look amazing!" Robin exclaimed, motioning for Kris to turn around. Kris turned in an awkward circle for Robin's perusal, tugging at the hem of the shirt. "I don't know. I've got a lot of skin showing and it feels a little drafty." Kris used her hands to cover the top of her breasts.

Robin grabbed Kris's hands and held them away from her body, eyes sparkling with excitement. "Girl, you are givin' them humps some air- and they are no joke! You. Look. Fabulous!"

Kris snorted and pulled away from Robin to check herself out in the three-way mirror.

Robin watched her, beaming. "A new hairstyle and a little bit of make-up, and the men in this town won't know what hit 'em."

Kris smoothed her hands over the curves of her waist and hips, turning left and right in the mirror. She couldn't deny that she looked good. She also couldn't deny that it felt good to be out of the heavy, oversized clothing she had hidden behind for years. The woman in the mirror was barely recognizable, with her curves, and skin, and...hope. For the first time in forever, she saw possibility staring back at her. Kris met Robin's eyes in the mirror and rewarded her best friend with a huge grin. "Okay, I'll take it."

••••

Rachel wiped down the top of the bar on autopilot, her mind miles away from the repetitive motion of her hands. She was struggling to concentrate. Discovering that Kim was having sex right under her nose left her shocked and unsettled, stirring emotions she believed her progressive mindset was immune to. The outfit Kim had sauntered out of the house in this morning was the final straw. It couldn't be avoided any longer. She needed to have a tough conversation with Kim.

Every conversation with her daughter lately ended in slammed doors and tears, making the prospect of this talk even more daunting. She had little patience these days with Kim, and her daughter ignited Rachel's temper faster than the snap of her fingers when they argued.

That bothered Rachel. She didn't know why her anger ran so damn hot when Kris and Tom seemed so docile all the time. Was her foul temper something she had inherited from their father? She'd likely never find out thanks to the circle of silence her mother and siblings had where her father was concerned. Kris and Tom claimed they couldn't remember anything about him, and her mother flat out refused to talk about him at all. All Rachel had was a few faded pictures and vague images of him from her own memory. The night he died remained a black hole in her mind.

She sighed aloud as she rinsed her rag in the disinfectant. No matter where the anger came from, it didn't change the fact that it was there, and Kim seemed to bring the worst of it to the surface every time.

When Rachel had gone through her own "sexual revolution" at Kim's age, Neva had remained calm and tried to talk with Rachel about sex and birth control. She offered to answer questions and had counseled her to guard her reputation. Rachel hadn't listened. Instead, she had hurled insult after insult at her mother. Once, she had even shoved her. She had been a venomous teenager with a terrible temper, but Neva had weathered it with as much grace as Rachel supposed was possible. Her mother never raised a hand to her, even though Rachel could tell there were times when she had wanted to. Instead, Neva had been quick with well-positioned verbal jabs. Those had stung. But looking back, Rachel knew she had deserved every one of them.

She hadn't felt that way about her mother's behavior back then, though. Hell, she hadn't felt that way about it two weeks ago. Funny how walking in someone else's shoes could bring things into focus. She would not share that revelation with Neva, though. Her mother wasn't being let off the hook for anything. Especially now, with this bribery scheme she was forcing on them all.

Rachel's distracted cleaning had reached the far end of the bar where a customer was seated. He lifted his glass and coaster good-naturedly so she could wipe the counter underneath. Rachel looked up from the bar top and met his blue eyes, which were sparkling with amusement. He smiled, and the way it made his eyes crinkle at the edges caused something in Rachel's core to resonate like a gong.

The man held out a hand to her. "Hi, Rachel. I'm Jim. Jim Masterson."

There was a deep, whiskey-and-cigarettes-tinged rasp to his voice. Minus the cigarettes, because there was no way this man smoked. There wasn't a hint of stale cigarette odor surrounding him. The only fragrance wafting off Jim Masterson was a slight hint of sawdust and aftershave that smelled like... what was it? Brut? Who wore Brut these days? He did, and it was working for him. It mixed with his man-musk in a way that made her want to climb over the bar and have her way with him. Rachel's eyes drifted to his smile, which was clean, white, and very inviting. Definitely not a smoker. She took a half step back to keep from catapulting across the bar into his lap. Damn her mother for passing that "clean teeth" obsession on to her.

A bit dazed, she wiped her hand on her blue jeans and hesitantly put it in his. His hand was warm and strong, and for just an instant, she wondered what it would feel like to have that hand moving down her naked back. The hair on her arms rose, and she snatched her own hand back. "How do you know my name?" she managed, in a tone that sounded almost normal.

Jim's smile became sheepish. He motioned to Lois, who was a few feet away, pretending to rearrange the drink cooler. "She told me."

Rachel stole a glance at Lois over her shoulder. Lois turned away and continued her ruse of cooler organization.

"I see," Rachel said with a sigh. She took Jim's glass and began refilling it.

Jim moved to a seat closer to her. "Anyway," he continued warily. "I was wondering if you'd like to get together sometime. Maybe grab a coffee?"

Rachel's hand shook as she finished filling his glass. She focused on steadying it as she put the beer on a clean napkin in front of him. "On the house."

Jim gave her another eye-crinkling, white smile and her knees threatened to buckle. Holy shit, dumbass, pull it together, she silently ordered herself. Taking a deep breath, she looked Jim in the eye. "No offense, Jim, but I'm really not in the market for a man right now."

Jim's smile faltered, and the sight shook her resolve a bit.

"Well," he said in that deep whiskey, smoky way. "I'm not trying to be your man. I was kind of hoping we could start by being friends."

Rachel wasn't sure why, but she felt disappointed by his words. She shook it off. "That's very nice, but I'm usually really busy. I don't have much time for friends. Thanks anyway." Before Jim could utter another word, she grabbed the bar towel and headed toward the other end of the bar.

Lois groaned and came to lean on the bar a few feet away from Jim. "Don't give up. She puts on like she's cold as ice, but she'll melt, eventually."

Jim pulled a five-dollar bill and a business card out of his pocket. He dropped them on the counter next to his beer glass. "If she does, my number is on the card." He gave Lois a half-hearted grin and walked away.

Lois watched him leave before snatching up his card and the five-dollar tip. Masterson Homes and Renovation was embossed in gold on a solid black background. Seeing Rachel wiping down a booth at the opposite end of the bar, she set her jaw and marched toward her.

• • • •

Rachel watched Jim leave out of the corner of her eye. His broad shoulders and confident stride made her feel worse about turning him down. She missed having a man in her bed, but the real reason for the ache she was feeling had more to do with wanting someone to share her life with. A man who cared about her, not what she could give him in bed or put in his bank account. She'd had her share of the latter type and had never felt loved by any of them.

She was done with all that. Done with men. She had sworn them off after the last one stole money out of her purse. They always disappointed her. Every damn time. She had decided four years ago that she was better off without a man. Then, someone like Jim walks in and rips open all the old wounds. Reminding her how lonely she really was. Attempting to shake it off, she wiped the table harder.

Lois stomped up beside her and slapped the five-dollar bill and business card onto the booth table. "This was left for you by the gentleman at the bar," she said, crossing her arms over her chest.

Rachel picked up the bill and put it in her pocket, leaving the card on the table. "Thanks," she said, meeting Lois's glare.

"Rachel Stevenson—" Lois began.

"Don't start, Lo. I'm not interested."

Lois threw her hands up in exasperation. "Not interested? Have you lost your mind? Jim is a good man. He's kind, intelligent, single, and has a job. Hell, he owns the damn company. And he's obviously interested in you."

Rachel's expression was stony. "That doesn't make him a good man."

Lois pinched the bridge of her nose and closed her eyes. "What is wrong with you Stevenson women? You sound just like your mother."

Rachel's back stiffened at the comparison. "Yeah, well, she oughta know."

Lois opened her eyes and focused on Rachel. "She oughta know what?"

Rachel lowered her voice to a low hiss as she leaned toward Lois. "Men leave, Lois. They die and leave you; they break up with you and leave you; they take your money and leave you; and they definitely leave you when you're alone and pregnant. Men leave. Hell, you should know that better than any of us Stevenson women. What man are you on this week, number twenty-four?"

Lois froze. She stared at Rachel for a long moment before untying her apron. "You know what, honey? If you'd knock that chip off your shoulder and pull that giant stick out of your ass, you might just notice how much livin' you're missin' out on." She dropped the apron at Rachel's feet, snatched Jim's business card off the table, and walked toward the back door of the bar.

Rachel's bravado drained from her as she watched Lois go. She looked down at the apron lying on the floor and scooped it up with a sigh. Lois was the last person she wanted to take her anger out on. How did everything get so messed up in such a short amount of time? It seemed to Rachel that her mother had started a chain reaction that was picking up speed by the day. She needed to have it out with Neva, once and for all. She had no right to blow up everybody's life with her ultimatums and then run away while the pieces rained down. Rachel was done with it all.

• • • •

Tom stood in the bathroom doorway, watching Patty style her hair. She eyed him in the mirror's reflection. "What?" she asked defensively.

Tom leaned against the doorjamb and looked down at his sneakers. "You're going out. What about AA?"

Patty sighed and turned to face him. "It's eighties night at Boomers," she whined.

Tom slipped his hands into his jeans pockets, meeting her eyes. "I wish you wouldn't go. It hasn't even been a week, and you promised..."

Patty wrapped her arms around him, nestling into his chest. "I know, honey, but you can't expect me to change overnight. You know how much I love Saturday nights at Boomer's. Just a few beers, and I'll be home early, okay?"

Tom sighed, enfolding her in his arms. "You promise?"

Patty stepped back and fluttered her mascara laden eyelashes at him. "Of course."

Tom hesitated before giving a curt nod. Patty purred with delight and threw her arms around his neck, pressing a firm kiss to his mouth.

• • • •

Trent stood at the dining-room window, watching the driveway for Robin's car. Headlights illuminated the tree trunks near the road, and he called out to alert his mother. "Mom! Hurry up! She's here!"

"Coming!" Kris called back as she hurried down the stairs.

Trent turned to see his mother burst into the foyer. He stared at her, wide-eyed.

Her smile faltered at his expression. She glanced down at the outfit Robin had helped her choose the day before, hugging herself self-consciously. "What? What's wrong? Is it too much?"

Trent shook his head, breaking into a grin. "No! You look great!"

Kris studied his face for any hint of dishonesty, then noticed his missing earring. Surprised, she gave him a quick once-over, noting his red t-shirt paired with black jeans.

"Thank you. You clean up pretty well yourself!" she said, gesturing at his outfit.

A loud honk from the driveway startled them both. Kris grabbed her purse while Trent held the door open, motioning for her to go ahead.

"Better hurry before she leaves without you."

Kris planted a quick kiss on the top of his head as she rushed out the door. "Lock the doors and don't wait up! I love you!" she called over her shoulder.

Trent waved to them both as Kris opened Robin's car door. "Just have a good time!" he yelled.

• • • •

Across town, Lois and Neva sat on the front porch of Lois's old farmhouse, gazing at the starry night. Two whiskey highballs and an ashtray rested on the wicker table between their rocking chairs. Lois lit a cigarette, taking a long drag in the silence before exhaling slowly. Neva waved the smoke away from her face as it drifted toward her. "You should quit smoking those stinking things," she remarked.

Lois chuckled and shifted the cigarette to her other hand, holding it away from them both. "You should stop drinking those nasty things," she shot back, gesturing toward the glasses of whiskey with her free hand.

"I plan to," Neva replied.

Lois paused mid-drag, exhaling the smoke she had taken in and waving it away. She turned to face her friend. "Seriously?"

Neva nodded, avoiding eye contact.

Lois stamped her cigarette out in the ashtray. "What's happened? What's made you decide to do that?" she prodded gently.

Neva sighed, finally meeting her friend's gaze. "Time."

Lois remained silent but attentive, inviting Neva to continue.

"I've been using whiskey to escape my life for so long that I forgot what it's like to truly live it. Now, Rachel's heading down the same damn road, and I'm telling her she has to change lanes, or I won't give her any money. I'm telling Kris to buck up and find another man, and I'm telling Tom to leave his abusive spouse. And the truth is..." Neva trailed off, lost in thought.

"What's the truth?" Lois whispered.

"The truth is...I'm a goddamned hypocrite," Neva finished.

"Mm hmmm..." Lois replied, nodding slowly.

At this, Neva looked directly at her friend. "I take it you agree?"

Lois offered Neva a tight-lipped smile and a one-shoulder shrug.

Neva snorted. "You think I should just give them a share of the money and forget the conditions?"

"Let me ask you this," Lois replied. "Do you wish you'd made different choices yourself?"

Neva scoffed. "You know I do."

Lois gave a curt nod. "Right. You're their mother. It's your job to try to keep them from repeating the same mistakes you made, from having the same regrets. Despite the heavy-handed way you're going about it, I think you're doing them a huge favor. They may not see that now, but they'll thank you for it later."

"Will they, though?"

Lois lifted her glass in a mock toast. "If they don't, tough shit. Being a mother is a thankless job. You're in good company."

"Amen, sister!" Neva exclaimed, lifting her glass and clinking it hard against Lois's. "Have you decided what you want to do with your share?"

Lois glanced at Neva and then back out at the night sky. "I've been thinking about selling this place. Maybe build a house in town."

Shocked, Neva set her glass down and gave Lois her full attention. "Are you sure? I thought you loved this place."

Lois shrugged, regret etched in the lines of her face. "We're not spring chickens anymore, Neevie. This place takes too much work for me on my own. I think I'd be just as happy with a little place in town." She lit another cigarette. Exhaling the first drag, she flicked her thumb against her pinkie nail, creating a repetitive clicking noise, a small smirk turning up one corner of her mouth.

Neva watched her with interest for a few moments before grabbing her hand to silence the clicking. "Lois Lorraine Evans—what are you not telling me?"

Lois chuckled. "Nothin', nothin'! I was just thinking that I know the perfect builder for my new house."

Neva's antenna immediately went up at this, and she straightened in her chair. "You don't say. And just how 'perfect' is this builder?"

Lois pursed her lips and tapped her cigarette on the ashtray, enjoying having Neva on the hook. "Real nice guy. Good-looking. Single. You'd like him. Strong hands. Nice white teeth."

Neva hummed in approval, her eyes riveted on her friend.

"I checked him out. Good reputation. Successful. He's been coming into the bar several times a week—just to see Rachel."

Neva's eyebrows lifted in silent question.

Lois shook her head. "Rachel won't give him the time of day. Says she doesn't need a man. Men leave." She slid a hooded glance at Neva.

A growling sound, dripping with exasperation and disapproval, rumbled from Neva as she closed her eyes.

"Yeah, I know. That's what she says." Lois stretched the last word, letting it hang between them.

Neva's eyes snapped open and fixed on Lois. "Go on," she urged.

"She says that, but she looks at him like he's the last bar of chocolate in the universe."

Neva slapped her thigh in pure delight. "Why didn't you tell me about this sooner?"

Lois raised her hands in a stop gesture. "Hang on, sunshine. It ain't gonna be that easy. She's convinced herself that she doesn't want or need him. It's gonna take some doing to change her mind...but I may have a plan."

Neva rubbed her hands together in excitement. "Let's hear it."

Lois leaned in. "His name is Jim Masterson, and he owns Masterson Homes, a house-building company. Seems to me he's exactly the kind of person I need to help me build my new house. Oh, and you know how good Rachel is at interior design. I think I might need her to work side by side with me and Mr. Masterson. You know, to make sure I have all the best design elements in place." Lois said, giving Neva a wink.

A slow, sly grin spread across Neva's face. "Ohhh, that is perfect. Well done, my devious friend. Well done. Where do we start?"

• • • •

Kris glanced around the loud, busy nightclub, and an anxious shiver ran down her spine. Men and women clustered in groups throughout the bar, attempting to talk over the music blaring from the dozens of speakers hanging on the walls. A large group of at least thirty people had taken over the dance floor. While some seemed to have a superb grasp of dance moves from the eighties, others adapted current moves to the classic tunes. Lights shone down from the ceiling, blinking in rhythm to the music and bathing the area in continuously changing colors. A long bar lined one side of the club, and bartenders worked quickly to refill drinks and fill trays for the wait staff. Tables and booths covered in black vinyl surrounded the dance floor.

Robin took Kris's arm and pulled her to one of the booths. "Isn't this great!?" Robin shouted over the music. She caught the eye of a waitress and motioned her to their table.

Kris nodded, giving Robin a wan smile.

When the unfamiliar song ended, the DJ announced a short break. Robin beamed at the waitress as she approached their table. "Hi! We'd like four Jell-O shots and two slow screws, please!"

The waitress nodded, jotting the order on her notepad, and hustled back to the bar.

Kris leaned into Robin. "What's a slow screw?"

Robin's eyes scanned the bar as she answered. "Sloe gin and orange juice. It's fantastic! You'll love it."

"Maybe I should start with something a little less potent," Kris said.

"That's what the Jell-O shots are for!" Robin announced with glee.

Kris watched Robin's face as her friend's eyes searched the bar behind them. She turned to follow her gaze and spotted a cluster of men standing near the bar. A tall, handsome blonde in the group made eye contact with her and smiled. Kris quickly snapped her head back around and scrunched herself lower in the booth.

Robin watched her reaction and chuckled. "Oh, it's too late to hide. He's on his way over here!"

At that moment, their waitress reappeared and hastily placed their order on the table. Kris slammed one of the Jell-O shots and was working on her second by the time Robin had paid for them.

"Whoa! Slow down, sister. Are you trying to break a record?" Robin teased.

Kris jerked a thumb over her shoulder as she downed the second shot. "Is he still coming?"

Robin rolled her eyes. "Kris, I was kidding."

A bit of orange Jell-O dribbled onto Kris's chin, and she wiped it with the back of her hand, her cheeks reddening with embarrassment.

"You've never been to a club before, have you?" Robin asked, studying Kris thoughtfully.

Kris's shoulders slumped. "No."

"Never?" Robin pressed.

Kris shook her head.

Robin stared at her in astonishment. "How did I not know this? How did you meet Carl—an arranged marriage?" She joked, attempting to lighten the mood.

"No! We met in the library. At college," Kris retorted.

Robin startled as if slapped, staring open-mouthed at Kris.

"Stop it!" Kris said, trying to kick Robin under the table.

Robin blinked several times, as if processing what she had just heard. "I did not know that. We've been friends how long? And I didn't know that. You met in a library. Wow! That's just so— you."

Kris laughed. "It's not that bad! It was actually very romantic."

Robin's teasing expression shifted to one of feigned horror. "Jeezus! He's the only man you've ever had sex with, isn't he!?"

Kris's eyes dropped to the table, and she shifted uncomfortably. "Sort of. It's complicated," she muttered.

Robin leaned forward, all teasing gone. "Sort of? What the hell does that mean? How can you 'sort of—'"

"Hi, Kris!" Patty interrupted as she approached their table. "I didn't know you partied!"

Kris's posture stiffened as she took in her sister-in-law's appearance. "Patty," Kris said. "What a surprise. AA didn't work?"

"A girl's gotta have a little bit of fun now and then!" Patty quipped back.

Kris's jaw tightened. Robin noticed.

"Excuse me—Patty, is it?" Robin interjected. "We were right in the middle of an important conversation. So, if you could excuse us."

"You got a problem with me?" Patty said, putting her free hand on her hip and narrowing her eyes at Robin.

Robin stared Patty down. "Yes, I do," she snarled.

Patty held Robin's gaze for just a moment before breaking eye contact to glare down at Kris. "Your choice of friends is as bad as your choice of husbands," she snapped, turning on her heel and stomping off toward the bar.

Robin downed a Jell-O shot. "So, that's Patty, huh? I see what you mean. Your brother deserves better than that bitch."

Kris claimed one of the mixed drinks and handed the other to Robin. "Yep. Too bad she left, though. I would have bought the next round if you had punched her."

"Look at you, getting all buzzed and cocky with your bad self!" Robin cackled.

Kris waggled her eyebrows at her. "Shut up and drink that, or I will."

Two hours later, the bar was packed, and the music was booming. Kris laughed hysterically at a joke Robin had made about two men staring at them from the bar. As she wiped tears from her face, "Burning Down the House" by the Talking Heads began playing.

"Oh my God! I love this song!" Kris squealed, jumping to her feet. She grabbed Robin's arm, attempting to drag her from the booth. "Come on! Let's dance!"

Robin allowed herself to be towed onto the dance floor, and Kris found them a spot in the middle of the dancing mob. She threw her arms into the air, swinging her head back and forth wildly. Robin watched in horrified awe as her friend jerked and swayed to the music, not caring or even seeming to realize that she wasn't in sync with it.

The song ended, and "The Safety Dance" began to play. Kris grabbed Robin's arms and twirled her like a ballerina. "Dance, robot, dance!" Kris yelled at her over the music. Laughing, Robin complied.

• • • •

Tom looked at the clock on the wall, then back out at the road in front of their house. It was midnight, and Patty still wasn't home. She hadn't called, either. Tom picked up the phone receiver and checked for a dial tone, just to make sure it was working. Should he call the bar to see if she was still there? What if she was? Should he demand she come home? Would she listen to him if he did? No, she wouldn't. Better to just wait. He'd give her another hour. Surely, she wouldn't stay until the bars closed—not after the fight and the promises she'd made last week. She said she would get counseling for her drinking and anger issues. That was a step in the right direction. Tom didn't want to cause more trouble by upsetting her tonight.

Ashlea's small voice interrupted his thoughts. "Daddy? Is Mommy home yet?" she asked sleepily.

Tom knelt in front of her and tucked a strand of hair behind her ear. "No, not yet, sweetie."

Ashlea frowned, causing the little anxiety lines between her eyebrows to surface.

"It's late. Why aren't you asleep?" he asked softly.

Ashlea brushed off his question with a half-shrug and stared down at her toes. "Are you and Mommy going to fight again?"

Tom was still for a moment, then he gently grasped Ashlea's chin and tilted her head up to meet his gaze. "No, honey. We're not going to fight again. Is that why you're still up? You're afraid Mommy and I will argue?"

Ashlea cupped a small hand to her mouth and leaned in to whisper in Tom's ear. "I packed a backpack for Meggie and me to take to Aunt Kris's. Just in case."

Tom closed his eyes, silently cursing himself for allowing his children to feel this way. He hugged Ashlea tight before scooping her up and walking toward her bedroom. "No Aunt Kris's tonight. It's okay to sleep in your own bed. I'll be right here, and I promise, no fighting."

Her little body relaxed with this reassurance, and he thought he could actually hear his heart break.

• • • •

Kris and Robin exited the convenience store, loaded down with packages of toilet paper, boxes of plastic forks, and a large bag of potato chips. They clamored into their waiting cab, giggling like second graders. The driver eyed them in the rearview mirror.

Kris tapped on the plastic divider and announced, "Diane Littrell's residence, please. 2525 Country Club Drive Southwest."

The driver nodded and pulled out of the parking lot as Robin ripped open the bag of Doritos and offered it to Kris.

Ten minutes later, the cab pulled up in front of a large Cape Cod-style home. "This shouldn't take long. Can you pull down to the corner and wait a few minutes?" Kris asked.

The driver shook his head. "Look, lady, I know what you're planning to do, and I can't be a part of it. I can drop you off here, but that's it."

Kris looked at Robin, eyebrows raised in question. Robin shrugged one shoulder and stuck another Dorito in her mouth. Kris grinned and fished a twenty-dollar bill from her purse. The driver took the twenty and nervously checked the rearview mirror.

Robin was already out of the car, a package of toilet paper under each arm.

Kris gathered the rest of their supplies, but the heel of her right shoe snagged on the floor mat as she attempted to exit the car, causing her to fall onto the grassy curb. The boxes of forks and the bag of potato chips flew from her hands, littering the ground around her.

Robin hurried to close the cab door before leaning down to help Kris up. The driver glanced one last time at the two women before speeding away.

"Wait!" Kris yelled after him.

Robin clamped a hand over Kris's mouth. "Shh! You wanna wake the whole neighborhood!?"

Kris looked up at Robin, wide-eyed, and shook her head. Robin removed her hand. "My shoe is still in the car," Kris whispered.

Robin looked down at her friend's bare foot. "We can't run in heels anyway. Take the other one off," she instructed, stepping out of her own heels.

Kris kicked off her other shoe, sending it sailing into the branches of a large oak tree. Together, they gathered their supplies and scrambled to the bushes at the edge of Diane's yard, peering over the top of them at the house. All the windows were dark.

"Is that the house?" Robin whispered.

"Yep. That's the one," Kris whispered back.

Robin opened the package of toilet paper and extracted two rolls. She hugged one roll to her chest and offered the other to Kris. "Let's get 'em!"

• • • •

Six blocks away, the cab driver pulled into a convenience store and parked next to a police car. Two officers exited the store and walked toward their vehicle. The driver rolled down the cab window and motioned them over. He told them about the two women he had just dropped off and what he thought they intended to do. One officer wrote the address down while the second spoke into the radio attached to his uniform.

• • • •

Kris and Robin darted around the Littrell property like maniacs. Over one hundred plastic forks, their white handles gleaming in the moonlight, stuck up all over the lawn. Robin jammed even more into the ground with amazing speed. Kris threw rolls of toilet paper up into the branches of the large oak tree closest to the road. Two other trees and several of the bushes were already covered with white streamers. She tossed the last roll to Robin, who went to work on Carl's car in the driveway. Both women were so focused that they failed to notice the two police cruisers that pulled up until it was too late.

Four police officers jumped out of the cars and ran toward the stunned women.

Kris dropped the toilet paper and shimmied up the bedecked oak tree as quickly as she could. Robin executed a near-perfect swan dive over a bush and tried to hide under the front porch of the house, her feet and legs still visible. Two of the officers seized them, and she was unceremoniously dragged back out, kicking and cursing.

The other two police officers stood below Kris at the trunk of the oak tree. "Ma'am? We know you're up there. We can see you. You need to come down from there right now," one officer called up to her.

Kris noticed lights coming on inside the Littrell house. Oh, God! It was bad enough that she was about to be arrested. To be arrested in front of fake-hair Carl and home-wrecker Diane was too much to bear. She had to get down. She had to get down right fricking now and try to escape before they saw her.

Kris glanced down at the branches right below her, trying to find a quick way down. She crouched, reaching out to grasp a branch a bit lower than the one she was standing on. With a shift of her feet, she managed to get one hand on the lower branch and tried to shift her weight. She lost her balance, both feet slipping off the limb, and she reached out, managing to prevent her fall by grasping the lower branch. Kris dangled there for a few moments, trying to find purchase with her feet, when the branch snapped. She fell, fast and gracelessly, out of the tree, landing hard on her stomach at the feet of the officers. The shoe she had kicked off into the tree's branches earlier also fell from the tree, hitting her in the back of the head. The wind was knocked out of her from the fall, and she gasped for air, her mouth opening and closing like a landed fish.

A deep, familiar voice cut through her panic. "Ma'am, are you okay? Are you hurt?" he asked.

Oh, no. No! You've got to be kidding me. It can't be him again! Kris thought in horror. Finally catching her breath, she rolled onto her back and looked up at the officer.

His partner shined a flashlight at Kris's face. She squeezed her eyes shut, but not before she saw the recognition on Officer Miller's face.

Officer Miller motioned for his partner to move the beam of the flashlight off her. He squatted next to her, chuckling softly as he scooped up her shoe from the ground. "Well, well, it's Ms. Walker. What a surprise finding you here."

Kris could feel her cheeks going red.

He held out the shoe to her. "I believe this belongs to you, Cinderella," he teased. "But I think you might be at the wrong castle."

Kris glared at him. "Don't you ever get a day off?"

Chapter 9:
The End of All Things

The sun was rising by the time Robin and Kris finally made it through processing and into a holding cell. Kris flinched as the heavy metal door slammed shut behind her. Her head was pounding, and she swallowed convulsively, trying not to throw up.

Robin sat down on a metal cot and motioned for Kris to sit next to her. Kris's bare feet felt like they weighed a hundred pounds as she propelled herself forward and sat down beside her best friend. She groaned as her headache intensified with the movement, leaning forward and cradling her head in her hands. "I swear, I'm never drinking again. I don't know how my mom and Rachel can stand this."

Robin motioned for Kris to lay her head on her lap. Kris obeyed with a small whine of pain. "Who'd you call?" Robin croaked.

Kris opened one eye and focused it on Robin. "My mom. Who'd you call?"

Robin sighed. "Michael."

His name sent a shock through Kris's system. She bolted upright, staring at Robin in horror. "Our BOSS? Of all the people in the world, you called—"

"A lawyer." Robin interrupted, placing two fingers over Kris's lips. "We're going to need one, and you know he's the best."

Kris fell silent as the realization of their situation sank in. Her shoulders sagged in defeat. She grasped the hand Robin was using to silence her and squeezed it gently. "I'm sorry, Robin. I shouldn't have dragged you into this."

Robin studied Kris's face, searching. "That's it?" she asked. "Just, 'I shouldn't have dragged you into it'?"

Kris swallowed hard. "Yes," she croaked miserably. "I'm sorry."

Robin snorted. "You're sorry you dragged me into it, but you're not sorry you did it?"

"No," Kris said flatly. "I'd do it again. I'd just leave you and the alcohol out of it."

Robin barked out a laugh and pulled Kris into a hug. "Congratulations, girl! You are officially over your ex."

• • • •

Tom sat at the dining room table with his head in his hands. He'd been up all night, thinking and worrying. Patty hadn't come home. He had watched every minute of the night tick by while his emotions knocked around inside him like the steel ball in a pinball machine.

The sound of a car door slamming jolted him from his reverie. Within a few seconds, the front door opened, and Patty stepped in. Her purse dangled from one hand while she grasped the straps of her stiletto heels with the other. She stopped and repositioned the purse onto her shoulder.

The morning light streaming in through the living room windows illuminated her face. Under one eye, a dark smudge of mascara was visible, and her lipstick was smeared beyond her lip line. Half the pins in her hair must have been missing, as random escaped tendrils hung limply around her face, the rest a tangled mass at the back of her head. She winced at the sunlight shining on her from the window and tiptoed across the room.

Tom stepped in front of her, blocking her progress through the dining room. "Where were you all night?" he asked quietly.

Patty startled, but quickly regained her composure. "I spent the night with a friend."

Tom raised an eyebrow. "Why?"

Patty huffed in exasperation and placed a hand on her hip. "I was too drunk to drive home."

"You could have called me to pick you up. Or called a cab."

Patty rolled her eyes theatrically before fixing him with an icy glare. "I'm here now, so just drop it." She dropped her shoes and purse on the floor. "Now, move," she barked.

Tom stepped to the side, but she bumped him hard with her shoulder as she pushed past him. "And don't wake me up until at least two o'clock. I'm exhausted," she said before slamming their bedroom door.

• • • •

Neva and attorney Michael Newburg waited in the reception area of the county jail. It had been an hour since Neva paid bail for Kris and Robin, and the young receptionist behind the bulletproof glass had informed them that the two women were on their way out.

Neva glanced over at Michael, sizing him up one last time. The man appeared to be in his late forties and looked distinguished in his tailored suit and dark GQ haircut accented with bits of gray. He had a lovely start on some beard stubble that Neva found very attractive. He wasn't tall, but he seemed well-built. Neva knew he was successful—one of the top attorneys in town, according to her own attorney, Richard Hastings. And single. No wedding ring in sight, and her gaydar wasn't raising any alarms. Like Neva, Michael had been up since dawn sorting out the mess Kris and Robin had gotten themselves into. He wasn't the type she would pick for herself, but he'd be a decent match for Kris. Not necessarily a replacement for Carl, but a solid rebound for her.

Hopefully, this arrest wouldn't be a serious strike against her. After all, Kris had worked for the man for fifteen years. Surely, he realized that being arrested was out of character for her. Just imagining her daughter drunk and vandalizing Carl's mistress's house made Neva want to laugh out loud with glee. She couldn't wait to hear the details.

Michael stood suddenly, looking toward the door connecting the lobby to the holding area beyond it. Neva followed his gaze as a loud clanking noise and a buzzer sounded before the door swung open.

A tall, handsome hunk of a policeman stepped into the waiting room, holding the door for Robin and Kris.

Robin rushed to Michael and threw her arms around him. The expression on Michael's face when he saw Robin quashed any notions Neva had of pairing Kris with the handsome attorney. It was obvious he was already spoken for. Sighing, she turned her attention back to the doorway as her daughter stepped through it.

• • • •

Kris shuffled forward, her eyes fastened on the floor. Neva enveloped her in an embrace, squeezing Kris tight and rocking them from side to side.

"Mom. Mom, stop," Kris moaned, pushing away from her.

Neva took a step back as Kris bent forward, placing her hands on her knees and breathing deeply. Neva rubbed Kris's back. "Is this one of your stress-breathing exercises, or are you trying not to puke?"

Kris glanced up at her. "Both," she answered flatly. "I don't know what's worse—the stress of being arrested or this hangover."

Neva chuckled and glanced at Officer Miller, noticing the look of concern on his face as he watched Kris. Neva cleared her throat, and his gaze shifted to her. She raised a questioning eyebrow at him. He shifted uncomfortably, but trained his gaze back on Kris. Neva ducked her head to rummage through her purse, hiding a smile.

Pulling a small can of tomato juice and a peanut butter Twix candy bar from the bottom, she bent to Kris's level. "I thought you might need these. It's not the hair of the dog, but it'll fix you up well enough," Neva said, waving them both in Kris's face.

Kris pushed the items away and stood up. "Can we just get out of here? I want to go home."

Neva smiled at her daughter. "Alright, but you're going to beg me for these later." She put the tomato juice and candy bar back in her purse. "We can't leave yet, though. Your boss needs to talk to you about all the legal hoopla before we go."

Kris placed her fingers to her temples and winced in pain. "I hope you're happy, Mother. I tried doing what you wanted, and now I have a criminal record!"

Neva took a step back in mock shock, a smile tugging at the corners of her mouth. "How is this my fault?" she asked innocently. Kris glared at her. Neva leaned forward and lowered her voice. "I don't recall ever suggesting that you go out and get yourself arrested," she said.

Kris's eyes widened. "Well, it didn't say anything in the contract about not getting arrested, so whether this disappoints you or not, I'm—"

"Honey, how could I possibly be disappointed?" Neva said, grabbing one of Kris's hands and squeezing it. "Not every woman can land in jail and land herself a handsome man all in the same night," she crooned.

Kris stiffened. She glanced at Michael, then back to the glint in her mother's eye. "What are you talking about!?" she hissed. "I didn't 'land' Michael! And keep your voice down, for Pete's sake."

Neva rolled her eyes and leaned in, whispering in her ear. "I wasn't talking about Michael, Krissy dear. Are you really that man-blind? He's obviously got a thing for Robin."

Kris placed a hand to her forehead. "Mom, just stop. I can't deal with your matchmaking delusions right now."

Neva smirked and took Kris by the shoulders, turning her toward Michael and Robin. "See for yourself, Helen Keller."

Across the room, Michael was leaning in close to Robin as they spoke in hushed tones. Robin was nodding and looking at him like...

"Oh my God!" Kris gasped. She glanced back at her mother. Neva gave a quick nod of confirmation. Kris narrowed her eyes and took a step closer to Neva. "If not Michael, then who did you think I landed?" Kris whispered.

Neva shot a pointed glance over Kris's shoulder. "I'll wait for you in the car, sweety," she replied with a wink.

Kris turned to see Officer Miller standing a few feet behind her. He gave her a small smile.

Michael approached Kris then, taking her arm and moving her toward the private area where he and Robin had been talking. "Are you okay?" Michael asked with genuine concern.

Kris swallowed hard and nodded.

He lowered his voice as he continued. "I was just telling Robin that the district attorney will drop the charges of resisting arrest and public intoxication, but you're still looking at a criminal mischief charge."

Kris hesitated before nodding again. "I understand." She could see Officer Miller over Michael's shoulder. She tried to steal a covert glance at him, but their eyes met. He dipped his head almost shyly, dropping his gaze from hers. Kris's toes tingled, and her belly fluttered. Her sick, alcohol-soaked belly actually fluttered, making her feel like a sea-sick passenger on the Titanic.

"Kris? Did you hear me?" Michael asked.

Kris's attention snapped back to Michael. "What? Sorry, I was distracted."

Sighing, he started again. "I said we might have gotten all the charges dismissed, but apparently, your husband wouldn't let Ms. Littrell agree to drop the criminal mischief charge just yet. Any idea why?"

Kris took a deep breath in through her nose and nodded. "Oh, yeah. I've got a pretty good idea."

Michael studied her for a moment. "Mm-hmm. That's what I thought. Well, I've hired a landscaping team to go over and clean up Ms. Littrell's yard, and I'm giving Robin a lift home. She's waiting in the car. We'll figure the rest out later, okay?"

Kris could see the concern in his eyes. A tidal wave of gratitude washed over her, and she pulled him into a hug. He froze for an instant and then patted her back awkwardly. She released him and took a step back. "Thank you, Michael. For everything. I'm so sorry you had to be involved in all this."

He chuckled. "It's what I do. Be a damn shame if I couldn't use it to help my friends and employees."

Kris grimaced. "Do we still have jobs to come back to on Monday?"

Michael laughed. "Let's just consider this on-the-job training. Check with your accountant; you may be able to write off the entire expense," he teased. "Go home and get some rest. We'll talk more on Monday." He gave her shoulder a quick pat of reassurance before turning and leaving the building.

Kris watched him go. The constant thumping in her head was becoming more persistent, and her need for a hot shower and a soft bed called to her like a siren song. There was still one more thing she had to do before surrendering to that call. Steeling herself, she walked over to where Officer Miller was standing. He smiled warmly at her.

"Officer Miller, I just want to say..." Kris started.

"Call me Dan," he interrupted, handing her a business card. "I see you more than I do my own family these days. No point in staying formal."

Kris grimaced and stared down at the card. It had his name on the front, along with the phone numbers for the police department and his extension. Turning the card over, she saw his cell phone number handwritten on the back.

"Although our last few encounters have been very exciting, the next time we see each other, I'd rather it be over a plate of good Italian food," he said with a smile.

Blood rushed to Kris's face, making her head pound even harder. Flustered, embarrassed, and sure she was suffering the worst hangover in history, she backed away from him, muttering, "Right. Well... thanks for, umm... thanks." Without waiting for his reply, she turned and fled the building.

• • • •

Three hours later, Kris was home, showered, and lounging in her favorite sweatpants on the sofa. She took a sip of the tomato juice Neva had given her and followed it with a bite of the Twix, marveling at how good the unlikely pairing tasted to her.

Trent stood in front of her, watching. "Is it helping?" he asked, his face screwed up in obvious disgust.

Kris studied the label on the back of the juice bottle, squinting as she tried to read it. "Surprisingly, it is."

Trent crossed to the window and opened the blinds, allowing a solid stream of light to permeate the dim room. Kris squeezed her eyes shut, holding her arms up in front of her face as if fending off a blow. "Close it, close it! You're killing me!"

Trent chuckled, tilting the blinds upward to decrease the amount of light. "How's that? Better?"

The sound of the front door slamming interrupted Kris's reply, and she sat up, alarmed.

Carl's voice bellowed from the entryway. "Kris!? Kris, goddammit, where are you!?"

Kris closed her eyes and sighed.

When she opened them again, Carl—red-faced and fuming with anger—was standing in the living room doorway. "What in the absolute fuck were you thinking!?" he yelled.

Kris set her tomato juice and candy bar on the end table with exaggerated care before standing to face him. She laced her hands in front of her in a show of contrition and forced a calm response. "I'm sorry for any trouble I may have caused Diane. I was drunk and angry, and—"

"Since when do you get drunk? I can't believe you'd pull such a stupid, juvenile, illegal stunt!" he sputtered, interrupting her.

Kris put both hands on her hips and matched his glare with her own. "I'm stupid? I'm juvenile? And what about you? What's your behavior been like, Carl?"

He looked at her like she had two heads. "What is going on with you? This isn't your normal behavior. Are you on drugs? Are you still drunk?"

Kris waved his comments away. "Of course not. Don't be an idiot."

His eyes narrowed. "Are you having some kind of breakdown, then?"

"No, I'm not having a breakdown. I'm having an epiphany!" she declared, punching the air with her fist.

Carl goggled at her, unamused.

"You know what last night really was?" Kris said, pulling her shoulders back. "I think it was my way of telling you and Diane to go fuck yourselves."

Trent let out a snort of laughter, and Kris glanced over at him.

He saluted her by punching his own fist in the air. "Yesss!" he whooped, grinning from ear to ear.

Kris couldn't help her own small smirk of satisfaction.

Carl's face turned an even deeper shade of red as he watched the exchange. "Well, congratulations!" he announced. "You've finally proven yourself to be a terrible wife and a terrible mother!"

Kris's face drained of color, but her back remained straight, and her chin raised in defiance. "Oh really," she bit out. "And just how do you think I've done that?"

"Do you really need me to point it out? Look at the example you're setting!" Carl motioned to Trent. "And just look at him! He didn't look like a freak when we were married!"

Trent's grin fell.

"We're still married, Carl," Kris answered with deadly calm. She moved to Trent's side and put her arm around his shoulders.

"You know what I mean! He wouldn't dress like that if I still lived in this house."

"Well, you don't live in this house, so—"

"And now you're drinking and getting yourself thrown in jail!?" Carl ranted.

Kris released Trent and crossed her arms over her chest. "What makes you think you have the right to come in here and say anything about what I do?"

"I'm still his father, damnit." He ran one hand through his hair and took a deep breath. "Listen, you're right. I have no right to tell you what to do, but Trent is still my son, and you haven't signed the divorce papers yet. So, technically, Trent's custody hasn't been settled. Considering the latest developments, I've talked with Diane and we've decided it would be best if Trent came to live with us."

Kris's stomach clenched as if Carl's words had been a physical punch. She gaped at Carl, unable to move or speak as the realization of what he was trying to do washed over her.

Trent took one look at her face, and before she could find her words again to stop him, he approached his father.

"No! If this is anybody's fault, it's yours," Trent said, his face twisted in anger.

"Trent, you're too young to understand this now, but..." Carl said, reaching out to grasp Trent by the shoulders.

Trent batted his hands away. "I understand more than you think. I understand you're a selfish asshole."

Carl closed his eyes and rubbed his temples as if relieving a headache. "I don't have time for this, Trent."

Trent lurched forward, pushing his father hard in the chest. Carl staggered back a few steps, eyes wide at Trent's reaction.

"That's just it, isn't it!?" Trent said, his breaths coming in angry pants. "You never had time for me or Mom! She worked forty hours a week, took care of me, took care of you, cleaned this house, and cooked your meals, and never asked you for a damn thing!" Trent bellowed. "And what did you do? You treated her like she was your servant. Like she was less than you! But guess what? You're the shitty one. She is so far out of your league; I don't get why she ever chose you! We're both better off without you."

Kris went rigid at the truth in Trent's outburst. In the span of thirty seconds, the final, and ultimate truth of the fifteen years she had spent married to Carl came crashing in on her. The blinders she had worn since meeting Carl were gone, and a rush of complete clarity washed over her. She could see Carl now. All of him. And she was disgusted and ashamed of herself for trying to hold on to someone who didn't love her, and had likely never loved her, or Trent. She crossed the room to her desk and, with a steady hand, signed the divorce papers.

Carl reached out to Trent again, but Trent stepped away. Carl held his hands out in front of him, as if pleading, and lowered his voice. "Trent, I know you're upset, and you may think I'm awful, but Diane is a good woman and—"

"You wouldn't know a good woman if you met one, and other than Mom, I doubt you ever have."

"Hey, that's enough!" Carl retorted. "I'm still your father, and I'm not putting up with your mouth!"

"I would never live with you. Never," Trent sneered, contempt emanating from every pore.

Kris stepped to Trent's side and thrust the signed documents at Carl's chest. "Aren't these what you really came for? They're signed. Custody is officially decided, and we are done. Now, get out of my house."

Carl looked from the bitter resignation on Kris's face to the disgusted glare his only son was giving him. He blanched, dropping his gaze to the divorce papers. Flipping to the last page, he scanned it for her signature. Satisfied, he rolled the document into a tube shape and tapped it nervously on one palm. He opened his mouth to speak, but Kris cut him off.

"Get. The. Fuck. Out," she said, in a tone that was a perfect imitation of her mother's.

Carl's eyes widened in surprise. Kris's steely gaze didn't falter, and Carl dropped his eyes to the floor. Without another word, he strode out of the room.

The sound of the front door slamming behind him triggered a loud exhale from Kris. She hadn't realized she had been holding her breath. She inhaled a lungful of air and bent over, putting her hands on her knees to steady herself.

Trent gently patted her back. "You okay, Mom?"

Kris let out a strangled laugh that was half sob and stood. "Yeah, buddy. I think I am. You?"

Trent nodded. "I'm good."

Kris ran a hand over her face as if scrubbing it. "I'm done putting up with his crap. We both deserve better."

"You know," Trent said, squinting at her as he pretended to stroke a fake beard in contemplation, "I think I like you with a hangover. Brings out the Grandma Neva in you."

Kris put a hand to her aching head. "Yeah? Well, I'm not so sure it's worth it, kid. I think I need to puke."

• • • •

Mondays were always slow at Lucky's, and Lois usually had them off. Rachel would be there, doing inventory and taking advantage of the lull to catch up on paperwork. It was too early for the regulars, and deliveries wouldn't start arriving for another hour or two. A perfect time for her to stop by and ask for help designing the new house. Convincing Rachel was going to be a delicate endeavor, but she couldn't wait to get phase one of her and Neva's plan in place.

Lois saw hundreds of people come in and out of the bar every week. Many of them were looking for love or looking for sex, but she couldn't think of one person she'd ever seen who needed to get laid more than Rachel did right now. If she had a hand in making that happen for Rachel, she'd feel pretty damn good about it. And if, by the grace of Aphrodite, that roll in the sack turned into a healthy relationship, she would consider it icing on the cake.

Lois had never been comfortable with Rachel's fixation on her dead son-of-a-bitch father. It wasn't healthy for Rachel to believe something about him that was such complete horseshit. It was equally messed up for Neva to keep the truth about him from her. Lois had this conversation with Neva many times over the years. Begging Neva to tell Rachel the truth about Robert and the night he died. Her friend always refused, claiming some nonsense about "preserving a positive memory" for Rachel. Neva's kids had been young when it happened, but Rachel had only been three years old—a tiny, fierce little thing. Lois loved all of Neva's kids, but if she was honest, Rachel had claimed the biggest piece of her heart, and she didn't want to see her get hurt. So, she had always let the subject go, hoping Neva was right and it would all work out somehow.

Then, when Rachel had turned thirteen and started obsessing over boys, wanting their approval, Lois had seen the train wreck coming and tried to warn Neva. "She's trying to make up for not having positive male attention in her life. She's got 'daddy issues,' Neevie. You need to sit that girl down and tell her about him. Talk to her about men, or you'll be a grandma before you're forty-five."

Neva would just laugh, shake her head, and say some dumbass thing about preserving memories and keeping Rachel innocent, which made absolutely no sense. Then, Neva would change the subject, and Lois would let it go. Again.

She and Neva had talked at length about this the night they created the plan to get Rachel and Jim working together on Lois's new house. It made Lois happy that her friend was finally planning to share the full truth with Rachel, but she was nervous about how Rachel was going to take it. Robert was a big lie, told for a long time. She prayed Jim might help lessen the blow when it came and keep Rachel from giving up on men altogether. Time would tell...but first they needed to put the "Jim" part of the plan in motion.

Lois pasted on a smile and stepped into Lucky's. A quick scan revealed she had timed her visit perfectly.

Rachel sat in the middle booth with invoices and the bar's accounting books strewn on the table in front of her. She looked up when Lois walked in. "Hey, Lo. What are you doing here today?"

"Here to see you about something super important," Lois chirped, joining Rachel in the booth. Both of Rachel's eyebrows went up in an expression so much like Neva's, Lois had to bite her lip to keep from laughing out loud. "I have a huge favor to ask."

Rachel stiffened. "What's up? Has something happened?"

Lois brushed her hand through the air as if waving something away. "No, no, nothing bad. Something good, actually."

Rachel's eyebrows and shoulders settled into their natural positions, and she put her pen down, giving Lois her full attention.

"I've decided to sell the farm and—"

"Sell the farm?!" Rachel exclaimed. "But you love that place."

Lois made a zipping motion across her lips. "Hang on. Hear me out."

Rachel clamped her mouth shut.

"I do love the place, but I'm getting older, and I don't love all the extra work of taking care of it. The truth is, I've been thinking of selling for a while now, and your momma offered to share some of her lottery money. So, I plan to sell the farm and use the funds to build a nice little house in town. I wanna be closer to your momma and the bar," Lois said, smiling at Rachel in a way she hoped conveyed excitement and happiness.

Rachel didn't seem pleased with the news. "Mom gave you money for a house?" she asked, her tone instantly setting Lois on edge.

"Yes, she did."

Rachel leaned back in the booth, crossing her arms. "What conditions did she put on you?"

Lois sighed, raising her eyes to the ceiling as if praying for help. "None. She gave it as a gift to her oldest and dearest friend. Jesus Christ, Rachel, can you drop the axe you have for your mother for ten damn minutes and process what I'm telling you?"

Rachel stared hard at Lois for a few seconds before letting her arms fall to her sides. "I'm sorry, Lo. Of course she should share some of the money with you. I'm not upset at you about it. Neva is just being such a controlling asshat; it's put me on edge."

It was Lois's turn to cross her arms and sit back. "Neva? She's Neva now, not 'Mom' anymore, huh?"

Rachel scrubbed her face with her hands. "Well, she's not acting much like a mother. Let's not talk about her," she said, trying to shift the conversation. "Selling the farm to build your own house, huh? I don't know whether to be happy for you or sad."

Lois reached across the table and took one of Rachel's hands, giving it a squeeze. "I had great years on the farm, but life changes, and you have to be willing to change with it. Holding on to things that don't fit you anymore will only hold you back. Your mom offered, and I knew it was my chance to move on to something new. Now, be happy for me, damn it!"

Rachel chuckled, the light returning to her eyes. "Okay! If you're happy, then I'm happy for you."

"Good, because I have a huge favor to ask, and you are the only one who can do it for me."

Rachel exaggerated a grimace. "Okaaay...what is it?"

Lois became animated with excitement. "Well, building a house is a huge deal. I wanna get it right, and I also want it to fit me. You know, be functional but also be built inside and outside in a style I like. To fit me. I never had that choice with the farm; it just was what it was. You're so good with interior design, and light, and making things functional and all that. I don't know a thing about any of it. So, I'd like you to help me—step by step, from the dirt to the finished product. You think you'd be willing to do that?"

Rachel's face lit up, and she beamed at Lois. "What? Are you kidding me!? Yes! Of course, I'll help! Do you have a design picked out yet? Who are you going to have build it?"

Lois beamed back at her. "Oh, thank you, honey! You don't know how happy that makes me! I have a builder picked out, but I was hoping you'd help me do something custom. You'll have to be the one working with the builder, though, because Lord knows it's all just gibberish to me."

Rachel nodded enthusiastically. "Yes! Absolutely. I can do that."

"I would rely on you to make sure everything is done right and ends up looking pretty in the end. It's a big commitment on your part, Hun, and you can't back out on me," Lois said, pausing to wait for Rachel's agreement.

"I would never leave you hanging, Lo. You know I've always wanted to do something like this."

"This is the biggest thing I've ever done, and I'd be counting on you." Lois said, laying it on thick.

"I'm in! I'm in! When do we start?" Rachel said, squirming excitedly in her seat.

Lois gave herself a mental pat on the back. It was done. She had convinced Rachel to commit to the entire project. Step one was firmly in place.

She looked at her watch, feigning horror. "Oh shit! I've got to vamoose," she said, sliding out of the booth. She stooped and gave Rachel a peck on the cheek. "I'll have my builder get in touch with you later this week. Thank you again, sweetie. I can't wait to get started!" Without another word, Lois turned and jogged toward the exit.

"Who's the builder?" Rachel called after her.

Lois just waved as she disappeared out the door.

Less than a minute later, she was in her car, calling Neva.

Neva answered on the first ring. "Well?"

"Step one was a success. I'm on my way to his office now."

"I'll meet you there in ten minutes," Neva replied before ending the call.

• • • •

Jim Masterson was working on a set of architectural plans when the two ladies strode into his office. He recognized Lois instantly and greeted her with a warm smile, extending his hand. "Ms. Evans, it's a pleasure to see you again."

Lois took his hand and covered it with her other one. "I was so happy you could see me on such short notice. Please, call me Lois," she simpered, adding a flutter of her lashes that made Neva want to roll her eyes. Instead, she squeezed Lois's elbow.

Lois gave a small start and turned to Neva. "Oh! Mr. Masterson, this is my dear friend Neva Stevenson. Neva, this is Jim Masterson. He's going to build my house."

Jim turned his full attention to Neva and offered his hand. His face clouded for a moment, puzzled. "I'm sorry, have we met before? You look so familiar."

"I'm sure we haven't, but I believe you've met my daughter, Rachel. She manages Lucky's Bar. I'm told we look a lot alike," Neva replied, studying his expression.

Jim snapped his fingers, as if it all just suddenly clicked. "Yes! That's it." He squinted at her suspiciously, "Wait. Did you say Rachel's your daughter? You look like you could be sisters."

Neva shot Lois a look of approval before rewarding Jim with her widest and warmest smile. "You'll do, Mr. Masterson. You'll do."

· · · ·

Having established that Jim Masterson was the right man for the job, not only for building Lois's house but also for breaking through Rachel's defenses, Neva felt more content than she had anticipated at this moment. She hadn't talked to her children yet, but the little information she had gathered suggested they were moving in the right direction. She couldn't put it off any longer; it was time for her to put her money where her mouth was and confront her own issues.

Getting her scar removed was a notion she had considered for years—decades, really. Something always stopped her from following through. In the years following Robert's death, she told herself it was too expensive. As a single mother raising three kids, it would be selfish to take what little savings she had and spend it on a surgery that was more vanity than necessity.

Then, when her parents passed away and left her a tidy sum of money, she convinced herself that remodeling the house was more important. After all, an expenditure like that would improve all of their lives, not just hers. Technically, she had enough money for both the surgery and the remodel, but she chose to put the extra funds away for emergencies instead. Later, when the kids had all moved out, she decided that she was too old for it to matter anymore.

But it did matter. It had always mattered. Neva had spent over twenty-five years hiding her scar. Never going swimming or undressing in front of anyone except Lois, and always wearing scarves and turtlenecks to cover it. Kris and Tom knew it was there; they had seen it the night she received it and understood that her fashion choices were solely to conceal it. But Rachel didn't know.

Rachel had been so young that night; she hadn't understood what had happened, or what a monster he really was. In the beginning, Neva covered the scar out of shame and to prevent questions from Rachel, wanting to hide what Robert had done until her daughter was older and could understand. When Rachel was fourteen, at the start of her boy-crazy phase, Neva had decided to tell her, but Kris and Tom pleaded with her not to. Neva's scar was visible, but Kris's scars weren't, and she had no intention of shining a light on them if Kris wasn't ready.

Neva had relented for Kris's sake, keeping both the scar and its story a secret for a while longer. She preferred bearing the pain herself rather than inflicting more suffering on Kris—or any of her children. After all, it had been her fault, not theirs. The scar became her cross to bear, her penance. A constant reminder of her poor judgment in men and her failure to protect her children.

For two and a half decades, Neva had lived with this reality. She'd denied herself any genuine relationship with another man, allowing only short, meaningless encounters. True intimacy remained a pleasure she wouldn't permit herself while her children continued to struggle. Yet, her self-imposed punishment had proved futile. Despite all her denial and self-flagellation, she couldn't prevent her children from suffering or stop them from making similar mistakes. Watching their missteps had inflicted far greater pain than her scar or loneliness ever could.

She was done with all that now. Done. The lottery winnings had offered them all a perfect opportunity. A chance to leave the past behind and forge a better future. How could she expect her children to make changes if she wasn't willing to do the same? So here she was, taking the first step on her list of changes. Today's mission: meeting with a plastic surgeon to schedule the removal of her scar.

Neva lowered the magazine she'd been pretending to read and scanned the waiting area. Her gaze landed on a young woman seated directly across from her. Oh, dear God, she thought, recognizing Roxxy, the cashier who'd sold her the winning ticket. She quickly raised the magazine to shield her face, but too late. Roxxy had already spotted her.

"Oh my God, it's you!" She exclaimed, rushing over to claim the empty seat beside Neva. "How are you?!"

Neva lowered her magazine and offered a polite smile. "I'm fine, just fine. And you?"

"I'm soooo great! Did you hear?!" Roxxy's face lit up with childlike excitement.

Neva barely managed a head shake before Roxxy continued in an eager whisper, "The winning ticket came from our store! Can you believe it?!" The cashier cupped her enormous breasts, giving them an unnecessary lift and thrust them toward Neva. "I'm here for my final check-up on the twins. That's what Rob calls them," she added with a giggle.

"Yes, I heard about the winning ticket." Neva waved vaguely at Roxxy's chest. "Those are... those are nice. Good for you," she lied.

Roxxy beamed. "Thank you!"

"Well, it was nice to see you again," Neva said, attempting to end their conversation.

"What are you in for? Face lift?" Roxxy pressed.

Neva fixed her with a hard look. "No."

"Boob job?"

Neva straightened, her irritation mounting. "No," she replied curtly, raising the magazine in an unmistakable hint.

Oblivious, Roxxy studied Neva for a moment before exclaiming, "Oh my God! Are you here for a sex change?!"

Neva slapped the magazine into her lap. "No! I'm here to get rid of this." She yanked down her scarf, revealing the scar to the ridiculous girl.

"Wow, that's a doozy," Roxxy marveled. "I bet that really hurt. How'd you get a scar like that?"

The door to the waiting area opened, and a nurse emerged. "Neva Stevenson?" she called out.

"Here!" Neva answered, relief flooding her voice. She stood and hurried toward the nurse without sparing the big-bosomed cashier another glance.

• • • •

Rachel had just finished restocking the beer cooler when Jim Masterson strolled up to the bar and claimed a seat in front of her.

Customers flowed through the bar all day, every day. Many were men, and they came in every type. Married, single, gay, and straight. None affected her heart rate quite like this one did. Until meeting Jim Masterson, she'd believed the last few years of staying away from men had made her immune to their allure. She wanted that to be true. Life was simpler when she stayed single and aloof—less drama, less hassle, less heartache.

But something had shifted the day she met Jim. She wanted to dismiss it as imagination. To convince herself that meeting him hadn't changed her resolve to avoid men. Yet it had changed, and that realization terrified her.

Now here he was again, standing less than two feet away with only the bar top between them. His smile flashed, that dimple winking at her, while a different scent radiated off of him today that was even more enticing than the last time she'd seen him. She inhaled deeply, trying to decipher what it was... Soap, sawdust, and some indefinable spice...

"Do I stink?" Jim asked.

"Wh-what?" Rachel stammered, jolted from her reverie.

"You were smelling me. Or at least I think you were. You were definitely sniffing 'at' me."

Rachel wiped the area in front of her. "No, sorry. I just smelled something odd and was trying to figure out where it was coming from. What can I get you?" she asked, her voice sounding unaffected. She met his gaze, and her traitorous heart began to beat in a quick, erratic rhythm.

Jim looked at her skeptically before surreptitiously sniffing his shirt and then his armpit. Rachel couldn't suppress the smile that ghosted across her lips. He noticed it and grinned sheepishly, shoving his hands into his front pockets and leaning toward her over the bar.

She could smell the mint on his breath when he whispered, "You could give a guy a complex, Rachel Stevenson."

Rachel glanced down at his lips, feeling a tug low in her belly. She was in big trouble with this one. Jim Masterson was like a magnet—an unavoidable force pulling her closer to him. She needed to create some space between them. She had to pull back right now, or she was going to...

Suddenly, Jim stepped back, pulling the chair away from the bar several inches before settling into it. "A Coke, please," he said, seemingly unaffected by how close they had just been.

Rachel cleared her throat, trying to ground herself in the moment. "Okay, Rum and Coke, Jack and Coke...?"

"No. Just a plain Coke. It's only eleven, and I'm working," he replied playfully.

"Must be lunch break then. Not into martini lunches?" Rachel bantered back.

"Generally, no. You've got to keep your wits sharp when you're working construction, and I'm on the clock."

"Ah, I see. So, you came into a bar for a Coke? There are cheaper options down at the gas station, you know."

Jim chuckled. "Yes, but I can't chat with my new client's project manager at the gas station." He handed Rachel his business card. "Lois said you're the woman in charge, so I thought I'd come down here to schedule a time for us to start working on her building plans."

"Wait, what? What do you have to do with Lois's house?"

Jim pointed at the business card in her hand. "Masterson Homes." He gestured to himself. "Jim Masterson. Builder."

Rachel grabbed the bar with her free hand to steady herself. The hand holding the business card began to shake. She tucked the card into her back pocket and grabbed the bar rag to hide her trembling. What had Lois gotten her into? She couldn't work with this man! She could barely take his drink order without feeling breathless. A vision flashed through her mind of them standing next to each other at a table, blueprints of Lois's house spread out in front of them. She imagined his body so close to hers that she could feel the heat radiating off him, smell the scent of soap, sawdust, and his mystery spice. In an instant, the vision shifted, and she was lying naked on that same table, with Jim between her legs. She jolted, snapping out of her thoughts as if burned by the image.

"Rachel? Are you okay?" he asked, genuine concern etched on his face.

Rachel sucked in a breath and looked up at him, waving the bar rag as if shooing away a fly. "Yeah, I'm fine. Fine. Just a bit surprised. Lois didn't tell me who the builder was, so you caught me off guard. I'll get you that Coke."

She snatched a glass from the shelf, trying to calm her racing mind as she poured the drink. What was she supposed to say to this? Damn Lois and her matchmaking! This was extreme, even for her. Or maybe not. Perhaps Jim was simply the best contractor for the job—or the only contractor Lois knew. Maybe it had nothing to do with Rachel and matchmaking.

Maybe she was making more of this than she should, doing what her mother always accused her of: making it "all about Rachel" when it should be about someone else. Comforted by the thought, she placed the Coke on a napkin in front of Jim.

"Lois works fast. She just asked me to help her two days ago," Rachel said in a friendly tone.

"Me too," he replied, flashing a dimple and throwing in a wink.

Rachel's stomach fluttered.

"I've never worked with someone else on designing a custom build, so I wasn't sure about taking the project at first. But Lois and your mother were very convincing. They raved about you and your design skills. So, I thought, what the hell? It might be fun. And here I am."

Rachel's smile tightened. "Did you say Lois and my mother?"

Jim took a sip of his Coke and nodded. "Yeah, Neva."

"Two days ago?" she asked.

Jim set his glass down and studied her face for a moment. "Yes..." he replied cautiously. "Is something wrong?"

Hell yes, something was wrong. Her blackmailing, meddling, horrible excuse for a mother was back in town and hadn't even told her. Lois hadn't mentioned it either! Of course not. If her mother had any part in this, Lois knew Rachel would never agree to help her build the house. Now, here she was, and here Jim was, and Rachel had no idea what to do about it—except to be honest with him. She shook her head and leaned against the bar. Lowering her voice, she said, "I hate to tell you this, but you and I are being played."

Jim held his hand up to his mouth as if sharing a secret and whispered, "I hate to tell you this, but I am well aware of that."

Rachel straightened in surprise. "You are?"

Jim gave a sharp nod.

Heat rose to Rachel's cheeks. "Well, it's not going to work. I'm not—"

"—Not interested. I know. Neither am I," Jim interrupted.

All the bluster drained from Rachel as she processed his words. He waited patiently as she regained her composure.

"You're not interested? Then why are you here?" she asked, attempting to hide her disappointment.

Jim sighed. "I'm interested in the project. I'm not interested in dating you, or ensnaring you, or whatever Lois and your mother have in mind. You made it pretty clear that you find me too repulsive to even have coffee with. I have no intention of putting my ego out there for another beating."

"I never said I found you repulsive," Rachel said, feeling shamefaced.

Jim laughed. "You didn't have to! The brush-off you gave me said it loud and clear. I took the hint. My romantic interest in you is done. Gone. You stabbed it to death. I told the two cupids that, too, and informed them I'm seeing someone else."

Rachel felt his words like a punch to the gut. She wasn't sure which part of his statement was worse: the fact that he had no interest in her or that he was seeing someone else. She should have felt relieved that he wouldn't pursue her and elated that he had beaten Neva and Lois at their own game, but she didn't.

For the first time in a very long time, she felt hurt and, somehow, abandoned. She wanted him, and that threatened her in ways she didn't want to think about. His declaration that he didn't want her only intensified her need for him. What was wrong with her? Why did she always want the guy who didn't want her? Was this one of those situations? After all, he had wanted her before she turned him down. And she had wanted him, even before she found out that he didn't want her anymore. Ugh! This was exactly why she didn't want a man in her life. It threw her off balance. He was her kryptonite. She needed to harden her defenses and stand firm against Jim Masterson.

"Kudos to you for outwitting Cruella and her sidekick," she stated flatly, "but I don't think it's a good idea for us to work together."

Jim sat back in his chair, crossing his arms over his chest as he studied her. She met his gaze, appearing outwardly calm while internally squirming under his scrutiny.

"I think I see what's going on here," Jim said. "You don't really have the skills to manage this kind of project."

Rachel's eyes narrowed, and her fists came to rest on her hips. "No, you don't see. My skills, which I do have, by the way, are not the problem."

"What's the issue, then?" Jim shrugged. "Who gives a shit what ulterior motives they have? This project is strictly business. Whatever machinations they may try to cook up won't work on me. I am immune—and you obviously are, too. Their attempt will fail, the house gets built, Lois loves it, and you and I go our merry way."

Jim's hand gestures while speaking, as if he were the lovechild of an Italian and a mediocre mime, made Rachel want to laugh. She liked this man. And yes, that was a problem, but she had been dying to take on a project this big. She'd spent the last nine years taking classes to prepare for it. Now, she had a real chance to put everything she had learned into practice and do something she loved. It would be great for her resume, too. He was right, and she would not let her crazy mother screw this up.

"Machinations, huh?" Rachel asked, fighting back a smile. "Do all construction workers have such large..." she trailed off, looking him up and down, "...vocabularies?"

A slow, panty-dropping grin spread across his lips, exposing his dimple yet again. "You bet your ass we do. Are you in?"

"I'm in," she said, grinning back at him. "Let's build a house."

· · · ·

Tom sat at Neva's dining room table, eating cake and drinking coffee. He had just spent a peaceful hour in his mother's presence and was basking in the novelty of it. Neva sat at the head of the table, as she always did, but was close enough to reach out and pat his hand from time to time as they talked. He hadn't seen her this relaxed or this open in a long time. Maybe getting away from them for a few weeks had done this for her. If so, he wished she had taken these breaks while he was growing up.

There were two versions of his mother that he remembered from childhood: the stressed and uptight Neva, and the drunk and carefree Neva. Living with both versions had been difficult. Navigating each day, never knowing which version of her would show up, had caused his anxiety to toss him about like a boat in a hurricane. He had tried hard to make his peace with the storm back then, though. After all, he had been the one to cause both versions of his mother, so he deserved whatever punishment came from it. But at this stage in his life, he felt exhausted by all the tumult and craved more tranquil waters.

When he was little, Tom came up with ways to make her happy when the stressed and uptight version of his mother showed up. He would draw pictures for her, bring her hand-picked bouquets, or clean the house. Sometimes, he would make up reasons for Kris to take him and Rachel away from the house so his mother could relax or, as Neva put it, "chill the fuck out and get her shit together."

The drunk and carefree version of his mother was a lot more fun, but she came with pitfalls as well. Neva would drink, laugh, and dance with Lois. When he and his siblings were around her during those times, Neva would sometimes include them in the fun—dancing them around the living room, bragging about them to Lois, and showering them with hugs and kisses.

Sometimes, though, she would look at them while drinking, and her mood would shift. In the blink of an eye, she would transform from drunk and happy to sad and weepy. When that happened, he knew his mother and Lois would be up very late. Neva would go through three cycles: talking, then yelling, and ultimately crying. These nights were always followed by two or three days of his mother being quiet and withdrawn.

Those days frightened Tom the most. He constantly worried that one day, after Neva had spent a night talking and weeping with Lois, he would wake to find his mother gone. He didn't want to be the cause of another parent hating him or leaving him and his sisters. So, sometimes he chose to stay away from her on the drinking days. Choosing to watch her secretly from his hiding places, praying that her laughter didn't turn into tears. He had gotten good at predicting her moods. Of knowing which drunk and carefree days would turn into sad ones... and he had become even better at being a good son.

But tonight, for the first time in twenty-seven years, he felt peace in his mother's presence. He was just about to tell her that when the tranquility was abruptly shattered by his sister storming into the house.

"Neva!" Rachel yelled from the entryway.

Tom's shoulders fell, and he sighed loudly.

Neva snorted and patted his hand. "Must be a full moon," she said with a wink.

Tom smirked back at her. "You wouldn't have any wooden stakes handy, would you?"

"That won't work. We'll need silver to kill this beast." She picked up the silver cake knife from the plate. "This should do," she teased, brandishing the knife.

Tom snorted.

Rachel stopped at the opposite end of the dining table and glared at Tom. "I see she had no problem letting you know she was home. Typical," she spat.

"I didn't know!" Tom replied defensively. "I was just driving by and saw the lights on."

Rachel ignored him, turning the full weight of her glare on her mother.

Neva made a show of checking the time on her watch. "Well, it's about time, Rachel. I've been home for a full seventy-two hours. I expected this tantrum two days ago," she said, smiling serenely at her daughter.

Rachel's eyes narrowed as she grabbed the back of the chair in front of her. "I've come to tell you that I have no intention of selling the bar or doing any other bullshit you want me to."

"Fine," Neva said, shrugging one shoulder.

"Whaddya mean, fine?" Rachel shot back.

Neva sighed. "I mean, fine. Do whatever you want to do."

Rachel was just opening her mouth to respond when Kris walked into the room, joining her at the end of the table.

Kris glanced back and forth between her mother and sister, noting Rachel's murderous expression before settling her eyes on Tom. "What's going on?"

Tom rolled his eyes toward Rachel. "Guess."

Rachel sucked in a breath to respond, but Neva interrupted her. "Well! If I knew all of you were coming, I would have baked a cake!"

Tom smirked. "You did bake a cake, mom."

Neva feigned surprise at seeing the cake on the table. "Oh! I guess I did, didn't I?"

Tom bit his lip, trying not to laugh.

Kris couldn't hold back a giggle, and Rachel turned to glare at her. "Mother says we don't have to do what she wants," Rachel reported.

"Is that true, Mom?" Kris asked, surprised. She took a tentative step toward Neva, as if her mother were a live grenade.

Neva rolled her eyes. "Of course, it is. You don't have to make any of the changes on your lists if you don't want to. It's your choice," she said, standing from the table and gathering her plate and cup.

Rachel leaned forward; her knuckles white on the back of the chair. "So, if we choose not to do what you want, you're still going to give us the money, right?"

"Wrong," Neva said flatly. "Make the changes, you get the money. Don't make the changes, no money. That's it. End of story. Thank you all for stopping by and have a lovely evening. I do hope we can do this again sometime!" she quipped.

A quick, alarmed glance passed between Tom and Kris before Rachel exploded.

"I can't believe you have the balls to tell us what to do and how to raise our kids! Kris raised us, not you! We hardly ever saw you, and when we did, you were either drunk or riding your bitch broom! You owe us that money as compensation for a fucked-up childhood and a lifetime of putting up with your shit!"

Neva remained stoic as her youngest daughter raged.

Tom moved closer to Neva. "Mom, you haven't told me about your trip. Got any pictures?" he asked, hoping to distract her.

Kris stepped between Rachel and her mother. "Rachel, that's enough. Calm down so we can talk," Kris began in a soothing tone.

Rachel was having none of it. She tried to push past Kris, but Kris grabbed her by the shoulders, holding her back.

"It's not enough!" Rachel yelled at her sister. "It needs to be said! She thinks she's so goddamn perfect, and she's not. She killed our dad! She fucking murdered him! She has no right to judge how we live!"

At this, Neva threw her dishes onto the table, shattering the coffee cup. Kris and Tom went still and silent, while Rachel continued to glare at their mother, her breaths coming in furious huffs.

Neva met Rachel's glare with one of her own. "I am well aware that I wasn't a perfect parent."

Rachel snorted, as if Neva's comment was the biggest understatement she'd ever heard.

"I'm not proud of some of the things I've done, but I had to protect and provide for you three, and I won't make excuses for it," Neva continued.

Rachel snorted again. "Protect us? Protect us from what? From Dad?"

"Mom..." Tom said. "Just let it go."

Neva stole a furtive glance at Kris, who shook her head slightly, her eyes pleading for Neva to stay silent.

Rachel noted their exchange. "Answer me, Mother!" she demanded. "What were you protecting us from?"

Neva closed her eyes for a moment, as if in prayer. "What happened with your father was horrible, but I'd do it again. You were too young, and you have no idea what he put us through."

Rachel waved her hands as if brushing Neva's explanation aside. "Every family has problems! You don't see them going around killing each other. You're just a fucking psycho!"

Tom saw the expression on his mother's face tighten and knew Rachel had gone too far. Instinctively, he stepped around his mother to get closer to Kris, who was standing like a statue a few feet away.

A low growl erupted from Neva as she untied the scarf at her neck and pulled it off, exposing her scar. "Look at this!" she hissed, pointing unnecessarily at the mark. "You want to talk about fucking psychos? You think this happened by accident? Just a normal family squabble?"

Rachel's eyes widened, and she gasped as she took in the gruesome red line across her mother's throat.

"Your father tried to kill me that night, and then he went after your brother!"

Rachel shook her head, as if trying to dispel what her mother was saying. "You're a liar! Dad would never do that. He loved us. Why would he—"

"Because I confronted him about molesting your sister!" Neva bellowed.

Kris flinched as her mother's words rang through the room. She let out a whimper, like a fatally wounded animal, as Tom put his arm around her shoulders.

Stunned, Rachel fell silent. Neva's hand flew to her mouth, her features contorting with regret as she saw the devastation on Kris's face.

Rachel looked from her mother to Kris, but neither of them would meet her eyes. Her gaze fell on Tom, and he nodded, confirming the revelations. Rachel swallowed hard.

Neva ignored her, raising a placating hand toward Kris. "I'm sorry, honey—but it's time she knew."

Kris stood very still, her head and shoulders bowed, saying nothing. Tom rubbed his hand up and down her arm reassuringly.

Neva turned back to Rachel. "I did the best I could. I only meant to stop him that night. To get you kids away from him. He wouldn't let me. I had no help, and he gave me no other choice. It was him or us," she said calmly. "You have a choice. All of you. You have a chance. It may be late, and maybe it's not enough, but I'm giving you that chance."

Neva blinked away the tears filling her eyes before straightening and clearing her throat. Her hand unconsciously rose to cover the scar. "I don't expect you to understand why I made the mistakes I've made, but I do expect you to learn from those mistakes and do a better job with your own lives and your own children."

"Incest and murder set a pretty low fucking bar," Rachel huffed.

Kris's head snapped up at the comment. Refusing to look at any of them, she snatched her purse and paperwork from the table and fled.

How could her mother betray her like that? She wasn't ready. Neva hadn't even warned her. And to yell it! The entire neighborhood probably heard how damaged she was. Kris let out a strangled moan as she flung the screen door wide and stomped across the porch.

Incest. Rachel had used that awful word. The word that branded her as a girl who had sex with her own father. It didn't matter that she hadn't wanted to. It didn't matter that she had begged him not to do those things. It didn't matter that she had endured it to keep him from hurting everyone else, especially Rachel. It was still incest, and it was still the reason that Tom and her mother were almost killed.

Molestation. Incest. Those damning words coming out of Rachel and her mother's mouths were like daggers through Kris's heart.

Kris needed to get away. She needed to get to her car, lock the doors, and drive. Get far away from her family, from Carl, from this town, and from all the poisonous memories that were reaching out from the grave, threatening to drag her deep underground with them.

She hadn't gone more than a few feet across Neva's front yard when Rachel called to her from the porch. "Why didn't you tell me?!"

Kris walked faster.

Rachel jumped off the porch and gave chase. "What kind of fucked-up person keeps information like that from her own sister?"

Kris stopped and whirled to face Rachel. "What kind of person?" she asked, her voice rising. "The kind that took care of you since you were three years old!" she shouted, throwing her purse and paperwork to the ground and stepping closer to Rachel. "The kind that's kept this horrible secret from you so it wouldn't screw up your vision of who he really was! So that you—YOU," Kris said, pushing a finger hard into Rachel's chest. "Wouldn't grow up with this horrible, poisonous truth! So you would have an easier time than me and Tom did!"

Tom stepped out onto the porch and froze at the scene in the yard. He had never seen Kris like this, and something about the tone in her voice made his stomach churn.

Rachel put both hands on her hips and sneered at Kris. "So I would have an easier time? Are you fucking serious right now? Oh yeah, you lying to me has made a huge difference, and being in this family has been a real fucking picnic! Nobody asked you to—"

In one fluid movement, Kris slapped Rachel hard across the face. Tom thought he heard Rachel's neck crack from the force of the blow. She stumbled sideways, her cheek already blazing red.

He jumped down off the porch and ran toward them.

"SHUT UP! Shut your mouth, you spoiled, selfish, immature bitch!" Kris screamed before lunging at Rachel with a raised fist.

Tom circled Kris with his arms and squeezed, trying to get her to calm down. Kris's eyes blazed with fury as she spat out a string of vile curses and insults at her sister, each word dripping with venom. Rachel hadn't moved an inch. She just stood there, staring, as she watched Kris struggle to free herself from Tom's hold.

Tom squeezed harder, speaking to Kris in a calming voice. "It's okay, Kris. It's okay. Just let it go. Let it go."

After a few more moments of struggle, Kris shook free of Tom's grasp and threw her hands up as if casting off a dirty shirt. "You know what!?" she ranted, pacing in a tight circle. "I'm done! DONE!" She stopped and pointed an accusatory finger at Rachel. "You grew up to be a clueless, hateful, narcissistic piece of shit. And you—" she seethed, shifting the finger to poke Tom's chest, "are a fucking coward for allowing your wife to abuse you and your kids! I guess the apples didn't fall very far from the fucking tree, did they?"

Kris shoved Tom hard and paced away a few steps before whirling to face them again, her arms waving, and a glint of madness in her eyes. "Mom's right about you both! Hell, she's right about all of us! But you know what? At least I've tried to make a decent life for myself. At least I tried not to be like them! Not you two, though. Nope! You two pissed your lives into the toilet for no goddamn reason!" she screamed. "She offered us five million dollars! Five million! To fix our shitty lives. And what did we do? We bitched, moaned, and rejected it! Who the hell does that?! WHO?!"

Kris snatched her purse and papers off the ground. "You two do whatever you want. I'm taking the money. I'm making those changes and putting all this shit behind me, and I don't want to hear another word about it from either of you! Not one word!" She fumed. "I'm not your mother. I'm not your fucking therapist. And I'm not your fucking doormat. Not anymore. I'm done! Deal with your own piece-of-shit lives and leave me out of it!"

With tears streaming down her face, Kris stomped toward her car. "Stay away from me. Both of you!" she snarled over her shoulder.

• • • •

Tom started forward to comfort her, but Kris held up her hand to stop him. He had never seen her act like this before. She had never been violent with him or Rachel. Ever. In fact, he'd never known her to be violent with anybody. And the swearing! Kris never swore, and the language she was using tonight was beyond anything he'd ever heard from her. Underneath it all, though, Tom could see how fragile she was—so close to the breaking point that it frightened him. There was nothing he could do. The truth was out. A lead weight settled in his chest as he watched his sister fall apart, her agony mirrored in his own helpless heart.

Sobbing, Kris unlocked the car and climbed inside, locking the doors the moment she sat down. Within seconds, the engine revved. Without a backward glance at either of them, she left rubber on the road as she raced away.

Tom turned to walk back to the house, but Rachel grabbed his arm. "Why didn't you tell me all this?" she asked, her tone more subdued.

"For the same reasons as Kris."

Rachel's eyes narrowed. "And Mom? Why didn't she tell me?"

"You've got it wrong about her. Always did," he said, shaking his head in exasperation. "She told you why. Later, she kept quiet because Kris begged her to. I think Kris didn't want you to know because you were too young to understand, and you looked up to her. I think she needed that." Tom took a deep breath and sighed. "Then, when you got older, it was different. You were different. I thought if you knew, you'd say nasty things to Kris or do, pretty much, what you just did. So, I begged Mom not to tell you."

"Figures." Rachel scoffed, still angry. "So, why'd Dad come after you that night, then?"

Tom's sad eyes met her skeptical ones. "Because I told Mom what he was doing to Kris."

Without another word, he shrugged her hand off and walked past her into the house.

Chapter 10:
Awakenings

Kris drove aimlessly for hours, each rotation of the tires a futile attempt at escape. She had contemplated driving straight out of the state. To keep driving until she reached the coast. It didn't matter which one. Maybe she would change her name and start a new life. Leave these painful memories and her screwed-up family behind her. Go somewhere far away and finally be able to breathe. She had a full tank of gas. She could have gone... but the thought of leaving Trent behind made her turn the car around.

Her heart and mind were still racing when she pulled down the long driveway to her home. Once inside, she checked on Trent, relieved to find him sound asleep in bed. Then she went directly to her bedroom. Once inside, she locked the door, grabbed the box of Kleenex from her nightstand, and stepped into her closet.

Kris's attempts to keep the memories of her childhood at bay were failing. Her breaths came in short, fast pants from the mental effort it was taking. Pushing her hanging pantsuits aside, she sank onto the floor, pulled herself into the fetal position, and focused on her breathing—deep and slow—until her heart rate slowed and her vision cleared.

Back in control, Kris examined everything that had happened that night. She tried to feel bad for slapping Rachel, but she couldn't muster an ounce of regret. Her younger sister had deserved that slap, and it had been more than a decade in the making.

When their father had been alive, Kris made sure that Rachel was sheltered from the undercurrents in their lives. Ushering her siblings out for walks or to the park whenever the shouting started. She'd held her breath through his assaults, so Rachel could sleep on, untouched and unaware, in the bed across the room. Kris thought she'd done it out of love. Now she wondered if it had been something else, too.

If she had known her sister would grow up to be such a selfish person, would she have done things differently? No, she probably wouldn't. But she may have confided in her mother sooner.

Kris had wanted to tell her mother right from the beginning. She had almost done so many times, but the threats her father whispered in her ear always stopped her. For their sakes, she always obeyed and promised to stay silent. She had endured that silent hell for over a year before the night that changed everything. The night Tom had stood in her bedroom doorway and witnessed her nightmare.

Kris didn't know what drew her eyes to the doorway that night. But there Tom stood, small and trembling, eyes wide with horror as he stared at her. She was already in pain and in the full grip of fear, but seeing Tom standing there had multiplied those feelings infinitely. Her panicked eyes met his, desperately urging him to leave. Tom had understood and vanished from the doorway so quickly, Kris wondered if she had imagined him there.

After her father left the room, Kris had pulled herself into a ball, certain something inside her had broken beyond repair. Every inch of her throbbed, pain radiating from her core to her spine. She needed the bathroom, but feared what would happen if she tried to stand. Only the thought of hot water—to soothe the ache and scrub him off her skin—coaxed her to move.

Kris eased herself off the bed, each step toward the bathroom a silent fight against the pain pulsing through her. She paused, folding over, arms wrapped around her middle as tears streamed. Once in the bathroom, she closed the door and turned the bath faucet to hot. Her trembling hands pulled her favorite bubble bath from the shelf and emptied it all into the rising water. Slowly, she stepped in, the heat stinging before it settled into her bones, dulling the ache. She drew the bubbles close and leaned back, eyes drifting shut.

Kris heard the creak of the bathroom door and her eyes snapped open to see Tom standing a few feet away. She sat up, startled, sending small waves of water and bubbles over the side. "Tom, what are you doing in here? You should be in bed," Kris whispered.

Tom didn't answer her at first. Instead, he grabbed a towel out of the dirty clothes hamper and mopped the bathwater off the floor. Kris sank back into the tub again, her mind racing to find a believable explanation for what he had witnessed earlier.

Once the floor was dry, he draped the towel over the rack and sat down on the toilet, facing Kris. "Are you okay?" he asked in a whisper. Kris looked away from him, unable to meet his eyes. "He was hurting you. I know what he was doing. I've seen animals do it."

Kris sat up, sending water dangerously close to the edge of the tub again. She reached out a bubble-coated hand as if to grab hold of Tom. "Sshh! Don't say that, Tommy. Don't ever talk about it." She added a belated, "Please," in a pleading whisper.

Tom stared at her a moment before shaking his head. "Dad is a bad man. He hurts Mommy and me, and he hurts you in a worser way than hitting. I'm telling the cops so they can stop him," he said solemnly.

Kris shook her head violently. Oh, how she wished it was that easy. Tom, with his superhero worship and kind heart, would be no match for their father's anger if anyone found out.

"No, Tommy. No, you can't. They won't believe us and if he finds out we told them…" she shuddered then, rubbing both hands over her face. "You cannot tell the cops. Promise me you won't do that. It'll be okay. We can pretend it was just a bad dream, okay?"

Tom shook his head again, brow furrowed in determination.

Tears welled in Kris's eyes. "Please Tommy. You can't tell the cops," she pleaded, her voice breaking.

Tom studied Kris's face for several moments before the furrow in his brow smoothed out. "Okay, Kris. I won't tell the cops."

The next morning, Kris stayed in bed, claiming she had a stomachache. She spent some of the morning curled into a ball, weeping quietly; the rest of the time, she stared blankly at the wall, contemplating her problem. She considered running away, wishing fervently that she was old enough to drive. If she was, she could drive away from her father and the fear that constantly smothered her like a weighted blanket.

She couldn't do that, though. Wouldn't leave her brother and sister here with their father. He would hurt Tom. She knew he would. The cast had just come off Tom's broken arm three weeks ago from the last time their father lost his temper. And then there was little Rachel. She was only three years old. What if her father did to Rachel what he had done to her? Kris shuddered convulsively at the mere thought of it.

No, she couldn't run away. She couldn't leave them here, alone, with their father. She was the oldest, and that meant it was her job to protect them. So, no matter what happened to her, she would save them from him. But who would save her? At that thought, the tears spilled again, and she cried herself to sleep.

When Kris awoke, her mother was sitting on the end of her bed. Neva, her jaw set in a grim line, brows furrowed in concentration, appeared to be studying a faded blue patch on Kris's quilt.

Kris sat up in bed, heart hammering. "Mom? What's wrong?"

Neva took a deep breath before she brought her gaze up to meet her daughter's eyes. Kris flinched inwardly at the fierce look she saw there.

"Kristin, do you know how much I love you?" Neva asked, her voice soft.

Kris's breath hitched, and she froze.

"Do you?"

Kris nodded.

"Good. Then you know that you can tell me anything and it won't change how much I love you. Right?" Neva said, giving her a reassuring smile.

Kris wrapped her arms around her middle as she tried to remain calm. What was going on? Did her mother know? Where was her father right now? Please God, please let him still be at work, she prayed.

Kris swallowed hard, replying to her mother with a quick nod.

"I want to ask you something, and I need you to be very honest with me. I promise I won't be upset or angry... I just need an honest answer."

A frantic rhythm pounded in Kris's ears as her heartbeat battered her ribs. She couldn't meet her mother's gaze. Her eyes flitted around the quiet room, searching for something, anything, to focus on instead of her mother's face. Neva placed a gentle hand on Kris's chin and turned her head, forcing her to look at her.

When their eyes met, Neva gently cupped Kris's cheek. "Kristin, has your father been touching you in your private areas?"

Kris's eyes filled with tears. Her mother held her gaze, silently imploring her to answer. Unable to hold back, Kris sobbed out one agonizing word: "Yes".

For the next hour, Kris confided the abuses she had suffered at her father's hands and the threats he had made to keep her silent. Her mother held her close, expressing her sorrow and assuring Kris that it wasn't her fault. Neva promised she would never, ever, let it happen again. Then, she dried Kris's tears and told her to pack a bag for herself and each of her siblings.

Exhausted and relieved to be free of her horrible secret, Kris hadn't asked where they would go. She knew they were going to drive away, and that's all that mattered.

Her relief had been short-lived. Her father had come home early from the bar and caught her mother packing. When he tried to stop her, Neva confronted him with what Kris had confided. He laughed, claiming that Kris was lying. The sound of his laughter made Kris's stomach churn.

Then came the terrible, silent pause when Neva revealed that Tom had witnessed him do it. After that, all hell had broken loose.

Kris jerked herself out of the memory and sat up. The whole truth had been revealed. She thought Rachel knowing the truth, or anyone saying it aloud, would make everything worse. She took stock of how she was feeling and realized that it hadn't. The shame and guilt hadn't incapacitated her. She no longer feared what the knowledge might do to Rachel. Her sister's selfish reaction had freed Kris from that burden.

Tonight's events were forcing Kris to face truths she'd struggled to accept. Yes, she had kept the truth from Rachel, in part to protect her from a harsh reality, but she had done it for her own selfish reasons, too. She had convinced herself that Rachel not knowing, and no one saying it aloud, would keep the abuse from being real.

In reality, the wall of denial had prevented Kris from confronting the truth and moving on. At eleven, she had shouldered the burden of that horrific night, convinced it was the consequence of her own weakness—her failure to protect her siblings. She had worn that mantle of shame and guilt like a suffocating woolen coat for decades...but she wasn't that helpless child anymore.

Through the years, whenever memories leaked through the mental barriers Kris had constructed, she would relive those events through her eleven-year-old eyes, experiencing the raw emotions from a child's perspective. Tonight had changed things. It had flipped some kind of switch. Severed some kind of connection. And now, she could see it differently.

The torment her father inflicted on her...on her mother, and her siblings, was never her fault. Had never been her fault. Robert wasn't a father; he was a vile, abusive predator who derived pleasure from the pain of others. That night, he would have murdered them all to protect his heinous secret if her mother hadn't intervened. Love had never been part of his vocabulary. Allowing Rachel to cling to that illusion for twenty-seven years was a mistake Kris deeply regretted.

She mourned, too, for the half-life she'd created while hiding from these truths. Years spent shrouding herself in plainness, striving for invisibility. Years of believing herself tainted and unworthy of genuine love. This distorted self-image had allowed Carl to manipulate and bully her, crushing her dreams beneath his demands. She had debased herself, begging for scraps of his affection. The sudden realization that Trent had witnessed this dynamic for fourteen years filled her with horror. What lessons had her son absorbed? Would he mirror her submissiveness in his relationships? Or worse, would he emulate his father's cruelty?

The revelation struck her with crushing force. She had never truly escaped her father. Carl was merely his echo, a different verse of the same toxic song. And she had married him. Another selfish tyrant who viewed relationships as transactions, and people as possessions. Tears streamed down her face at this realization, and she allowed them to flow freely. It would be the last time.

• • • •

After Kris's departure, Rachel couldn't bring herself to re-enter her mother's house. Tom's validation of her mother's devastating revelation was finally hitting her, doubling her over as waves of nausea crashed through her. She retched violently until her stomach emptied, yet the spasms persisted, her body purging itself of more than just physical contents.

When the convulsions finally subsided, she collapsed onto the cool grass, her eyes fixed on the vast night sky above. The weight of deception pressed down on her chest as she realized how blind she had been to the decades of carefully maintained lies. Fury blazed through her veins at the thought of the years she had spent building her life around them.

The need for movement overwhelmed her; she had to channel this tempest of emotions somewhere, needed space to process the seismic shift in her reality. On unsteady legs, she pushed herself up and retrieved her Jeep keys from her pocket. After grabbing her purse from its floorboard, she began walking.

• • • •

Tom stayed with Neva until he was sure Rachel was gone. Once Rachel processed the information about their father, he didn't know how she would react. Whether she would be angry and blame Neva, or him, or all of them. If she did, there was no telling what she might do, and he didn't want to leave his mother to deal with the fallout alone. Not that he thought Neva couldn't handle Rachel. He knew she could. He was just as much to blame for keeping the secret, though. So, if Rachel was going to go postal, she would have to take them both on.

Tom was done hiding from it all. Done with keeping his mouth shut. He needed to make changes, to prioritize himself and his kids. He hated the way the truth had emerged, and his heart ached for Kris, but it had lifted a massive weight from his shoulders. Whatever happened now, he vowed to straighten his spine and deal with it.

• • • •

As Rachel walked, her mind spun with the revelations of the night. She was still furious they had kept so much from her, but she was also physically sick and horrified at the thought of what her sister had endured. The specter of what her father had done—what he might have eventually done to her—sent violent shudders through her body. Bile rose again in her throat, and she willed herself not to retch.

She had very few memories of their father, and her family had refused to talk about him. Every question she'd asked about him over the years drew only short yes-or-no replies. Now she knew why. The truth had been too monstrous to utter, too hideous to revisit. He was a depraved predator who had violated her sister and attempted to murder both her brother and mother.

Jeezus, her poor mother! That scar was horrible. Rachel couldn't believe Neva had kept it hidden from her all these years. It seemed impossible that she hadn't seen it. She tried to remember a time she'd seen her mother naked but couldn't think of even one. Never saw her in a swimsuit, either. Always dressed and always wearing a scarf or turtleneck. Why didn't she have the scar removed? How many times had Rachel mocked her mother for what she was wearing? And the whole time, Neva had been wearing it to shelter her from this ugly truth.

All those years believing her mother loved her less than Kris and Tom. Interpreting her siblings constant defense of Neva, and their shared glances, as a conspiracy against her. She had twisted everything to fit her narrative of being an outsider in her own family. Her mother's frequent accusation echoed in her mind: she had indeed made everything "all about her". Constantly inflicting fresh wounds on an already scarred family. Kris was right. She was an arrogant, selfish bitch...and worse. She groaned in anguish, quickening her pace as her mind continued to sift through two decades of her life.

• • • •

Neva watched Tom drive away in his beat-up car, making a mental note to take him car shopping over the weekend. This idea would have brought her joy just days ago. Tonight, it felt hollow. The lottery winnings would allow her to take care of their material needs, but money couldn't heal the emotional wounds that ran so deep.

The memory of Kris's shattered expression carved fresh pain into Neva's heart. She hadn't meant for Rachel to learn the truth that way. She'd planned to share it with her daughter privately so she could shield Kris from Rachel's unpredictable reaction. The careless emergence of the truth had ended up wounding both her daughters.

It made her realize how much power Robert's sick, sadistic soul still held over them all. That power needed to end. This was their chance to end it. The truth was now exposed and it would either heal them—or shatter them. They would each have to choose. This realization twisted like a knife for Neva, but she finally knew she needed to let go.

• • • •

Rachel wasn't aware of the time, or her location, as she continued to walk, her mind lost in the details of the past few hours. She had no conscious plan for where she was going, but it didn't surprise her to find herself at the cemetery, standing over her father's grave.

A bouquet of withered flowers lay across the top of his tombstone, her offering from four weeks prior, when she'd come to share news of her mother's lottery ultimatum with him. She had come here many times over the years to talk to her father, sharing news and complaining about her mother. Rachel's stomach roiled at the thought.

"I complained to you about her," she said, in a voice thick with disgust. "I always defended you, like you were the fucking victim." The thought of it made her feel even sicker. She bent over, clutching her stomach, waiting for the retching to start. Instead, a different bodily urgency made itself known. After a moment's panicked thought about finding a bathroom, a darkly satisfying solution presented itself. What better way to express her newfound contempt? Without hesitation, she turned, lowered her jeans, and squatted over her father's grave, conveying exactly what she thought of him.

It was nearly seven a.m. when Rachel had reclaimed her Jeep and finally made it home. After she left the cemetery, she had walked all night, thinking about what she had learned. Thinking about all the nasty things she had said to her mother over the years, and the hell she'd given her siblings. She had been horrible to all of them and hated herself for it. She hated them for it too, though. Maybe, if she had known the truth, she would have been a different person. Would have made different decisions or made fewer mistakes. She may have tried to make something more of herself. Might have followed her dreams of having a career in architecture and interior design instead of buying the bar out of a desire to keep her father's memory alive. That thought made her shutter. She would never look at the bar the same way again.

Maybe she wouldn't have searched for love and attention in all the wrong places, ending up pregnant at fifteen. Her mother's words about "daddy issues" echoed with painful accuracy now. Neva had been spot-on about that one. And Kim had been the result.

Kim. The thought of her daughter stirred complicated emotions. How many times had she wished she hadn't gotten pregnant so young? A hundred? A thousand? Countless nights she'd lain awake, wondering how different her life might have been. It had been so hard raising Kim on her own. She had been clueless about raising a child. Neva had helped, as much as Rachel had allowed her to, but her spite and pride had caused her to stumble through raising Kim with very little grace.

Yet now, with fresh perspective, Rachel couldn't imagine erasing Kim from her story. Kim hadn't always been the sullen, mouthy creature she had been lately. She had once been a sweet, funny, loving little girl who would cling to her legs at goodbyes. Kim had been her shopping buddy and cuddle bunny. Kim had taught Rachel what unconditional love meant, both giving and receiving it. She would do anything for her daughter and would always do everything she could to make sure she was safe and happy.

And there it was—the revelation she'd been circling all night. Her mother's decades of silence now made perfect sense. Just as she would do anything for Kim, Neva would do anything for Rachel and her siblings. She had proven she would. Neva had gone to the ultimate extreme to keep them safe. She had killed for them.

Rachel opened her front door and stepped inside, taking care to close it quietly behind her. She stood still, listening for any sign that Kim was awake. The house was silent. With a sigh, Rachel headed to the master bath. She would get to the bar early today. Maybe get enough done so she could leave and go see her mother to get the rest of the story. She grabbed the Bismuth from the medicine cabinet and took two big gulps from the bottle. She stared hard at her reflection in the mirror, unsure of what she was hoping to see. A younger, slightly rounder, darker blonde version of her mother stared back at her. And for the first time in her life, Rachel thought that wasn't such a bad thing.

• • • •

Kris woke early, still lying on her closet floor. She waited for the familiar weight of depression to descend—that terrible sadness that had been her companion every morning since Carl left. It didn't come. She braced herself for the previous night's revelations to overwhelm her. That pain, too, remained absent.

Despite only four hours of sleep, she felt rested. Rising from the floor, she stepped out of the closet and took stock of herself in the full-length mirror. Her hair had come loose from the bun, hanging in tangled tendrils around her face and neck. A pin was poking painfully into the back of her head, and she removed it, watching the rest of her hair come loose and fall around her shoulders. Her eyes were puffy and red-rimmed from the hours she had spent crying. She removed her clothes, viewing her naked form through her new untainted perspective, as if seeing it for the first time. Robin had not been lying when she told Kris her body was beautiful.

Fresh tears welled as she realized how cruel she had been to herself. For decades, she had hidden and hated her body, refusing to acknowledge herself as beautiful and valuable. Those days were over. Today was her rebirth. Everything was going to change, and she couldn't wait to get started.

Flinging open the back door, she stepped onto the deck. Sunlight filtered through the trees in beams of beautiful golden light that spilled onto the wood, warming it under her bare feet. She imagined the energy and warmth of those rays seeping up through the soles of her feet and into her bones, flowing through every cell, flushing out any pain and lingering baggage that remained. She drew in a deep breath of the fresh morning air and smiled.

Certainty and excitement pulsed through her veins. The mere thought of the different ways her life might change made her dizzy with anticipation. Spreading her arms wide, Kris tilted her face skyward, letting the golden sunlight touch her face. She was ready.

Chapter 11:
Walking the Walk

Rachel showered and dressed in a fog. She hadn't slept, and her head hurt from chasing her racing thoughts all night. It was an absolute wonder that she had managed to start a pot of coffee. She took in a deep breath of the rich aroma filling the small space, noticing the bit of unexpected comfort it brought. The vodka and orange juice hadn't called to her as it normally did. She hadn't even considered making a drink this morning, which was a surprising but welcome development.

Determined not to think about the vodka, Rachel searched the cabinet above the coffeepot for the powdered creamer and felt an absurd amount of satisfaction when she found it. She was spooning healthy amounts of it into her travel mug when the pot finally completed brewing. Sighing with relief, she filled her mug, gave it a quick stir, and walked out the front door, her mind still mulling over the events of the last twenty-four hours.

Rachel was still lost in thought, fifteen minutes later, when she unlocked the door of Lucky's and began flipping on the lights. She startled, dropping her coffee mug, when she saw Kim sitting in a booth a few feet away. She scrambled to pick up the cup and then stared at her daughter in wide-eyed surprise.

Kim was slumped into the corner of the booth, her face stained with tears and smeared mascara. Her swollen, red-rimmed eyes met Rachel's startled ones.

"Mom..." The word barely escaped before Kim dissolved into sobs.

Rachel dropped her things on the corner of the bar and rushed to the booth, sliding in across from Kim and clasping her daughter's hands. "Honey, what's wrong? What are you doing here?"

Kim could only shake her head, avoiding her mother's concerned gaze.

"I thought you were asleep at home. How long have you been sitting here?" Rachel pressed.

Wiping her runny nose with her sleeve. "Since about three," Kim managed, her lip quivering.

"Three?!" Rachel's voice rose in disbelief. "What were you doing here at three in the morning?"

"You didn't come home," Kim drew in a shaky breath. "So, I thought you'd still be here. I needed to talk to you."

"Why didn't you just call me?"

"I tried. Texted like a hundred times," Kim's accusation carried through her tears. "You never answered me."

"Oh God, I forgot. I turned my phone off last night," Rachel groaned. "But when you saw I wasn't here, why didn't you call a cab and go home?"

Kim's expression crumpled further. "I don't know, I just... couldn't."

Unease crawled up Rachel's spine. She straightened, squeezing Kim's hand while seeking her daughter's eyes. "I'm here now. Tell me what's wrong."

Kim's gaze dropped to the table.

"Kim?" Rachel's voice climbed an octave with her growing anxiety.

Rachel's heart stuttered at Kim's expression, an achingly familiar look of childish contrition, as if silently pleading for mercy. Once, that expression had been cute and endearing, always quick to melt Rachel's resolve. Now it twisted her stomach into knots.

Am I seriously going to start puking again? Rachel thought, fleetingly. She needed to steady herself. She wasn't a weak person. At least, she'd never considered herself a weak person, but then again, everything else she believed was a lie. That might be, too. The thought made her anxious, and she unconsciously tightened her grip on Kim's hands. "Tell me what's going on!"

Kim flinched, pulling her hands free from her mother's desperate grasp. "You're going to be so mad," she mumbled, swiping at her tear-stained face with her sleeve.

"Your silence is freaking me out, Kim. That's what's going to make me mad. Just take a deep breath and tell me. We'll figure it out together."

Kim nodded, drawing in a trembling breath. She released it in a rush, swallowed hard, and met Rachel's anxious gaze. "I'm pregnant."

Rachel stared at her daughter for a long, silent moment, her brain scrambling and stuttering as it tried to process the weight of those two words. Kim stared back, eyes filling again with tears, lip trembling.

Then it all snapped into place and vertigo swept through Rachel as alternating waves of heat and cold ran the length of her. She pressed a trembling hand to her forehead, fighting the urge to faint. Seeing panic bloom across Kim's features, she arranged her face in what she hoped was a look of calm. She planted both palms flat against the table's surface, and carefully measured her words: "How do you know? Have you taken a test?"

"Three," Kim whispered.

Rachel closed her eyes, inhaling deeply. "How far along?"

"I don't know." Kim said in a voice barely above a whisper. "Maybe six or seven weeks."

Rachel's eyes snapped open, fixing on her daughter with sudden intensity. "Who's the father?"

Kim covered her face with her hands.

"Kim!? Who's the father? Is it that little son-of-a-bitch you were screwing in my bed because—"

"I don't know!" Kim slammed her fists on the table, tears streaming down her face.

Rachel's spine went rigid. "What do you mean, 'you don't know'? You don't know the name of the guy you're having sex with!?"

"No. I don't know because..." Kim's throat worked as she swallowed. "Because..." The words died as she covered her face, shaking her head.

Rachel felt the bottom drop out of her stomach. "Because why?" she pressed, her patience evaporating. "Kim? Because why!?"

Kim dropped her hands and looked up, fixing her swollen eyes on the ceiling. "Because there's three guys," she whispered, the confession barely audible.

Rachel exploded out of the booth, unable to contain herself. "Three guys!? Three fucking guys!?" She began pacing, her voice rising. "Oh my God! I can't believe you did this. Of all the stupid, selfish, irresponsible things to do, you had to fucking do this one."

Storming behind the bar, Rachel grabbed a highball glass, muttering as she poured a double vodka and topped it with tonic. She drained half the glass in one gulp. "Jeezus, Kim! If I knew you were out whoring around the whole damn city—"

"You did know! You just didn't care!" Kim yelled, her face flushing crimson. "You'd rather hide behind your precious bar, and drink your vodka, than actually give a shit about me or what I'm doing!"

The words struck Rachel like physical blows. She stared at her daughter, stunned. "I don't hide behind the bar, Kim. I need to provide for us. This is the only way I have to do that."

"I don't care how much money we have!" Kim's voice cracked with hysteria. "I'm all alone, mom! You just leave me out there, all alone! You never care if I'm okay. You never want to be with me or even talk to me. The only thing you care about is this place!" she bellowed, sweeping her arms in a wide gesture meant to encompass the bar. "You don't want me. You never wanted me! Now nobody else will want me either! I'll end up just like you, and I don't even have a stupid fucking bar to run away to!"

Rachel's heart shattered as she realized the depth of loneliness and abandonment Kim must have been feeling. She mentally stabbed herself in the eyeball for her explosive reaction to her daughter's news. Most of Kim's outburst had been accurate, and she recognized with growing horror the parallels between Kim's situation and her own teenage years.

She remembered her own pregnancy at fifteen...the feelings of devastation. Like Kim, she had felt the bitter conviction that her mother didn't love or care about her. Felt that Neva had abandoned all her children for the bar and its whiskey. She'd felt adrift, angry, and completely alone. Now, with the truth of her past laid bare, she understood how wrong she'd been about everything. It suddenly struck her, with brutal clarity, how those distorted perceptions had affected her relationship with Kim. Even worse, it seemed that she had somehow transferred those malignant beliefs to her daughter. Duplicating and imprinting her own issues into Kim's psyche like some kind of ugly genetic birthmark.

Rachel stared at the drink in her hand, self-loathing flowing through her veins like poison. What a shitty mother she was. A shitty mother, a shitty daughter, and a shitty sister. But no more, and never again. She wouldn't allow alcohol, her dead monster of a father, or this bar to create barriers between her and her family anymore. With sudden resolve, she poured the remaining vodka down the drain, then circled the bar to gather Kim into her arms. She rocked her daughter gently, stroking her hair as she sobbed, while tears of regret tracked down Rachel's own face.

Eventually, Kim's sobs subsided. "Can we go home, mom?" Kim asked in a raw, exhausted voice.

Rachel pulled back, brushing Kim's tear-dampened hair from her eyes. "Yeah, honey. Let's go home." She stood and helped Kim to her feet, both of them startling when the bar door swung open, flooding the dim space with morning light.

Lois stepped inside and gave a yelp of alarm when she saw the two of them. "What's happened!?" she demanded, hurrying toward them. "Are you okay? Are you hurt!?" she questioned, hands fluttering anxiously as she scanned them for injury.

Rachel caught one of Lois's fluttering hands. "We're okay. We're okay, Lois. But can you handle the bar without me today?"

Lois took in Rachel's tear-stained face and Kim's bowed head and frowned, concern creasing her brow. "Yeah, sure honey, but what—"

"Thanks, Lo," Rachel cut in firmly, putting an arm around Kim's shoulders.

As they moved toward the door, Lois called after them, "Are you sure you're alright? Want me to call Kris, or your momma?"

Rachel retrieved her purse from the bar, turning back to Lois with a shake of her head. "No, we're fine." She motioned to her father's photos and memorabilia behind the bar. "Will you take all that shit down, today?"

Lois followed Rachel's gaze, and her expression softened, one hand rising unconsciously to cover her heart. "She finally tell you?" she asked, in a tone so warm and rich with sympathy it caused tears to sting the back of Rachel's eyes.

Rachel could only manage a tight nod.

"Sure, baby girl. I can do that. What should I do with it all?"

"Burn it," Rachel rasped, before guiding her daughter out the door and into the bright sunlight.

• • • •

Kris emerged from the shoe store, with two more bags to add to her growing collection. Her steps were quick and lighter than usual, despite her three-inch stilettos. Duplicates of the ones she'd worn on her infamous night out with Robin.

The old Kris never would have worn heels to go shopping. The old Kris never would have dared to cut and highlight her hair either. She smiled, holding her head a little higher. She was a new woman. Transformed. There was no other way to describe it. She had felt freer in the past three days than she had in...well, ever. Like a chrysalis finally breaking free of its cocoon, this new version of herself was ready to spread her wings and fly.

Pausing to admire her reflection in a storefront window, a glimpse of color from inside caught her eye.

A wall inside the shop displayed a kaleidoscope of colorful illustrations, but one image captured Kris's attention—a striking butterfly design. Stepping back, she read the shop's sign: New You Tattoo and Piercings. Kris looked through the shop window again, this time noticing the chairs and other furnishings inside. A young woman reclined in a chair, getting her navel pierced.

Kris stood back, studying the storefront. She had been down this street countless times in the past year, but had never noticed this place before. Then again, she probably wouldn't have paid any attention to it if she had. The old Kris wouldn't have given it a second glance. Would the new Kris? Are tattoos and piercings a change she would consider? She dismissed the thought immediately. No. Absolutely not. New clothes and highlights were one thing, permanent changes were quite another. She adjusted her shopping bags, ready to move on, when the implications of her previous thought stopped her. Was she afraid of making her transformation permanent? Was she somehow leaving the door open, like an escape route back to her former self? As she wrestled with these questions, her gaze drifted back to the butterfly design on the wall: nature's ultimate symbol of irreversible transformation.

• • • •

Officer Dan Miller strolled down Grant Street, enjoying the sunshine and savoring his Frappuccino. This was his first day off after eleven straight days of duty, and the sheer freedom of this casual stroll was bliss. Being short-staffed and breaking in two new police officers meant a lot of overtime and few days off. He and his buddy, Jeff Coggins, were the only two officers without a wife, husband, or kids. So, when one of the other officers begged him to take their shift so they wouldn't miss a birthday, date night, or little Johnny's baseball game, Dan felt like an ass if he refused. So, he usually didn't. His sister frequently pointed out that he would never find a wife of his own if he was always working so his buddies could hang out with theirs. She had a point, but he believed the right woman would come along, eventually.

A woman's squeal came from the shop he was passing, and Dan instinctively stopped to investigate. Kris Walker stood on the other side of the glass, one hand hiking her t-shirt up to her bra line, the other pulling the edge of her jeans down below her right pelvic bone, to reveal the fresh and colorful tattoo of a butterfly. He watched as she examined her new ink. Her face lit up with a huge smile, and she threw her head back, letting out another squeal of delight.

She whirled to look at the tattoo in the mirror behind her and caught a glimpse of Dan reflected there. Kris's demeanor shifted instantly as she slowly turned around, dropping her shirt back into place to cover the tattoo. Her earlier confidence was evaporating right before his eyes, as she fumbled to gather her purse and belongings. A flush of embarrassment crept up her neck and face as she avoided his gaze. Her smile was gone.

Dan's stomach tightened. He could not, would not, be the reason for the joy leaving her face. He leaned forward and knocked on the window—once, twice, three times—before she would finally meet his eyes. Dan smiled, pointing at her midsection. He raised his voice to carry through the glass. "It's beautiful."

The smile she graced him with nearly stopped Dan's heart.

• • • •

Tom pulled into a parking space in front of Lucky's, shifting the car into park with a heavy sigh. Every fiber of his being resisted being here. He didn't want to see or talk to Patty. What he wanted, more than anything, was to be back at his mom's house with the girls. He adjusted the rearview mirror so he could see them in the backseat. Megan was absorbed in a picture book she held open in her lap, while Ashlea's solemn gaze met his in the mirror's reflection. If his mother had been home, the girls could have stayed with her and he wouldn't have had to bring them along to witness this mess.

He should have refused Patty and called her a cab or something. Instead, here he was, doing whatever she asked, while exposing his daughters to the emotional turmoil she was sure to inflict on them all. The muscle in Tom's jaw tightened as he ran a hand through his hair, exasperated by his own weakness. It needed to stop. He needed to "cowboy up" as his mother would say, and stop being a willing participant in his alcoholic wife's chaos.

This was it. This was the last time he would answer Patty's call. The last time he would deal directly with her, at all, until the divorce was final. He refused to be a victim anymore, and he refused to allow his daughters to suffer the way he had as a child.

Tom looked into the rearview mirror again and cleared his throat. "Girls, I'm going into Aunt Rachel's work to get Mommy. I'll only be a couple minutes, okay?"

They both nodded.

"Stay in the car. Do not get out or unbuckle your seat belts for any reason. I won't be long and we'll get back to Grandma's as soon as we can, okay?"

Megan nodded enthusiastically. "Okay, Daddy! Back to grandma. Yes, yes, yes!"

Tom winked at her and turned his gaze to Ashlea. "'Okay, punkin'?" he asked.

She hesitated. "You promise? Take Mommy home and then back to grandmas?"

"Absolutely," Tom said, forcing a reassuring smile. "Keep an eye on your sister for me while I'm in there. I'll only be a minute."

Ashlea nodded, but he could see the doubt in her eyes. Strengthening his resolve, he stepped out of the car.

The bar's darkness momentarily blinded him. At two o'clock on a Tuesday afternoon, an hour before happy hour, business was slow. Two old farmers sat at the bar, arguing over what sounded like politics; a couple huddled close together in a booth near the door; and a middle-aged man sat at the end of the bar, nursing a Busch Light and staring at a game show on the TV overhead. He noticed Patty sitting on the last stool at the far end of the bar, a tall glass of beer in front of her.

Lois was at the bar sink, a few feet away, cleaning glasses. She shut the machine off when she saw him walk in. "Hey there, handsome! How's my baby girls doin' today?"

Tom smiled, stepping up to the bar next to Patty. "Hi, Lo! The girls are great, how are you?"

"I'm still kickin'. Did your sister tell you about the house I'm-"

"S'bout time!" Patty slurred, interrupting Lois. "I called you half'n hour ago!"

Tom shot an apologetic look at Lois. "Well, I'm here. Come on. The girls are waiting in the car," he replied, already turning away.

"Hold up." Patty demanded, grabbing the back of his shirt, pulling him toward her. "I havint fin'shed my beer."

In one fluid motion, Lois snatched the glass of beer from Patty's napkin and poured it down the sink. When Patty moved to grab her glass, her hand closed on empty air.

"Oops! I'm sorry, honey, were you still drinkin' that?" Lois asked with false concern.

Patty's eyes narrowed into slits. "I'll take a new one."

"No can do," Lois said, shaking her head. "You're too impaired, and by the power vested in me by the state of Iowa liquor license commission, I'm cutting you off."

Patty glared, while Lois batted her eyelashes innocently back at her.

Tom had to duck his head to hide his smile. Another example of why Lois Evans was at the top of his list of favorite people.

"Fuckin' shit was flat, anyway. Let's go." Patty spat, sliding off her barstool.

Tom followed in her wake as she staggered toward the exit.

Outside, Patty lurched to the driver's door, leaning heavily against it, as she thrust her hand toward Tom. "Gimme the keys."

Tom shook his head. "I'm driving. You've had too much to drink."

"Gimme the damn keys!"

"No. Go get in on the other side." Tom said, putting a hand on her shoulder to guide her away from the driver's door.

Patty's attack came out of nowhere. She shoved Tom hard in the chest and then reared back, kicking him with her pointed flats. The impact felt like being stabbed in the shin with an ice pick. He dropped the keys and cried out, hopping on his good leg while cussing and rubbing the wounded one. Patty scooped up the keys and planted herself in the driver's seat before Tom could recover enough to stop her. His attempt to reach into the car to retrieve the keys was met with a savage slam of the door against his arm. He screamed, as searing pain exploded through the limb and radiated to his shoulder. She had broken it— he was sure she had broken it.

Tom limped around to the passenger side of the car as quickly as he could, his injured arm cradled against his chest. As he reached for the handle, the sound of the door locks engaging stopped him cold. He slammed his good hand against the window.

"Patty! Patty, unlock the door!"

She was laughing as she stretched across the passenger seat to place her raised middle finger against the glass.

His eyes darted to the back seat. Megan had her eyes squeezed shut, her little hands covering her ears as she shook her head back and forth. Ashlea sat paralyzed, tears streaming down her face as she stared at him. His panic level rose to dizzying heights. "Patty! Let me in goddamnit! You can't drive, the kids are in there!"

The engine roared to life, and Patty cranked up the stereo, drowning out his pleas. Tom pounded on the window again. She ignored him, lurching the car backward out of the parking space.

Tom staggered into the street, positioning himself in front of the car. Passing cars slowed, drivers gawking at the unfolding drama. The car lurched and stuttered as Patty wrestled with the gears—reverse, brake, reverse again, then a hard stop that threw her forward in the seat. When the parking lights flashed, hope flickered in Tom's chest. Surely, she would stop now and let him drive. That hope fizzled when, a moment later, Patty shifted the car into drive. She grinned out at him through the windshield, her foot still on the break.

"Please, stop!" he yelled, waving his arms.

He watched in horror as Patty's smile turned predatory. Then she took her foot off the brake and stomped the gas. Time seemed to slow, and in that moment, Tom saw everything with crystalline clarity: his wife's face twisted with malicious intent, his daughters' terror-stricken expressions as they screamed for their mother to stop.

He tried to leap clear at the last moment, but he was too late. One second, he was airborne as he leapt, and in the next, he felt the impact of his side colliding hard with the windshield. The momentum rolling him up and over the top of the car before depositing him hard onto the street. As his consciousness faded, the last image he saw was Ashlea's horrified face in the rear window, as Patty sped away.

Chapter 12:
Aftermath

Neva had blown through two stop signs and doubled the speed limit on her way to the hospital. Despite Kris calling her first, and Rachel starting from a greater distance, she watched in disbelief as her daughter's Jeep cut across a four-way intersection to screech into the hospital parking lot ahead of her.

"Holy shit, Rachel!" Neva shouted at her windshield. The mental calculation of just how recklessly Rachel must have driven to beat her to the hospital sent her blood pressure soaring. Once Tom and her grandchildren were confirmed safe, she would throttle Rachel for such dangerous driving.

Pulling into the first available space, she grabbed her purse and emerged to find her daughter already sprinting toward the building. As if sensing her mother behind her, Rachel turned, catching sight of Neva.

"Mom!" Rachel called, waving frantically. "Hurry up!"

• • • •

From the hospital window, Kris watched her sister's Richard Petty imitation as she entered the parking lot, her mother's car only a few seconds behind. Fresh tension knotted in her neck and shoulders. She checked her watch. How long would it take them to get up here...two minutes, maybe three? The thought of explaining what had happened made her stomach clench. There was no way she could tell them the full story in the hospital room. Her mother was going to lose it, and God only knew what Rachel's reaction would be.

Massaging her tight neck muscles, Kris closed her eyes, searching for the peace and strength she would need to get through the next hour. She hadn't seen or spoken to Rachel since the night at their mother's house, and she wasn't ready to. Kris was finally letting go of the past and embracing her new future. She wasn't ready for Rachel's snide comments or bitchy attitude to try and ruin it. Though she felt more emotionally grounded now, there was no guarantee that she wouldn't slap her sister again if provoked.

Kris glanced at her watch again before returning to the bed nearest the window where Megan lay sleeping. Tiny drops of sweat beaded at the little girl's temples. Kris placed a palm on Megan's forehead, checking for fever, before gently removing one of the blankets, careful not to jostle the cast on her left leg. She pressed a light kiss to the bruise marking her niece's cheek, and moved to Ashlea's bed.

Even in sleep, Ashlea's face held a troubled frown. The bandage wrapped around most of the top of her head, hid a gash that had required seven stitches to close. Her right arm rested in a protective sling, while her left hand clutched the blankets in a white-knuckled grip.

The sight of Ashlea's clenched fist brought tears to Kris's eyes. She recognized what it meant. Knew that the traumatic events of the past few hours would be hard for this sweet, strong little girl to deal with in the coming days. She silently vowed to do everything she could to help them get through it. Kris gently loosened Ashlea's grip on the blankets, brushing the fingers of her hand into a more relaxed position, before moving to the recliner positioned in the corner of the room.

Tom lay reclined in the chair, finally resting after the doctor had put him out with a heavy sedative. He had refused to be placed in his own room, insisting on staying with his daughters. Afraid that Tom would do himself more damage if forced to be away from Ashlea and Megan, the doctor had relented.

Kris winced as she looked down at his battered body. The usually playful features of his handsome face were grotesquely swollen and discolored, barely recognizable. A neck brace supported his head, while his right arm was encased in a cast from wrist to shoulder. If she lifted his hospital gown, she was certain she would find massive bruises peeking out from under the bandages around his torso. Fighting back tears, she ran a hand over her face. Rachel and her mother would be there any second. She needed to get herself together and try to appear calm.

Drawing a steadying breath, she stepped into the hallway just as the elevator at the end of the corridor chimed. Rachel and Neva emerged, breaking into a jog at the sight of her. Kris put up both hands and patted the air in a gesture meant to slow them down, while composing her features to convey reassurance. It had no effect. Their concerned voices crashed over her like a wave, with Neva's "Those poor babies! Is Tom alright!?" colliding with Rachel's, "What's going on!? What the hell happened!?"

"It's okay. It's okay," Kris began, striving for calm. "Tom is fine, but he's pretty banged up. No internal bleeding, but serious bruising of his liver and kidneys, and three broken ribs."

Horror transformed Neva's face as her hand flew to her mouth. Kris caught her mother's free hand, squeezing it reassuringly, while Rachel unleashed a creative string of profanity.

"It's okay, Mom. He's going to be okay, but I need to tell you about their injuries, so you're not surprised when you see them. Tom is wearing a neck brace—more as a precaution than anything else. The impact caused severe whiplash. They'll run more tests later to be sure they didn't miss anything. His right arm is broken in two places, so he has a cast from wrist to shoulder. Other than that, he's okay. The doctors expect a full recovery. They're keeping him twenty-four hours for observation and, if everything looks good, he can go home tomorrow night."

Neva let out a sigh of relief, returning Kris's reassuring squeeze. "Thank God. What about the girls?"

Before Kris could answer, Rachel added, "And where are they? Is this their room or Tom's?"

"They're all sharing this room," Kris said motioning behind her. "Ashlea suffered a concussion that required stitches and has a dislocated shoulder, so she's in a sling. Megan's face is bruised up pretty bad, and her left leg is broken."

Neva gasped. Rachel ran her hands through her hair, pulling it away from her face and holding it there, which gave her the appearance of a furious, slant-eyed cat. Sensing their composure beginning to slip, Kris rushed on.

"The doctor says they'll be okay. He gave them sedatives to help calm them down and allow them to get some healing sleep. So, when you go in there, you can't be loud or cause a fuss. You have to stay calm and let them rest."

Neva dropped Kris's hand, squinting at her suspiciously. "What do you mean, 'stay calm'? What are you not telling me, Kris?"

Rachel stepped closer to Neva and leveled Kris with an identical squint. "What's going on? What the hell happened!?"

Kris took a step back and sent a silent prayer to Jesus for backup. "From what Tom told me before they sedated him—Patty was drunk, down at Lucky's. He came to pick her up, and the girls were with him. When Patty got to the car, she wouldn't let Tom drive. She took the keys, locked him out, and attempted to drive off. When Tom tried to stop her, she hit him with the car."

Neva inhaled sharply, her expression hardening to stone.

Rachel gaped bug-eyed at Kris. "On purpose!?" she boomed.

Kris put a finger to her lips, motioning with her head toward the door behind her.

Rachel clamped her jaw shut, but her nostrils flared with anger.

Kris nodded in confirmation of her question. "According to the police, she was on the highway a few minutes later and passed out at the wheel. She went off the road and rolled the car, with the girls in the backseat."

While Neva stood frozen, Rachel stalked the hallway like a caged animal. "Fucking bitch! They could have been killed!" She halted abruptly. "Was Patty hurt?"

"She better be dead." Neva said, her voice carrying the arctic chill of absolute hatred.

"Just cuts, bruises, and a ruptured disk in her back. She'll live," Kris reported.

Without a word, Neva turned and strode toward the elevators.

"Mom?" Kris called after her. "Mom? Where are you going?"

She and Rachel watched uneasily as Neva jabbed the elevator button and disappeared behind the closing doors.

Kris turned to Rachel. "That wasn't good."

"Nope." Rachel agreed, eyes still fixed on the elevator's sealed entrance.

"I better go after her. She had that look in her eyes-" Kris started, but Rachel grabbed her arm.

"No. I'll go. You stay with Tom in case he wakes up. He'll want you here, not me."

Kris opened her mouth to deny it, then closed it again. If she was going to be honest with herself, she was going to be honest with her family, too.

Rachel grinned ruefully. "The gloves are completely off then, huh? I get it."

Kris shook her head. "No gloves. Just honesty. We shouldn't have kept the truth from you. From now on, honesty is all you're getting from me."

Rachel stared at her sister for a long moment. Kris stared back; the silence heavy with unspoken truths. Finally, Rachel surged forward, wrapping Kris in a fierce embrace. Hesitantly, Kris returned it. When Rachel finally pulled back, she looked at Kris with eyes full of pain and remorse.

"I'm sorry. I'm so, so sorry. About everything. All those years I bragged about him—acted like he was a fucking hero. You must have felt so..." Rachel swallowed hard, unable to finish the thought. "You were right. I was such a bitch. Such a selfish, fucked-up, bitchy, little bitch. I just want you to know—" Her voice cracked as her eyes welled with tears.

Kris gripped Rachel's shoulders, giving them a reassuring squeeze. "You didn't know. It's out now and everybody's on the same page. We can finally put it behind us. I'm fine. You're fine. Let's just focus on Tom and the girls." She nodded toward the elevator. "Now, go find Mom before she lights Patty on fire or something."

Rachel's involuntary snort of laughter caused a tear to overflow, spilling down her cheek. She sniffed, and Kris wiped the tear away like she had done a thousand times when they were younger.

"You were always the best one of us," Rachel said softly, as two more tears fell.

Kris wiped those away too, before pulling her sister close. "Go find Mom, or I'm blaming whatever she does on you," she whispered into her ear.

With another snort of laughter, Rachel drew back to meet Kris's eyes, tears still gathering. "I love you, you know."

"I know. I love you, too. Now go!" Kris urged, giving Rachel a gentle push toward the elevator. Without hesitation, her sister turned and jogged down the hall.

• • • •

Back in the room, Kris smoothed Tom's hair from his forehead, another familiar gesture from their childhood. What kind of person could do something like this to their spouse and children? The answer chilled her: she knew exactly what kind. The same kind their father had been. Sick. Selfish. Abusive. They'd all recognized Patty's true nature long ago, yet they had done nothing meaningful to stop her.

Oh, they had begged Tom to leave her countless times. Had despised Patty privately and lobbed passive-aggressive barbs her way publicly. But that was the extent of it. Not one of them had confronted Patty directly. None of them had sat down with Ashlea and Megan to discuss their feelings and needs. She, of all people, should have at least done that...and more. But she hadn't. Neva hadn't. Rachel hadn't. Why?

None of them had ever admitted it out loud, but Kris was way past hiding from the truth now. Patty was an abuser. She was a smaller, female version of Robert Stevenson, with the bonus of a drinking problem...and that type of monster still scared them. Still held power over them. Over her, Tom, and Neva, at least. She had no idea why her Pitbull sister hadn't confronted Patty. It didn't matter, anyway. Whatever the reason, none of them could escape the ugly truth. They hadn't helped Tom get free of that drunken psychopath, and their inability to act had resulted in devastating consequences for her brother and nieces.

Kris studied Tom's sleeping battered face, guilt weighing heavily on her chest. But it wasn't too late. They were alive. Bruised and broken, but breathing. There was still time to make this right. She pressed her palm gently against his cheek. "You saved me once, Tommy. This time, I'm going to save you."

• • • •

Rachel stepped out of the elevator onto the first floor, scanning the hallway for her mother. She had found out Patty's room number and had gone there first. Her mother wasn't there. Where would she have gone? Did she leave? Rachel walked out the sliding doors to the emergency parking lot and checked for her mother's car. It was still parked in the same spot. Maybe the cafeteria? No, Mom never ate when she was upset. Did the hospital have a bar? She laughed aloud, causing a passing doctor to eye her suspiciously.

She continued walking, trying to imagine where Neva might have gone. She noticed a sign that read: Gift Shop, with an arrow pointing down the hall. Yeah, she's probably buying a stuffed animal or something for the girls, she thought, picking up her pace as she followed the signs. When she got to the Gift Shop, though, it was closed. As she wandered back down the hall, she saw a sign on a large, ornate door that read: Chapel. She doubted her mother would be in there, but she had run out of options and decided to check it out, just in case.

The wooden door opened silently into a miniature sanctuary that took Rachel's breath away. At the front of the room, stained glass windows flanked a large effigy of Jesus on the cross, while skylights let in softened beams of sunlight from above. White lilies and mixed blooms filled massive urns, their overwhelming sweetness triggering uncomfortable memories of funerals. A central aisle divided rows of chairs and wooden pews, leading to where Neva sat alone in the front row, head bowed in prayer.

Rachel moved silently down the aisle, settling beside her mother. She watched, fascinated, as Neva's lips formed silent words of supplication. In all her years, she'd never witnessed her mother pray, hadn't known she even knew how. But lately, everything Rachel thought she knew about Neva was being rewritten. This moment was just another revelation to add to her rapidly growing list.

Neva finished her prayer, crossed herself, and opened her eyes. Her body jerked at Rachel's presence, as if jolted by a sudden shock. "Jesus Christ, Rachel! You scared the hell out of me."

"Mom!" Rachel scolded, gesturing toward Jesus' image, scandalized.

Neva glanced at the crucifix, crossed herself again, then fixed Rachel with a scowl.

Rachel suppressed a laugh. "You look just like Kim when you do that. Why are you in here? You've never been to church a day in your life."

"Oh yes I have!" Neva bristled.

"Really? When?"

"My mother dragged me to church twice a week, from the time I could crawl, until I married your father." Neva replied with satisfaction.

Rachel's eyebrows shot up. "Why'd you stop going, then?"

"Because my mother dragged me to church twice a week from the time I could crawl, until I married your father," Neva echoed dryly.

"So, you stopped going out of pure spite?" Rachel grinned.

Neva chuckled. "I was every bit as rebellious with my parents as you are with me."

Rachel's gaze dropped to her lap. "And Kim is with me."

"Circle of life, and all that shit." Neva said, patting her daughter's knee.

"I should have listened to you about her." Rachel's voice softened. "She's pregnant, Mom."

Neva studied her daughter with gentle eyes, but remained silent.

"What? No 'I told you so'? No ranting and raving?" Rachel prompted.

Neva sighed. "Honey, if you recall, I already went through this sixteen years ago with you. Ranting didn't help then, I doubt it'll help now."

"What do you think we should do?"

"There is no 'we'. This is Kim's decision. You can love her, and support her, and help her any way you can...but this is her life. It's her decision." Neva stated firmly.

"She's fifteen! She doesn't know anything about life!" Rachel huffed.

"So were you. Did you want me to make the decision for you?"

Rachel collapsed against the pew, letting her head fall back as she released a tortured moan.

"Just be there for her and offer advice when she asks. That's all you can do. It's hard, but it's the Mother's Code," Neva said, patting Rachel's knee again.

Rachel's head snapped forward, fixing her mother with a sardonic look. "Did you read that code before or after the five million dollar ultimatum?"

Neva snorted, bumping shoulders with Rachel. "I know the code. I didn't say I always follow it. Besides, that's different anyway, and you know it."

"Mmmhmm," Rachel teased. They settled into comfortable silence for a few moments before she turned to her mother again. "Mom... I'm sorry about the other night. I just...it's so shitty that you—I just feel so—"

"Rachel," Neva interrupted softly, "I know you haven't always felt it, but all I ever wanted was for you and Kris and Tom to be safe and happy. No matter how old you get, you're still my children. That wish, that need to make sure you're okay—it never goes away." She paused, laying her palm on Rachel's cheek. "Everything I've done, everything I do, is because I love you. Maybe not how you want me to, or need me to, but it's the only way I know how."

Neva looked away, but not before Rachel caught the glimmer of tears in her eyes. "Are you sure it's not because you enjoy being a giant pain in the ass?" Rachel teased, trying to lighten the moment.

Neva's laugh echoed in the chapel. "Well, maybe a little of that, too," she offered with a sheepish grin as she rose from the pew. "I'm going to go check on your brother," she announced, striding purposefully up the aisle.

"Mom?" Rachel called after her.

Neva turned, the skylight's rays creating a halo around her face and hair. She's so beautiful, Rachel thought, wanting to voice this revelation. Needing to express all the kind words she'd withheld through years of spite, hurt and anger. Instead, she simply said, "I love you, too."

Neva winked and blessed Rachel with a radiant smile before gliding through the chapel door.

· · · ·

Kris eased the door to Patty's hospital room open and peeked inside. Finding her sister-in-law alone and sleeping, she glanced down the empty hallway once more before slipping through the door. This room differed from the room Tom and the girls were sharing. It was spacious and private, providing her own bathroom and park view, unlike Tom and the girls' shared space overlooking asphalt. Patty's parents had obviously made sure she was getting the best care the hospital offered, while leaving their son-in-law and grandchildren to fend for themselves.

Somehow, seeing Patty laying in the upgraded hospital bed with no casts and no bandaged head, without a visible scratch on her, made Kris even angrier and more determined than she already was. It wasn't right. Patty laying here looking like she didn't have a care in the world. Sleeping peacefully while her children were struggling with physical and emotional pain. While her husband lay sedated, bruised, and broken because of what she had done to them. The wrongness of it, the sheer unfairness, solidified Kris's resolve. She wouldn't stand by and let it happen ever again.

She approached the bed, shaking Patty's shoulder. "Patty?" she hissed. "Patty, wake up." Nothing. Disgust roiled through her as dark thoughts surfaced. *It's too bad she can't stay like this forever. Fall into a coma of some kind and just never wake up. Never darken our doors again. Then the girls would be safe, and Tom would be free. No more danger. No more abuse. If she just wouldn't wake up...*

The IV pump's beep startled her, and she took a step toward it to get a better look. One of the IV bags hanging from the machine had a morphine label. Kris froze, gaze moving between the machine and Patty's sleeping form. *If she just wouldn't wake up...* She could do this. She could make sure Patty didn't wake up. Could make sure Tom and the girls were safe from her forever. Without another thought, Kris grabbed the IV pump and began pushing buttons. The numbers under "dosage" climbed, and the machine beeped twice more as she poked and prodded the screen.

"Kris! What are you doing!?" Neva's harsh whisper cut through the room from the bathroom doorway.

Kris spun to face her mother, both hands in the air like she was being held at gunpoint.

Neva rushed forward, grabbing Kris's hands out of the air and staring at them as if searching for answers in her palms. "Dear God, please tell me you weren't doing what I think you were doing," she moaned.

Kris's silence spoke volumes.

Lifting her daughter's chin, Neva forced eye contact. "Kris? Please tell me what you were doing."

Kris's gaze darted wildly around the room, attempting to elude her mother's scrutiny, but Neva held firm until their eyes finally met.

"Tell me," Neva whispered.

Tears welled in Kris's eyes. Neva closed hers in pained recognition before snapping them open again to focus on her daughter. "So, you came in here to kill her."

Kris lifted her chin in defiance. "Not at first! I just...I don't want Tom to be unhappy. I owe him this."

Neva pressed a hand to her forehead, pacing away before wheeling back. "You don't owe anybody anything!" she whisper-hissed.

"Yes, I do. You know that I do," Kris said softly, pleading for understanding. "He'll never leave her. He's not strong enough and I can't just—"

"—Yes, he is. He is strong enough, and he has left her," Neva said in exasperation. "That's what we were discussing at the house before you and Rachel arrived that night."

Kris's eyes widened. "He did? He left her?"

Before Neva could answer, the door to Patty's room cracked open and then closed again. Neva pressed a finger to her lips, pulling Kris into the bathroom. She positioned Kris behind her, leaving the door cracked just enough for surveillance. Kris's anxious breath burned against Neva's neck as they waited.

A few moments later, the room's door opened again, and Rachel slipped inside. Neva watched through the narrow crack of the door as her youngest daughter scanned the room before crossing to the window and lowering the shade.

Neva felt Kris's urgent sleeve-tugging and turned, pressing a finger to her lips.

"Who is it?" Kris mouthed.

"Rachel," Neva silently replied.

Kris's eyes went wide, and she quickly wedged in next to Neva so she could see for herself. They both watched, fascinated, as Rachel paced back and forth around Patty's bed for a few moments, before crossing back to the door. She opened it just enough to poke her head out, then pulled back and closed it again. Returning to Patty, Rachel's face twisted with revulsion. "I think it's time for you to meet your father-in-law, in hell," she snarled, before yanking the pillow from beneath Patty's head and pressing it over her face.

Kris recoiled in shock.

"Jesus, Mary, and Joseph", Neva muttered as she pulled the bathroom door open. "Rachel Stephenson!" she whisper-barked. "Stop that right now!"

Rachel's body stiffened at her mother's voice, but instead of backing off, she leaned forward, putting even more of her weight on the pillow.

Kris scrambled to her feet and pushed past her mother. Grasping Rachel by the shoulders, she tried to pull her away. Rachel grabbed the frame of the bed, hanging on like a barnacle.

Neva joined the struggle, wrapping her arms around Rachel's waist and yanking forcefully. The Heimlich-like movement knocked the breath from Rachel, breaking her grip.

Kris snatched the pillow away, anxiously monitoring Patty's breathing. Assured of her survival, she spun to face her sister. Rachel was red faced with anger.

"You two need to get out of here and let me finish what I started," Rachel said, fighting her mother's restraining grip.

Neva released her. "You aren't 'finishing' anything," she stated firmly. "You're coming with us, out of this room, right now."

"No, I'm not."

"Oh yes you are!" Neva fumed. "What is wrong with you two?"

"That bitch almost killed Tom and—" Rachel paused, her eyes narrowing. "Wait, what do you mean 'you two'?"

Neva threw up her hands. "I don't know what possessed you girls to think murder is the answer to dealing with—"

"—A manipulative, violent psycho that abuses her kids and tried to kill my brother?" Rachel interjected.

Kris aligned herself beside her sister. "Yeah. Sounds very familiar to me, Mom."

"Listen. There's a big difference between what happened with your father and what almost happened here," she hissed, deploying her best disappointed-mother glare. "Didn't I teach you that violence isn't the answer? Didn't I?"

"Not really," Rachel replied, unfazed.

"Mom, I understand, but we can't just let her—" Kris began.

"—Apparently, what I failed to teach you..." Neva continued, as if they hadn't spoken, "is that there's more than one way to deal with a slime ball."

The sight of Neva's devilish grin sent a chill down Kris's spine, but Rachel fist-pumped the air and she whisper-yelled, "Yesss!"

Neva snapped her fingers at Kris. "Go get a warm, wet, paper towel. Rachel, put that pillow back behind Patty's head."

The girls snapped into action as Neva took a quick peek into the hallway. Seeing that the coast was clear, she re-joined the girls. Kris handed her the paper towel and Neva began wiping down the screen of the IV machine.

"Krissy, help me here. Use your foot to move the IV closer to the bed. Rachel, watch the door."

Rachel rushed to the door, taking another quick peek into the hall. "Coast is clear," she said over her shoulder.

Neva gave her a thumbs up and continued wiping the machine as Kris nudged it closer to the bed. "Just our luck, she'll die now on accident," Neva mumbled.

Kris glanced at Patty, seeing the rise and fall of her chest. "She's still breathing. I only pushed the buttons a couple times. I doubt it was enough to—"

"Yeah, well, great minds think alike." Neva huffed.

Kris stared at her mother, aghast. "You pushed them, too?"

"Shhh!" Neva warned. "I changed my mind in the middle of it because I thought of a better plan, then you came in here with your eighty-words-per-minute fingers and—"

"I didn't know!" Kris hissed, panic rising.

"I know, I know. Don't worry about it. We'll go to jail together if she croaks," Neva said.

Rachel took a few steps toward them, hand raised. "Me too! I'm going with you for aiding and abetting," she added with enthusiasm.

Kris and Neva exchanged alarmed looks.

"Is she enjoying this?" Neva asked. She looked over her shoulder at Rachel. "Please tell me you're not enjoying this."

"A little, yeah," Rachel confessed.

"Jeezus, Rachel," Kris huffed.

"What?! You are too, and you know it," Rachel shot back.

"Shush!" Neva commanded. "Kris, steady the machine with your foot while I finish."

As Kris braced the IV pump, Neva extracted Patty's hand from beneath the sheet, carefully positioning two of her fingers on each button.

"What are you doing?" Kris whispered.

"Protecting my children," Neva answered.

. . . .

Kris had been relieved the next afternoon when Neva left her a voice message informing her that Tom and the girls were being released that night. Her relief morphed into instant panic when Neva's second message informed Kris to come to the hospital right away and meet them at the nurse's desk on Patty's floor. There was no explanation or even a hint of what was going on. Kris was shaking so violently when she got in the car; it had taken her three tries to get the keys into the ignition. The drive to the hospital became a blur of anxiety as she wondered if what they had done the night before had somehow been discovered. By the time she stepped off the elevator onto Patty's floor, her stomach was roiling, and she had to keep reminding herself to breathe.

She spotted Tom at the nurse's station, deep in conversation with a doctor. Neva leaned against the wall a few feet away, arms crossed, concern etched on her face. Kris's gut clenched tighter as she approached her mother. "Sorry it took me so long. What's going on?" she managed, voice unsteady.

Neva eyed her, raising an eyebrow with a look that meant "get your shit together". Kris gave her mother an imperceptible nod and willed herself to take a deep breath. Neva held up two fingers, and Kris obeyed, taking a second steadying breath.

Satisfied, Neva answered Kris, her voice low. "Patty refused the psych evaluation."

"Psych evaluation?"

"Yep. Doctors say she nearly overdosed on morphine last night. Would have succeeded if the drip hadn't been almost empty," Neva replied pointedly.

Kris's heart thundered as she pressed a trembling hand to her chest. Glancing toward Patty's room, she froze. Two police officers stood guard, and one of them was Officer Miller. Her heart plummeted to her feet, taking all of her blood with it.

Neva's throat-clearing pulled her attention back to her mother.

"As I was saying," Neva went on, her voice dripping with meaning, "the hospital suspects either a suicide attempt or drug-seeking behavior. Either way..." She twirled a finger near her temple in the Universal sign for crazy.

"What's Patty's story?"

"She's denying everything. Blames hospital incompetence."

"Why are the police here?"

"I called them," Tom answered, limping to Kris's side. Despite the swelling and bruises, his eyes held unprecedented determination.

"You called them? Why?" Kris glanced nervously between Tom and her mother. Neva's answering wink did little to calm her nerves.

Before Tom could respond, Officer Miller approached, flashing Kris a grin. "Fancy meeting you here," he teased, before turning to Tom. "You ready?"

Tom nodded.

Officer Miller nodded toward the door to Patty's room. "We'll be right outside. Just call when you want us to come in."

. . . .

Tom paused at Patty's door, looking back at his mother. Neva's sharp nod and thumbs-up steadied him. He nodded back, pushed open the door, and limped inside.

Patty perched on the edge of the hospital bed, deep in conversation with her father, Ed, who sat in the nearby recliner. Patty's demure mother, Helen, sat in the straight-backed chair in the corner, purse clutched like a shield in her lap. Helen noticed Tom first, offering a timid smile that he acknowledged with a curt nod. He felt sorry for Helen. She was married to a man who was every bit the nasty piece of work his daughter was, and just as eager to embarrass, belittle, and bully his spouse. Though he lacked proof, Tom always suspected Helen suffered physical abuse from Ed, too. What a sad life she must have had. Married to an asshole like Patty's father, and then to have her only child turn out just like him.

Patty's head snapped up. "Well, it's about damn time. I'm ready to leave. Where are the girls?"

"They're waiting with Rachel, in their hospital room," Tom said, with ice in his tone.

"I'll get them," Ed announced, rising.

Tom's raised hand stopped him. "That won't be necessary, Ed. They're coming home with me and my mom. I'm filing for divorce and full custody today."

Ed's face went red and contorted with anger. "Just you wait a damned minute", he fumed. "Who do you think you are? You aren't taking custody of anything but yourself."

Tom kept his gaze locked on Patty. "Your daughter is a drunk and an abusive mother and spouse. She nearly killed me, and your grandchildren. I'm making sure she never comes near them again."

Patty's face flushed to match her father's as she rose. "You aren't taking my kids anywhere," she seethed.

Tom retreated a step, turning his head toward the door. "Come on in!" he called, then faced Patty again. "Watch me."

Patty drew back her fist and punched Tom in the face, bloodying his lip. The two police officers stepped into the room just in time to witness the assault. They wasted no time, grabbing Patty by the arms as she reared back to deliver another blow.

Tom grinned at Patty, teeth red with the blood oozing from his split lip. "I'd like to press an additional assault charge, Officers. And I think I'll need that restraining order."

Patty let out a guttural howl of outrage as the officers placed her hands behind her back. Helen met Tom's eyes for a moment, offering him a small smile and a nod of approval. Ed, his face now a dangerous shade of purple, blustered and seethed as the police began reading Patty her rights.

"Patty Stevenson, you are being placed under arrest for drunken driving, three counts of vehicular assault, two counts of domestic assault, and attempted murder. You have the right to remain silent..."

"Attempted murder!?" Ed bellowed. "Helen, call our attorney. This is ridiculous! I won't stand for it!" Ed raged, as spittle foamed at the corner of his mouth.

Without another word, Tom turned and limped toward the door. He had just opened it to leave when Patty called after him. "Tom! Tom, I'm sorry! I made a mistake. I won't drink anymore, I promise. I need a psyche evaluation!"

He stepped back into the hallway, letting the door close hard behind him. Kris was pacing the hall, while his mother stood motionless a few feet away, watching her. At his entrance back into the hallway, they both turned to him with matching expressions of concern. He gave them a thumbs-up and a broad, bloody grin.

Chapter 13:
One Year Later

Rachel bounced baby Jack on her hip while Kim finished stuffing diapers and baby wipes into the bag. The baby's fine blonde hair floated up and down with each bounce like a miniature toupee as he gazed at his grandmother with pure adoration. She lifted him to nuzzle his neck, making him squeal with delight.

"If you make him puke again, you're cleaning it up this time." Kim warned. "Where are we headed?"

"Stopping by Grandma's to show her the kitchen paint swatches. Yes we are, aren't we, Jack?" Rachel said in baby talk, drawing an exasperated huff from Kim as she wrestled the diaper bag under the stroller.

"Wait!" Rachel said in her normal voice. "Did I put the swatches in the bag?"

"Yes, I saw them in there. Is Jim completely done with construction, then?"

"Finishing on Monday."

"Are you telling Gramma about the ring?"

Rachel glanced at her engagement ring, smiling. The Charleston weekend had been perfect. Jim's surprise proposal, in one of the city's architectural masterpieces, had left her breathless. Besides Kim, he was the greatest gift life had given her. Her "yes" had been immediate and certain.

"I want to wait until I can get mom and Lois together to tell them."

"That'll be fun to watch!" Kim giggled. "So, Gramma is having Jim build her a house close to Lois, but what else did she buy with her money?"

Rachel lifted Jack into the air and blew a raspberry on his belly. His giggles made both women laugh. "I don't know. I don't think she's really bought anything else except the surgery to remove her scar," she answered, moving to the stroller with Jack. "Great Grammie's just a tight wad, isn't she Jack? Just a pickled old tight wad!"

"Not nice, Mom!" Kim scolded, extracting Jack from her mother's arms and fixing Rachel with an admonishing look.

"I'm just kidding! Jeez, motherhood has made you such a grump. Mom told Kris she was going to get something she's wanted for a long time, but she wouldn't tell Kris what it was, and I haven't seen anything so..."

"Okay, so what has she wanted for a long time?" Kim asked as she finished securing Jack in the stroller.

"No idea." Rachel answered, grabbing her purse and the bottled water off the sofa table. "Let's get going and maybe we can tag team her for answers."

• • • •

Kris paced the kitchen, cell phone pressed to her ear while Officer Dan Miller calmly took a bite of his ham sandwich as he sorted through the daily pile of mail. She ended the call in frustration. "Still can't reach Mom, Dan. She's not answering either phone."

"Maybe she's got the ringer off on her cell." Dan said in a reassuring tone.

Trent slouched into the kitchen, dropping into the chair beside Dan.

"About time you got up, slacker!" Dan teased, ruffling Trent's short, undyed hair. "You ready to get your ass kicked at some basketball?"

Trent scoffed, dodging the ruffling attempt. "In your dreams, old man."

Dan lifted an eyebrow in an expression like The Rock. "Old man? Did you just call me an old man?"

Trent crossed his arms over his chest and grinned. "Sure did," he taunted.

With a speed belying his old man status, Dan snatched Trent into a headlock, playfully applying a nuggie to the top of his head. "Oh, it is on! I will show no mercy!"

Trent broke the hold, dancing away, laughing. "You're on, Gramps!" he taunted.

"Dan," Kris said quietly, reaching out to touch his arm. "I'm seriously getting worried. It's not like mom to not pick up my call."

Dan's playful expression evaporated, and he enveloped Kris in his arms. "Honey, I'm sure Neva's fine. She's probably just busy."

"Busy with what? We were supposed to go shopping this morning. No call to cancel. Nothing. It's not like her. I think I better call Tom. See if he's heard anything."

• • • •

Tom stepped out of the psychology building and into the bright assault of spring. He paused, squinting slightly as his eyes adjusted. The spring term was almost over, and he had just aced one of his last two exams. Soon, it would be summer break, and he and his daughters had big plans for travel and fun.

The first few weeks after the hospital had been rough, but Kris had been their anchor. She had partnered with Tom during that crucial conversation with Ashlea and Megan, helping them understand everything that was happening and reassuring each of them that they were not to blame for any of it.

Ashlea had embraced their new lives with courage and determination, tackling first grade with a vengeance. She had become one of the best readers in her class and was often chosen for leadership responsibilities. Two achievements that had become fierce points of pride for her.

Megan's pre-school year had followed a rockier path. After the accident, she had developed an intense car phobia, refusing to ride in a car, or even sit in one. Being forced to do so would trigger full-blown panic attacks, complete with screaming, sweating, and tears. It had broken Tom's heart to see her so traumatized. Even worse, though, was her overwhelming fear that something would happen to him.

For the first three months, Megan would not let him out of her sight. Clinging to him like a small squid, refusing to release him, even for bathroom breaks. Through patient support from Kris and his mother, they had gotten through it, and over time, she gradually regained more of her previous personality. Perhaps quieter now, and more watchful and contained, but each day she made more progress.

Tom was a psychology major and, although he was just getting started, he understood enough to know that the damage and trauma Patty had caused would leave a permanent mark on his daughters. He had accepted that awful truth but was determined to shield them from any additional damage. He was committed to ensuring they had wonderful childhoods and would grow up to be well-adjusted adults. This summer was about creating happy new memories and, bit by bit, Tom was hopeful that their new life would help them heal their wounds for good.

Patty was serving a fifteen-year sentence in the women's state penitentiary, with no chance of parole for at least nine years. She also had a strict no-contact order, preventing her from reaching out to him or his daughters. He had at least nine years to prepare them for whatever would come after her release. He intended to make the most of them.

As Tom crossed the campus lawn toward the parking lot, his phone vibrated in his pocket. He answered it while continuing his stride. "Hello?"

"Tom, have you heard from Mom yesterday or today?" Kris's voice came through the line, tinged with concern.

"No, why?" Tom replied, his pace slowing.

"I can't get a hold of her. She's not picking up her cell or the phone at the house. We were supposed to go shopping this morning and...nothing. Not a word."

Tom stopped walking and frowned down at his sneakers. "I don't have my last class until this afternoon. You want me to swing by and check on her?"

"Would you? I'm starting to get a really bad feeling about this. Maybe we should both head over there."

He could feel Kris's anxiety beginning to infect him, too. He started walking again, this time at a much quicker pace, toward his car. "Okay, I'm leaving now. I'll meet you there."

· · · ·

Kris threw her cell phone into her purse and started for the door.

Trent stepped in front of her. "Mom, what's going on? What's up with Grandma?"

Kris shook her head. "I don't know, honey. Tom and I are going to go check on her."

Dan grabbed his keys off the table. "We'll all go. I'll drive."

A few minutes later, Kris twitched with anxiety in the passenger seat. "Go faster, Dan! She's probably sick. She could have fallen and been hurt, or— oh my God, what if somebody broke in!? Do you have your gun!?"

In the backseat, Trent was wide-eyed, chewing nervously on his thumbnail.

Dan glanced at him in the rearview mirror, then over at Kris. "God help the idiot who tries to rob your mother," he teased, earning a bark of laughter from the backseat.

Kris glared at him. "Not funny."

Dan cleared his throat and summoned his calm police officer voice. "I'm sorry, honey. Look, I'm sure everything is fine. We're not going to need a gun. She probably just accidentally turned the ringer off on her phone."

"Both phones?!", Kris said, leaning forward to check the speedometer. "Drive faster, Dan!"

• • • •

Tom arrived in his SUV just as Kris and Dan were stepping out of their car. Without waiting for Tom, Kris hurried toward Neva's front door. Tom, giving a quick wave to Trent and Dan, followed her at a more measured pace.

Kris rang the bell and waited only a few seconds before attempting to open the door. Finding it locked, she frantically searched her pockets. "Damn it! I didn't bring the key!" she exclaimed. "Mom!? Mom, are you in there!? It's Kris, open up!" she yelled, pounding on the door.

Tom approached the large picture window, cupping his hands around his eyes to peer inside. "I can't see anything. The curtains are closed."

Kris ceased her pounding. "She never closes the curtains, even at night," she said, with an edge of alarm in her tone.

"I'll check the garage to see if her car is in there," Tom said, quickly descending the porch steps.

On the sidewalk, Trent and Dan paused as they noticed Rachel and Kim approaching with the stroller.

"What's going on!?" Rachel called out, quickening her pace.

"Kris hasn't heard from your mom in a couple of days, and she isn't answering her phone. I'm sure everything is fine, we're just checking in," Dan explained, trying to maintain a calm tone. His attempt had the opposite effect.

"What!? Why didn't somebody call me?" Rachel said, sprinting up the walk to join Kris.

Trent shrugged, offering Dan a sympathetic grimace.

"Did you bring your key?" Kris asked Rachel urgently.

Rachel shook her head.

Tom reappeared from around the corner of the house, his expression tense. "Her car is here, but the back door is locked too," he reported.

Kris and Rachel exchanged panicked glances.

"Let's just break one of the windows," Rachel suggested with calm determination. "Kim or Trent can climb through and unlock the door."

Before anyone could respond to her suggestion, the front door swung open abruptly. Neva stood in the open doorway, her expression fierce and her hair a tousled mess. She was wearing a short bathrobe of purple silk belted loosely at the waist. The front of the robe hung open slightly, giving them all a view of the lacy black corset underneath. Three-inch stiletto heels completed her ensemble.

"You will do no such thing," Neva growled, staring at her daughters with an expression so murderous, they both took a step back.

"Mom! I have been calling you for hours! Why didn't you answer your phone?" Kris asked, exasperated.

"The better question is, why are you dressed like a hooker?" Rachel asked.

Neva took a deep breath through her nose and looked down it at them. "Because I've been busy!"

"Busy?" Kris exclaimed. "You had me scared to death. We were all worried something had—"

Her words trailed off as a man, who was considerably younger than their mother, appeared in the doorway at Neva's side. He was wearing nothing but a towel. He grabbed Neva around the waist, leaning in to nibble playfully at her ear. The gesture caused Neva's robe to fall open even wider, giving them all an eye-blinding show.

Dan coughed and turned away, suddenly occupied with surveying the neighborhood. Trent stared open-mouthed and transfixed, his face turning a scalding red. From the sidewalk, Kim whistled under her breath in admiration.

"It's okay, invite them in," the man said to their mother, with a familiar ease. "I can finally meet everybody," he continued, grinning at all of them.

Kris choked on her saliva, gasping and sputtering. Rachel patted Kris's back helpfully, but her gaze remained fixed on Garrett's towel.

"Everybody, this is Garrett. We met in Florida," Neva said. She turned, running her hands over his chest. "I'm not up for a meet and greet today, sugar. What I'd really like is for you to get your gorgeous ass in there and start that hot tub. I'll join you in a minute, okay?" she said, giving him a quick peck on the lips.

Garrett chuckled and lifted a hand in a casual wave to Neva's family. "Can't wait to meet you all," he said, then shifted his attention back to Neva. He kissed her passionately on the lips before disappearing into the house.

Neva watched him go before turning back to the shocked faces of her family.

Tom was bright red with embarrassment. "Holy—Mom, close your robe!" he said, placing one hand over his eyes and waving wildly at Neva with the other.

Rachel clapped her hands together in delight. "Let me guess! This is the thing you've wanted for a long time, isn't it?"

Neva responded to her daughter with a sly smile.

"Holy shit, mother! You're a modern-day Mrs. Robinson!" Rachel exclaimed.

"Who's that? What does that mean?" Kim asked, with excited curiosity.

"It's from an old movie about an older woman who seduces a younger man. Like Stifler's mom in American Pie," Rachel explained.

Kim's gaze whipped from her mother to Neva and back again, her eyes wide. "Grandma's a MILF?!"

"A MILF?" Trent said, looking horrified.

"More like a cougar, probably," Dan offered. "He's older than college age."

Kris shot Dan a dirty look.

Tom closed his eyes and covered his ears. "I do not want to hear this or see this. Jeezus, now I'm scarred. Permanently scarred."

"Way to go, Grandma!" Kim called from the bottom of the porch steps. "He's smokin' hot!"

Neva lifted her chin, beaming at her granddaughter's approval.

Kris stared at her mother in shock and horror. "Mom! Are you telling me that you've been in there having— you can't possibly think that he—" she sputtered, incoherently.

"Think that he what? Loves me?" Neva replied, rolling her eyes. "Honey, I am not naive. I know money can't buy me love, but what it can buy me ain't too shabby," she added with a wink.

"I don't think you should be—" Kris started, but Neva cut her off.

"Kris, I know what I'm doing, and I am perfectly fine. Now, go home and let me get back to—cougaring," she said, shimmying her shoulders and making cat growling noises.

"Oh, dear God," Kris muttered.

"Lighten up, prudie pants," Rachel chimed in, bumping shoulders with Kris.

"Listen to your sister," Neva said. "And get off my porch." She blew them all a kiss and shut the door in their faces.

Leaning against the closed door, Neva eavesdropped on her family's chatter as they departed the front yard. What a difference a year had made.

Kris and Tom were out of their failed marriages, and Kris had found genuine love with Dan. Rachel was finally in a relationship with a truly good man. Trent and all her granddaughters were thriving, and the addition of baby Jack had made her a great-grandmother. While she wasn't crazy about broadcasting the great-grandmother part, she was finally in a place where she could enjoy being a grandmother, and Jack was her pride and joy. Lois was happy and settled into her new house, just three blocks away from the house Neva was having built for herself, and everyone was healthy and happy.

Sure, there were bumps and hiccups. There always would be. They still bickered like most families do—but even that was less frequent now. No longer fueled by the specter of their past.

It hit her all at once how blessed she was. Perhaps it was time for her to have a chat with "the man upstairs" and let Him know how grateful she felt. And maybe, while she was at it, she would ask forgiveness for a few dozen things. Both conversations were long overdue. She released a contented sigh as Garrett stepped into the room, offering her a sensual smile.

"Come here, you sexy cougar," he said.

"So, you heard," Neva chuckled. "Now is your chance to run."

"No way. I like cats." He let his towel fall to the floor and beckoned her with a crooked finger. "Here, kitty, kitty."

"Who's seducing who?" she asked, swaying her hips seductively as she sauntered toward him.

"Join me in the hot tub, and let's find out," he teased.

With a slow, deliberate movement, Neva ran a finger down the sizeable length of him, feeling him shiver. "Change can be so damn good," she purred.

And it was.

Can't get enough of Neva and the Stevenson family?

Join my Inner Circle at LAarbuckle.com! Come along on my writing journey, uncover bonus scenes, dig deeper into the characters, snag exclusive giveaways and be the first to get a sneak peek at my next book!

LAarbuckle.com[1]

---

1. https://laarbuckle.com/

About the Author

L.A. Arbuckle is an award-winning producer, screenwriter, and novelist who loves weaving complex characters into twisty plots you can't put down. Conditional Love first turned heads as a screenplay, nabbing finalist spots in international competitions before becoming her debut novel. Although born an Iowan, she now writes from Florida, fueled by chai lattes and 80s tunes. Want to learn more about L.A.? Join her "Inner Circle" and she'll spill the tea... LAarbuckle.com

Read more at https://laarbuckle.com/.